TREATY

Also by Davis Bunn from Severn House

The Rowan Trilogy

THE ROWAN
NO MAN'S LAND
STAR CIRCLE

Other Novels

PRIME DIRECTIVE
ISLAND OF TIME
FORBIDDEN
THE SEVENTH SPELL
QUANTUM CAGE

TREATY

Davis Bunn

SEVERN
HOUSE

First world edition published in Great Britain and the USA in 2026
by Severn House, an imprint of Canongate Books Ltd,
14 High Street, Edinburgh EH1 1TE.

severnhouse.com

Cover and jacket design by Piers Tilbury

British Library Cataloguing-in-Publication Data
A CIP catalogue record for this title is available from the British Library.

ISBN-13: 978-1-4483-1992-3 (cased)
ISBN-13: 978-1-4483-2064-6 (paper)
ISBN-13: 978-1-4483-2063-9 (e-book)

All Severn House titles are printed on acid-free paper.

Typeset by Palimpsest Book Production Ltd., Falkirk, Stirlingshire, Scotland.
Printed and bound in Great Britain by TJ Books, Padstow, Cornwall.

The manufacturer's authorised representative in the EU for product safety is Authorised Rep Compliance Ltd, 71 Lower Baggot Street, Dublin D02 P593 Ireland (arccompliance.com)

Praise for Davis Bunn

"A swift-paced narrative, sympathetic characters . . . will appeal to a wide range of readers"
Booklist on *The Seventh Spell*

"A deep look at how a transition can help heal past personal traumas"
Booklist on *No Man's Land*

"Impressive . . . Bunn keeps the suspense high"
Publishers Weekly on *The Rowan*

"I absolutely loved this story! *The Rowan* is a powerful political thriller that delves both into sci-fi and fantasy. The result is a mesmerizing page turner"
David Lipman, producer of the *Iron Man* and *Shrek* films, on *The Rowan*

"A wild ride"
Kirkus Reviews on *Island of Time*

"A fast-paced, retro-feeling sci-fi mystery. Bunn offers readers a sure guide through his far-future setting . . . A pleasure. This is good fun"
Publishers Weekly on *Prime Directive*

About the author

Davis Bunn's novels have sold in excess of eight million copies in twenty-six languages. He has appeared on numerous national bestseller lists, and his novels have been Main or Featured Selections with every major US bookclub. Recent titles have been named Best Book of the Year by both *Library Journal* and *Suspense Magazine*, as well as earning Top Pick and starred reviews from *RT Reviews*, *Kirkus Reviews*, *Publishers Weekly*, and *Booklist*. Currently Davis serves as Writer-In-Residence at Regent's Park College, Oxford University. He speaks around the world on aspects of creative writing. Davis also publishes under the pseudonym of Thomas Locke.

This book is dedicated to
Clint and Leslie Bruce
Friends For Life

ONE
Kirra Barret

Kirra was born in a frontier zone swamp. She was orphaned that very same day. All because of a scientist her clan called the dragon lady. Kirra's mother had been a clan member, her father a scientist in the frontier lab. The clan assumed the dragon lady had forbidden their love because Kirra's clan came from the city-state's poorest district. Kirra did not need to know the woman's name to hate her.

Her mother was the first of the Barret clan to graduate with a higher degree. She was by all accounts as intelligent as she was lovely. And Kirra's mother was very beautiful indeed.

Kirra grew up shielded from the surrounding threats and dark ways for the same reason her mother had been granted a chance. The clan Barret took care of its own.

For an orphan like Kirra, lovely and alone, the clan was everything.

It did not mean her life was easy or even pleasant. This was, after all, the mining community of Fifth Ward, a region known to all its inhabitants as the Stretch, named after time in prison. As in, trading one stretch for another.

On the bad nights, and there were any number of these, Kirra had the dream. The one that was actually not a dream at all, but rather a genuine memory rendered and twisted by time and slumber. Sometimes the dream made her six years old, the age when the event occurred. Other times she was her current age, and in those she often switched from observer to combatant. Those were the worst dreams of all.

The day the event actually happened, the Black Watch made another raid. Police, federal agents, whatever the badge they wore, there was only one name for the uniformed might keeping an iron grip on the Stretch. They always wore black, the Watch did, and swarmed in great numbers. Always with the loud alarms and megaphones blasting threats and weapons on the ready. Only this time had been different because the clan was celebrating. Kirra and four distant relatives had all reached the age of six, which was known in their community as the Milestone. This was a sign from past ages that the threats of infant death were behind them. Today's party marked their first rite of passage, and something more besides. Their clan was almost unique, how they and protected the innocent, the infirm, the vulnerable. Their Milestone festival celebrated how the clan Barret had defied the Black Watch and the city-state's Council and the mines and the passage of eons. The clan cared for their own.

But the Black Watch came hunting that day. And the clan had lined up in the building's central corridor with their faces to the wall, like always, everyone from Elder Barret to the youngest able to stand. The Black Watch invaded their homes and smashed things as was their habit. Ruining the celebration.

When the Black Watch departed, the clan tromped back inside and silently began cleaning up the debris. Kirra let her four cousins weep over the celebration that was no more. Even at her young age Kirra recognized a bitter rightness to their tears. But for Kirra, what happened that day marked a transition.

Something inside had shattered.

In her dreams, every single one, the sound inside was loud as an explosion, the snapping of an internal component far deeper than the level of bone and sinew.

Kirra always woke after that sound, and lay in her bed and relived what happened next. The six-year-old child had followed the clan back into the corridor, where her two favorite relatives, men of twenty-one and the dearest of friends, were fighting. The clan watched, silenced by the fury these two normally cheerful men showed the world. Kirra was astonished by the brawl, for she had always assumed she was the only one filled with such futile rage.

When Elder Barret started to end the fight, her husband

halted her by saying, "You know as well as I do, they need to let it out." Elder Barret's husband was almost always silent. When he spoke that day, his wife listened. So, they stood and watched two good men beat themselves to bloody pulps.

Kirra's dreamscape always faded the same way. More vivid than the fight was what came from that internal breakage. Standing in the fetid corridor, surrounded by her clan, watching them fight. She saw clearly how these good people were stained by exhaustion and wasted lives. Kirra knew she was going to get out of there. Six years old, this became the mark of her own private Milestone. Whatever it took. If she failed, she died. It was that simple.

One of the clan's unbreakable rules: Everyone worked. If they could draw breath, they could do something useful. Kirra had been assigned duties since she was old enough to stand upright and hold a broom.

Her first paying job started at age twelve in the mines' front office, where Elder Barret served as a depot manager. Kirra was assigned duties as a tea girl. Because she was good with her letters and loved her studies, she was granted time to continue schooling until her seventeenth year. That was later than most, and offered Kirra months of futile hope. But when the gradient arrived on her eighteenth birthday, Kirra was designated a Five, same as virtually everyone in the Stretch.

The city-state's authorities claimed in speeches, declarations, advertisements, school meetings, family gatherings and so forth that gradient assignments were both fair and without prejudice. All of which made for acid-laced humor in the Stretch. Offspring of the poorer districts rarely if ever rose above a Four. Kirra had never even met a One. Her assignment as a Five, the lowest gradient, was a lifelong condemnation. All official doors leading to a better life were shut and locked. Permanently.

Elder Barret took a personal interest in this lovely orphan, and did what she could to ensure Kirra's mathematical abilities were put to good use. Barret pretended to ignore the tears Kirra allowed no one else to see, and when further schooling was forbidden, the clan's elder personally arranged for tutors. In return, Kirra thanked her as Elder Barret expected, by working hard and learning fast. In time, when Kirra was assigned responsibilities over the mines' incoming supplies, Elder Barret showed her how to fiddle the records. Not a lot, but enough to permit a certain amount of pilfering.

Elder Barret made sure a small portion of the proceeds were passed back to Kirra. She saved everything.

By her twenty-first birthday, Kirra was dying inside. Fading away to nothing. Gradually slipping into a solitary and ghost-like existence.

Elder Barret noticed, of course. She was as watchful as she was wise. Finally, the heavyset woman took her outside, to the plaza where they could be seen and yet remain private. She told Kirra, "You're miserable."

Kirra found no need to respond.

"I was hoping your attitude would change with time. But I see now it was a futile expectation."

That was how this unlettered woman always spoke. Using a precise diction and careful wording, as if she intended her words to show that she was indeed separated from clan members by a gulf wider than merely her title. The label that in time had become her only first name.

Elder Barret continued, "We've had offers for your hand. One Fourth Ward clan in particular—"

"No."

"If we insist?" It was always "we" with Elder Barret. Never I.

She had been fearing precisely that. Kirra rose from the bench. "Thank you for the warning, Elder. You've always been kind—"

"Sit down, lass."

"Madame Silver has offered me a position."

The news about the Fifth Ward courtesan shocked Barret. "You'd sell yourself to that woman? Spend your short life whoring?" When Kirra remained silent, the older woman's voice rose a notch. "Forsake the clan?"

"I want out." Because it was Elder Barret, the woman who

had sheltered her for years, Kirra added, "A man of power will have me as his mistress."

"You trust Silver's word?"

"She's arranged a screen-meet. Day after tomorrow. And offered me refuge while I decide."

"When were you aiming on telling me?"

"I'm telling you now. And yes, I trust her because I suspected it would come to this. Having my life bargained away. Being chained by rite and marriage law—"

"Enough." Elder Barret indicated the empty space beside her. "We're not done."

Kirra wanted to bolt. She could hear the cage door swinging shut.

Elder Barret reached out and gripped her forearm, but gently. "You owe me a few moments more."

The Stretch was divided into a series of five-story blocks. They formed a concrete forest that curved slightly as it followed the Fifth Ring. Rings were the names applied to the city-state's circular walls, the first having been constructed over a thousand years earlier, each marking a major expansion of the city-state's reach. On the Fifth Ring's other side stood the mines' central offices. Beyond that was an elongated stretch of wasteland, almost twenty kilometers wide, extending out to where the mines began. Far beyond the most distant wall rose the Sixth Ring, the wall that now formed the city-state's furthest boundary.

Kirra knew the royals and their Council were now planning a Seventh Ring. The clan was tapped into the mining offices' newsfeeds, and often received information before it became public knowledge. Elder Barret had used a recent clan gathering to explain how the new development would not impact the Stretch at all. Instead, the Seventh Ring would merely expand Florian's opposite side. Florian's population now totaled nearly seventeen million citizens, and the city-state was bursting at the seams. New Seventh Ward developments would center around hydroponics and high-tech manufacturing and mineral refineries. All the new residences would be upscale, pristine, and connected to the First Ring via a luxurious high-speed transit system. Seventh Ward was to become an expansion of the city-state's wealth and power. The poorer wards in between would simply be shadowy blurs as the privileged few swept back and forth in safety.

The Stretch's residential buildings were more or less identical. Three blocks of grey concrete rimmed an interior courtyard where nothing grew. The clan maintained their own space as a graveled park and children's playground. Kids from other blocks could visit so long as they behaved. Older clan members were assigned park duty, dawn to dusk. Entry after dark was forbidden. The clan's night patrols made certain of that.

Once Kirra was seated again, Elder Barret told her, "Your mother was like my own daughter."

Kirra nodded. She had heard pretty much those same words all her life.

"I can't let you sell yourself, no matter how nice Madame Silver dresses it up."

"Because it's you, Elder, I'll answer this one time. This is no longer your decision to make. I am leaving. Try and cage me, I'll—"

"Don't say it."

Kirra might have swallowed the words. But she showed Elder Barret the grim determination and bleak rage she had spent years hiding away.

"The dangers are out there, waiting. You're a smart lass. You know what I'm saying is the raw truth."

"I can't stay. I won't."

"All right. I see you mean it." Elder Barret levered herself up in stages. "Put Silver's screen-meet off a day. Let me see what I can arrange."

The unexpected gift of hope was genuinely painful. "What good can come from waiting?"

"Maybe nothing." Elder Barret started away. "Mind what I say. Three days."

As always, the diddybirds waited until Elder Barret was well removed from the park bench. When Kirra was alone and evening shadows almost blanketed the empty playground, three of the flying beasts fluttered down to join her.

These were the only alien creatures who dared enter the human zones. They were shy, skittish animals. Which was good in a way, because they appeared very dangerous. Scary.

They were not really birds at all. They most resembled some form of flying reptile, except for their beaks, which were long and ended in a sharp point. This same protuberance extended in a bony ridge between their eyes, and formed a second spear-like blade at the back of their heads. Their bodies were two of Kirra's hands in length, yellow with orange streaks. These same stripes extended over their wings, which were broad and leathery and the color of rust. Their rear legs were cocked for springing, their forearms long for such small bodies. All four limbs ended in claws with sharp yellow talons. The locals called them rats with wings.

Kirra thought they were beautiful. Even as a young child, the diddybirds had used moments of solitude like this to come close. She had never known them to do so with anyone else, never heard of such a thing. Her clan had of course noticed such times, and made jokes of how the winged rats were drawn to her beauty like all those men walking dark ways.

As long as Kirra could remember, diddybirds appeared from nowhere as soon as she was alone. For years they had remained her silent and precious friends.

As usual, three settled on the bench while others circled overhead or perched on the surrounding rooflines. They never crowded. Kirra always carried something to offer those who approached. Today it was bread and a slice of apple from her lunch. They accepted her gift with almost dainty gestures. They did not eat. They never did while Kirra watched. She often wondered if they took her offerings merely to be polite.

Eventually Kirra turned her attention back to the approaching shadows. She had no real interest in the life Silver offered, no matter how finely the woman dressed it up. Whenever she thought of Silver, the recollections were marred by the jangle of the gold bracelets that Silver rattled with her exaggerated gestures. Kirra started a silent dialogue with the watchful diddybirds. How she had once heard Elder Barret describe a clan member's suicide as a call for help that no one heard in time. That was precisely how she felt about Silver's proposal. She couldn't see what Barret could possibly do to change things. But she was glad to have a reason to wait and look away from that dread prospect.

Three days.

For two days, nothing happened except Kirra could not sleep. The mining office remained just another cage, the hours an endless treadmill that took her nowhere. Elder Barret vanished, calling in sick, appearing for brief moments inside the clan's residence, then gone. Kirra almost hated the older woman for the offer of futile hope.

On the third morning, Elder Barret appeared as Kirra was preparing for work. "You're coming with me."

"I'm due at the office."

"Your days at the mines are over." When Kirra still did not move, she added, "You were leaving anyway, yes? Now let's go."

They took the rattling, smelly Fifth Ward inbound transit, away from the mines. When their transport passed through the Fifth Ring, two Black Watch entered, inspected the riders, snapped a few pictures, eyed Kirra, then departed. That was the one brief moment when Kirra felt joined to Elder Barret. United by a loathing for everything that held them down.

Their destination was a nondescript office building on the Fourth Ward market's northern boundary. Kirra often spent her free afternoons strolling the boisterous lanes. Everything was said to be for sale in the Fourth Ward market, legal or otherwise. A broad avenue kept the shops and stalls from further expansion. On the thoroughfare's other side stretched a wall of warehouses and ratty structures and sidewalks filled with pedestrians and pushcarts.

The building's entrance was scarred and flanked by a pair of dirty windows. The brass nameplate was pitted and filthy and illegible. Kirra declared, "I'm not working here."

The older woman did not bother turning around. She pressed

a buzzer and lined herself up so as to face a camera imbedded in the side wall. The door opened, only to reveal a second portal of what appeared to be solid steel. It slid silently to one side. As Elder Barret stepped in, she told Kirra, "Your job is to stay quiet and do what you're told."

The office was an astonishment. They entered a high-ceilinged antechamber, freshly carpeted and well lit, with comfortable chairs and benches lining two walls. An empty desk was flanked by credenzas holding an array of electronic equipment, much of which Kirra did not recognize.

Elder Barret called, "Arno?"

A man's voice spoke from the inner office, "Come on through."

The interior office was grand and very large. Original artwork adorned the walls. The room was lit by a trio of chandeliers. Two young men and a woman stood watching as a fat bald gentleman in a stained jacket and mismatched shirt sat behind a massive desk, examining a half dozen gemstones. He scrutinized each jewel in turn, then slipped the largest into some sort of device and studied the screen. He asked, "You mentioned a bracelet?"

"And ring." One of the men handed over a felt envelope.

Arno spilled the contents onto the desk, examined both briefly, then said, "All right, Quinn. Pay the gentlemen what they've requested."

Only then did Kirra notice the man standing in the corner. Which was frightening in and of itself. She had been trained from an early age to notice anyone who treated shadows as their allies. It was how a lovely young woman survived.

The man was sleek, middle-aged, and moved like flowing liquid. Kirra had met a few like this one. Not many. The kind who were brethren with dark ways. Who killed with silken pleasure.

The two men accepted their money, thanked the old man profusely, and fled.

Arno told the woman, "Best you stay." He examined Kirra with eyes the color of wintry mud. "You did not mention her looks."

Barret replied, "I told you she was attractive."

"This one's beauty goes far beyond such an empty word. A single gesture from such as this and the dead would gladly rise from the grave."

Kirra had never met such a man, whose look carried no desire or anything like a real emotion. His gaze was as impersonal as the way he spoke to Elder Barret. As if Kirra was not in the room at all.

Arno asked, "You are absolutely certain we can trust this one?"

"All the items we've brought to you during the past year and a half, she's the one covering our tracks."

When Arno continued his examination, Elder Barret pressed, "Can you make this work?"

"Before, I was uncertain. Now, yes. Definitely." A long pause, then, "We should forge her counterfeit identity and gradient as a Three."

"No," Elder Barret countered. "We planned a Four Plus. We should stay with that."

The woman standing beside Arno's desk spoke for the first time. She was blonde and youngish and incredibly pale, like she had never in her entire life stepped into sunlight. "Four will hamper this one's placement."

"She's young," Elder Barret said. "She'll have no idea how to fit in."

"She can learn," the woman said. "I'll teach her."

"In time, yes," Elder Barret said. "But at first, with the world watching . . ."

"Yes, true," Arno said. "All right. Three Minus. And you say she's willing to work hard?"

"I've yet to determine her boundaries."

Both Arno and his assistant looked pleased. The old man said, "We'll start her training tomorrow morning."

"I and the clan thank you," Elder Barret said, and motioned for Kirra to depart. "Until tomorrow.'

Elder Barret spent the transit back describing Arno Held and the role he played in maintaining the clan's singular position. Arno was a master at gaining both power and wealth, yet staying all the while in the shadows. He held no official position, he made no grand alliances. Instead, Arno lived and worked in stealth, finding partners he could trust, and doing whatever it took for them both to succeed. By the time they left the transport and walked toward home, Kirra had pretty much accepted the opportunity as real, and she could genuinely see this as her chance to escape. Finally. At long last.

As they approached the residence Kirra thought Elder Barret looked so very sad. The older woman had gotten exactly what she had intended. Kirra remained firmly linked to Elder Barret and the clan. Just the same, Barret's expression was tragic. It was not until they approached the central playground that Kirra forced herself to say, "Thank you. So much."

Elder Barret directed them to the same bench they had occupied three days earlier. "I thought you would someday become vital to our clan. Perhaps even take my place."

Kirra's gut reaction was to shout at the rising second moon, scream her revulsion to the idea. She clenched down tight, toes to hairline, and buried the response deep.

Just the same, Elder Barret nodded understanding. "You'll let me handle Silver?"

Kirra released a cautious breath. "With pleasure."

"Arno's assistant is named Dell. She was a Fifth Warder. You can trust her."

"All right."

"Any questions, any concerns, you come to me. Not them. To Arno and Dell you show a silent compliance. Nothing more. They may appear pleasant enough. But the threat is always there. The danger. You understand what I'm saying?"

Kirra nodded. "The man who didn't speak."

"His name is Quinn. Think of him as the hidden blade."

"How long will I be held to this agreement?"

The older woman nodded, clearly approving of the question. "Three years is the plan. But I'd suggest you aim on four. If Arno insists, you'll have no choice but wait."

Given the alternatives, Kirra knew without question she

could hold her breath that long. She said, "I owe you everything. And I always will."

Elder Barret rose to her feet. "I suppose that will have to do."

Kirra spent the next forty-six days preparing.

Much time was given over to corporate manuals. This new position required her to have successfully passed the company's in-house training exams. Most days she went back to Arno's office, where specialists taught her or tested her or both. All of these instructors were somehow tied to Arno. Most of them liked and trusted the man. Even revered him, in a few cases. All were frightened by the killer, the man who rarely moved from his corner position and never spoke.

Afternoons were spent transforming Kirra into a Three.

Not *appear* like one. Enter the Three gradient and *become.*

The dress and hair and cosmetics were easy enough. She was a pretty girl; those words had been blathered about since childhood. A gorgeous lass. A young lady made for fun and the high life. Enough of her clan had taken that easy road for Kirra to know exactly what it meant. Silver had made sure of that. Kirra had spent years dulling down her looks, at least a little, hiding the shimmering edge as best she could. Dell's first task was to make her erase those urges and shine. Arno's assistant spent countless hours working on the talk, the attitude, the manner of standing and acting. All that took serious work.

Dell was a slender woman with skin the color of chalk. She tromped about in low heels with no grace whatsoever. But she was intense and as intelligent as she was perceptive. When Kirra showed a genuine determination to break her self-imposed mold and build a new persona, Dell became an ally, perhaps even a friend.

She had been born a Five, and gained Three status illegally, same as Kirra. She revealed this the same day Kirra's new ID arrived. The chip imbedded in Kirra's wrist was shifted, her retina scanned and attached to this altered ID, and Kirra Barret officially became Kirra Eblon.

Once the technician had departed and the two of them were drinking tea and sitting as Kirra would soon be required, Dell told her, "Most of the female Threes you meet will be interested in one thing above all else."

"Becoming a Two," Kirra guessed. Dell had a cynic's attitude toward the entire gradient system. Fueled, Kirra suspected, by a rage similar to her own.

"Rising up," Dell corrected. "To most of them, being graded a Three is bland as gruel. A few are content, not many, and among them you might make friends, or at least allies. The others, if they have any ambition at all, they want out. Promotions big enough to raise them to Two status. A chance to enter higher society. Something."

"How should I treat them?"

Dell glanced at Arno, who stood in the office doorway. The old man was scarcely taller standing than when seated. A fleshy shapeless gentleman who cared little for dress or appearance or what the outside world thought. Arno said, "A mask would be best. You understand what I'm saying?"

"I've been wearing one my entire life," Kirra replied.

"You're different from most of the Threes you'll find inside that company," Dell said. "And it's not just your looks. You're smart, and you're intensely aware. Whatever you do, you're going to stand out."

"The ones who would give a limb to add a plus to their gradient, they're potential enemies," Arno said.

"They'll assume you're after bigger game," Dell said.

"Which makes you someone to quash, eradicate, dispose of as fast as possible," Arno said.

"To them I show the mask," Kirra said, understanding.

"Bland, calm, totally untouchable," Dell agreed.

"Don't try to make friends," Arno said. "Don't react when they offer their version of verbal knives."

"Let the men protect you," Dell said.

Kirra disliked that intensely. "I can protect myself."

"You probably can," Arno said. "But let the men do it anyway."

So, she studied and she learned and she flat aced her

unofficial exams. Four times during that period, Kirra met with her boss-to-be. Boaz, the company's divisional director, and Arno were clearly friends. Kirra's time with the elegantly dressed manager always followed a lunch where the two men returned slightly glazed of eye and smiling. But there was nothing humorous in the way Boaz quizzed her. He was clearly stressed by her coming entry into his group, and his questions probed deep. Yet by the third session he was convinced she could do what was required. He and Arno then began instructing her in the true purpose of her job.

She was being prepped to steal. Which Kirra had assumed all along.

The company owned and operated almost a third of the city-state's hydroponics farms and food-processing facilities. And two of Florian's largest distilleries. And a major factory producing pharmaceuticals.

Five trucks of food, two of booze, one of drugs. Four times each year. Kirra's job was to make them disappear. As far as the company's records were concerned, those items never existed. Factory records, transport, warehouse, right down the line. Poof. Gone.

Arno waited until the last day to finally ask the question that had been hanging in the office air. "Are you going to be OK with this?"

"Yes."

Her immediate response seemed to reveal a tension he and Dell had both been carrying. Arno said, "I'm not talking about your first day. Elder Barret told you this is a three-year stint, correct?"

Kirra nodded. "She said it might be four."

Dell said, "There are risks involved."

Kirra had become accustomed to the way those two traded off each other. Emphasizing the importance of any topic. Especially when Quinn appeared in the background. Watchful. Silent. Like now. She replied, "There are risks in breathing."

"A third of all profits from this venture flow back to your clan," Arno said.

She found it curious that he would find it necessary to

mention this. "Barret said this as well." And a tenth of these proceeds would go to her. The elder had wanted Kirra to be rewarded. Prepare her for the day of liberation. Three years, four, she would wait. Happily. It was almost real now. Some mornings on the transit ride to Arno's office, she could taste it.

Arno said, "These dangers will most likely increase with time."

They had both repeatedly stressed this. And how Kirra needed to keep a watchful eye on any signs this was happening. "Piece of cake."

Company records were maintained in thirty-day segments. Arno and Boaz had decided on holding off their first trial run until Kirra had been imbedded for two full cycles. Her arrival was easily explained: The company was shifting to a new accounting system. This was where Kirra's training had been most intense. Her job was to serve as an additional assistant to the director during the transition. Boaz let it be known that he hoped Kirra would prove a solid enough temp to be rewarded with full-time employment.

The initial fifty days went well enough. Very long hours. Sullen to hostile co-workers. Especially after some of Kirra's male colleagues began clustering like flies around honey.

Kirra could not decide which group, her new female foes or those men, made her feel lonelier.

Even so, Kirra experienced secret moments of pleasure so intense they felt explosive. The work was both challenging and exhilarating. Time after time, she became so involved in what she was doing that the exterior world melted away. The fact that her true duties remained clandestine, utterly unseen by everyone except her boss and Arno and Dell, carried an unexpected side effect. Often during the long commutes Kirra found herself bonding with Quinn. She silently wondered if the assassin melded so easily with shadows because it was necessary for his work, or because it came naturally. She eventually decided he actually liked moving through hidden ways. As if the act fed a mysterious component of his nature.

Kirra took her midday breaks in a park three blocks from the offices. The buildings were uniformly designed and somewhat similar to the Stretch. Only here the exteriors were colorfully tiled, and their courtyards dressed with fountains and paving stones and blooming shrubs in matching planters. The park where she ate lunch contained a small lake with a central fountain. The lake was rimmed by a walking path. Further back were benches set within tight clusters of trees. The setting was pleasant and fragrant and as groomed as the people who strolled the graveled paths. This was a world removed from the Stretch. A universe. Kirra found two benches which were almost hidden, allowing her to watch the passers-by and remain unseen.

Birds transplanted from distant Earth flew and sang from the branches overhead. She knew their names from childhood lessons, robin and swift and thrush and skylark and wren and the occasional hummingbird. Sometimes the difference between her new existence in the Fourth Ward and the Stretch was simply too much. Great lonely waves rose up and threatened to crush her, surging currents of all she did not have and probably never would. A job where she could grow and thrive, one that was not founded upon her ability to walk dark ways. A life she could truly call her own. A man. And love. Whatever love was.

She often thought about the clan in such hard moments. Kirra watched couples stroll around the lake, saw others sprawl on blankets and laugh and chatter and flirt, and thought about people she knew in the Stretch. Good people in their grim way, who walked with a listless shuffle, weighed down by work and exhaustion, who had given up on any prospect of knowing a better life. Or hope.

Whenever those bleak moments struck, her solace came in the same way it had since childhood. Diddybirds fluttered down to perch alongside, their fore-claws reaching out as if asking to help. Kirra always responded by offering them food, and they always accepted. But she became increasingly convinced they were merely being polite. In truth they were asking for something else. What that might be, she had no idea. Only that these shy and skittish alien creatures made her feel better. Almost whole.

The diddybirds vanished whenever passers-by approached her bench. Even feathered birds caused them to flee. But so long as the dark moods held her, they always returned.

On longer days, Kirra often didn't reach the Fourth Ward transport depot until well after the last Fifth Ward vehicle had departed. Elder Barret and Arno had both fronted her cash. A lot of it, by Kirra's standards. Even so, it felt like losing blood to pay for a private hire to take the last long leg of her homeward journey.

Worst about the commute, though, was the depot itself. The Fourth Ward main depot was well removed from Kirra's safety net. The station held three buildings set in a wide paved area where passengers were discharged and collected. The passenger terminal was a vast, dirty place with uncomfortable seats. It and the adjoining café were generally closed when Kirra most needed shelter. The third building was a massive warehouse where transports were stored and repaired. Late at night, when the café was shut and the terminal empty and Kirra felt most exposed, drivers who clustered by the repair depot's bay doors tracked her every move.

She confessed her fears to Elder Barret, who immediately demanded a meeting with Arno. Kirra could not find the words to express what it meant to have the clan chief take her concerns so seriously. Not that it helped.

Arno was courteous and heard them both out. As did his assistant Dell. What Quinn thought of it Kirra had no idea. She had never heard the shadow-man utter a sound. Arno told them, "We are looking. You know we are. But in living memory the housing market has never been this tight. And it's going to stay that way until Florian completes work on the Seventh Ring."

"No questions are asked about your situation because many other young staffers are forced to live in Fifth Ward," Dell said.

"A room," Elder Barret insisted. "A space shared with other young women."

"You know that can't happen," Arno replied. "Kirra doesn't work normal hours. She can't, not and do what we need."

Dell said, "Some of the most important components of our plan require her after-hours routine to go unobserved."

"Say the authorities catch wind of our project. Say they start sniffing around. And here is this lovely young lady whose longest days are timed to when the loads go missing." Arno shook his head. "You don't need to look any further to know what real danger looks like."

"We're scouring the Fourth Ward," Dell said.

"And the Third," Arno said. "Though I personally think that's stretching our credibility. Even a Third Ward studio costs more than a woman of her status could possibly earn."

Elder Barret said, "So send her private transport."

"No." Arno and Dell together. Dell added, "Sooner or later someone is bound to notice."

"A lovely young woman leaving her cubicle and slipping into a private hire? Night after night? We're asking for Kirra to be brought in for questioning."

Elder Barret didn't like it any more than Kirra. She was sour and worried in defeat, and departed with the command, "Look harder."

The nine days leading up to their first theft, Kirra did not leave before midnight. Except for the commutes, she actually liked these run-throughs. Far more than the tampering of records and rerouting of goods was required. Kirra served as the fulcrum upon which everything depended. She loved the responsibility, her first truly vital role. Success relied on smooth actions in tight sequence. These practice runs granted them the opportunity to erase weaknesses. They became a team.

But her late-night transfers at the depot became increasingly tense, the drivers calling to her, the words and their attitudes frightening.

That final night Kirra insisted on leaving early enough to arrive at the depot and catch the last Fifth Ward transport. No matter what her boss said, she watched the clock and when it came time Kirra raced out.

As usual for such late-night transports, she was the only passenger. Three times during the ride, the driver used his commlink. Talking softly and watching her in the overhead mirror.

Twice the driver halted at empty stops. And lingered. Kirra knew at gut level what was happening.

There was no way she could make the last ride home.

Despite the hour, Kirra contacted Arno. He was closer than Elder Barret and his reach went further. Midway through her recap, he demanded, "Where are you?"

"Three stops from the depot." She saw the driver observing her, and watched as he accelerated past the next stop. "He's just raced past the shelter. Two stops now. And he's speeding up."

Arno muted the link, then came back and told her, "Quinn is leaving now."

"What about a private hire?"

"If there's any trouble, they'll just send the driver away. Listen to me. You stay on the line."

Her hand shook so hard she dropped the communicator. She leaned down, picked it up, heard Arno shouting. "I'm here."

"Soon as the transport halts, you get out and find a place in the open. Stay in the lights."

There was such a palpable tension inside the transport Kirra could actually taste it. Like the charred remnants of hope. She clenched the commlink with both hands and felt her world close in on the sheer intensity of this moment. As if the entire world was conspiring against her. It had been like this since alien lifeforms had murdered her mother and father. Orphaning Kirra when she was just a few hours old. So long as she had accepted the clan's cage, she had remained protected. But one step beyond those confines, one brief glimpse of different life, and now this.

When the transport slowed and entered the vast empty station, Kirra knew Quinn would not make it in time.

As if in confirmation, the driver caught her eye in the rear-view mirror. And he smiled.

The driver did not stop in front of the depot. Instead, he drove straight through an open bay door and entered the repair garage. Nine, ten, eleven men stood around the vast space. So many Kirra could not count, not with her heart yammering in her ears and all her muscles jerking in pure unadulterated fear.

The driver cut the motor and half turned in his seat. His grin revealed yellowed, uneven teeth. "End of the line, pretty lady."

Kirra dropped the commlink into her pocket, lowered herself into a crouch, and gripped the forward seat's metal frame with all the strength in her body.

The driver opened all four doors and called, "Little help here. The lady's not cooperating."

The man who entered was so huge he had to crouch and twist his upper body to manage the doorway. He was not muscular so much as a giant slab of human flesh. He looked down at Kirra and smiled like the driver. "Good."

He gripped the chair back she was using as refuge and ripped it from the floor. The metal bolts shattered in a series of loud pops. Kirra did not release her hold in time. She was flung forward with the chair and landed hard. Some component of the broken seat stabbed her in the ribs. She cried out in pain.

The man gripped her hair and wrenched her back, the force so brutal he could well have snapped her neck if Kirra had not released the seatback.

When Kirra screamed a second time, he jammed an oily rag in her mouth, stuffing it down so far she gagged.

He flung her over one shoulder and carried her from the transport. He ignored her struggle, took three steps from the transport, and made a slow circle, giving her a good look at all the grinning men.

He asked, "Where are we doing this?"

That was when she really screamed.

The fact that her shout was utterly soundless only added to its internal force. A mental barrier became shattered by this silent yell. She actually felt it happen. One moment she was isolated and helpless and being carried by this animal.

The next, *she joined.*

The bonding was so instantaneous and complete and visceral Kirra felt it with every fiber of her being.

Now the scream had a focus.

Help me.

The first response was a sound, soft as whispering death.

Kirra heard the flutter of wings.

One of the men shouted. Another.

Now it was the men who screamed.

Hundreds of silent diddybirds swarmed into the depot, so many the overhead lights flickered and danced. Gone was the alien birds' shy and skittish nature. These creatures were made savage by the same fearsome rage that filled Kirra's being with purpose.

Her rage.

The giant dropped Kirra to the concrete floor. She landed hard, taking the impact on her fractured rib and the side of her head. Kirra scarcely felt it.

Her lifelong fury now possessed a cloud of wings and talons and predatory beaks. The men screamed high and fought their way outside, or tried to. The diddybirds swarmed, tore, attacked.

Killed.

The giant slammed into the side of the transport, blindly searching for the door. Kirra could not see his face—so many birds encircled his head and upper body. He roared and swatted and struggled. Then his strength gave way. He slumped down beside her, sobbing now, then moaning, then silent.

Kirra waited until the wings were the loudest sound. That and her own rasping breaths. As she gasped her way up and crouched on all fours, a single thought took full hold of her brain.

All this had to remain secret.

Her secret.

She shot out two messages, meager and silent shouts. The first was, Thank you for saving my life.

The second contained just one word. Flee.

Soon as the thought formed, they were gone. Poof. All of them.

The night was utterly still as Kirra groaned to her feet. Her head and ribs throbbed terribly. Each breath stabbed her, every moan.

The floor was stained dark and very slick and covered with gore. Kirra's limbs trembled so hard she could only move by reaching for the next available support. But the stench was as terrible as the sight. She had to get outside.

She could only use one arm. Lifting the other was agony. It took forever to stagger into the night, but she made it.

Then she tripped over an inert body and fell face-first into a warm black puddle.

Kirra screamed with the pain, or tried to, only to choke on the mess now coating her face and hair.

She sensed the diddybirds returning, called back by this new calamity. She choked and coughed and spat and yelled aloud, "Stay away!" Or at least she tried to.

The birds vanished into the night.

And just in time, for an arriving vehicle's headlights illuminated the brutal scene.

Quinn rushed up, hesitated, then took a firm grip of the arm not holding her ribs. "Are you hurt?"

Suddenly she was trembling so hard she could scarcely choke out, "A little."

"Is any of this your blood?"

She shook her head, and winced at the agony. She would have fallen again had it not been for his strength. She had none of her own.

He started back toward the vehicle, their every step a squishing tread through the encircling blood. Quinn stopped twice to inspect the inert bodies. Or what was left of them. "Where are you hurt?"

Opening her mouth to speak only heightened the horrid taste. "Ribs. Head."

He eased her down on the rear hold's floor, then stripped off his jacket and used it to support her head. "Kirra, who did this?"

But she was already gone.

TWO

Eva Fourier

When Eva was four years old, her mother's bedtime reading became the exobiology primer that she had authored. Even then, Eva knew it was a strange way to send her daughter to sleep. But Maxine was a very strange woman indeed.

Eva's mother lived for her work. Maxine ran the only lab in what the world's human inhabitants referred to as the frontier zone. This solitary research center was the only permitted base from which the human race might study the original planetary inhabitants. This agreement governing humankind's place and restrictions had been agreed upon a thousand years earlier, and was not some mere piece of paper. Maxine drilled the facts into her daughter along with the exobiology text. Throughout the entire Stellar Empire, this treaty between humans and the planet's original inhabitants was the first and only of its kind. So important it gave their planet its name.

Other than these lab scientists and technicians, the only contact Treaty's human inhabitants had with the planet's original life forms was a glimpse of the occasional diddybird. Most people who called Treaty home had no interest in what lay beyond the outer ring. The aliens had their world, humankind had another. End of story, for all save a very few like Eva's mother.

Maxine was naturally thrilled when her only child's mathematical abilities came to the fore. She took a smug pride in discussing this with her own mother, who could hardly add.

Maxine worked in cycles of ten days away at her frontier zone lab, the only such outpost permitted on Treaty, then five days at their apartment. Her five days back in their Second

Ward home were mostly spent writing up lab reports and meeting with government officials. Throughout her childhood Eva repeatedly asked what was out there beyond the city's mines, where the treaty territory ended and true alien life began. But Maxine never said.

Every question the young Eva posed regarding life beyond the city's boundaries was met with silence. Such discussions were forbidden, was Maxine's only response. When Eva begged to go out with her mother, witness this second world for herself, Maxine's answer was the same. If Eva was truly interested, she would need to complete her training as an exobiologist and join Maxine at the lab. The right to enter alien territory had to be earned.

After a time, Eva stopped asking.

While Maxine was away, Eva lived with her grandmother. Salma's apartment was two floors above theirs. Maxine and her mother did not agree on almost anything. But they maintained a shaky truce because of Eva. Maxine's only alternative was to give Eva up for adoption. Which neither woman wanted.

Eva adored her grandmother. Salma was a very difficult woman in her own right, strong and mostly silent and stern and as perceptive as a cop walking her beat—which Salma once had been. At least, that was how Salma described her former occupation. Eva knew Salma's true position had been deputy head of the city-state's interior guards, known by inhabitants of the outer wards as the Black Watch. Maxine made a point of describing how she had lost her father, another senior officer, in the same skirmish that had wounded Salma and eventually forced her into early retirement. Eva's grandmother always left the room whenever Maxine talked about that incident. Whenever she was alone with her grandmother, Eva never saw any reason to mention the subject. The last thing Eva wanted was to make her grandmother sad.

The one instance when Eva asked her mother about her father, Maxine replied that she detested lying. So Eva should never ask again. Because that was how Maxine would respond the next time and every time after that. She would lie. Her grandmother was equally silent, saying merely this was a topic she had to leave to her daughter, for better or worse.

When it came to weights and speech and distance and time, most planets within the Stellar Empire held to two systems—their own, and what was known as Earth Standard. Treaty's situation was unique in this way as well. Its rotational day and solar year were so close to humanity's homeworld that the original settlers adopted Earth Standard for almost everything, time and metric measurements and much else besides. Which made things much easier, because this Earth-based secondary system was used for all interplanetary communications.

Citizens of Florian were normally assigned their official gradient on their eighteenth birthday. During their nineteenth year on rare occasions. Twenty, well, hardly ever. Eva had never known anyone who waited past then. Never heard of such a thing.

Eva's mother was naturally a One.

When her eighteenth birthday came and went, and Eva was not assigned a gradient, her mother's moans and accusations became so insufferable Eva waited until Maxine transferred back to her frontier zone lab and then moved in permanently with her grandmother. The transition went so smoothly Eva wondered afterwards why she had not done it years back.

While transferring her belongings upstairs, Eva discovered her grandmother's gradient status by way of a framed document hidden at the back of her closet. Salma had originally been assigned a flat Two, neither good nor bad, and rarely holding any potential for a raise in grade. The framed certificate raised her to One Plus, and described some heroic effort that had saved lives and perhaps the city-state of Florian itself. At the bottom were the Regent's insignia and signature. Eva never mentioned what she had found. There was no need.

Months passed, and still no word came from the authorities. Salma became the rock upon which Eva clung. The older woman insisted that all was well, and with patience everything would become clear. Just the same, this absence of a gradient left Eva feeling bodiless. Her early teenage years had been framed by sports and studies and friends and the occasional wild night. All that was lost to her now, the friends gradually drifting into lives and activities barred to her. Former acquaintances who considered social standing important all shied away. She could not go for higher studies. Most professions were cut off. Opportunities, almost none. Travel, social life, the chance to fit in or belong . . . with each passing day and no gradient, Eva mentally envisioned another door slamming shut. All such avenues were bound by the same decrees that established and maintained the gradients. The silence made for a sad, lonely, and futile existence.

Her grandmother remained as she had always been, calm and stoic and highly aware. She did not discount the utterly tragic nature of Eva's empty hours. Instead, she offered an alternative. A dear friend, a colleague from her days on the force. A man who owed Salma a lifetime debt. He had led the division known as forensics, which Salma explained meant the gathering of evidence pointing to a crime. This man's specialty was something called forensic accounting. Eva had always loved numbers. Why not see if this held an interest?

The man was stuffy and pedantic and had an irritating nasal voice and tended to sniff with disdain at her work. He dribbled dandruff. His fingernails were long as broken talons and stained yellow. He wore the same clothes for days on end. And he smelled. Eva wondered how the man had survived long enough to retire.

Just the same, the man and his work became Eva's lifeline.

Forensic accounting was a simple term for a highly complex series of actions. Eva learned accounting, auditing, and investigative techniques, all aimed at detecting and analyzing cases of fraud and other financial crimes.

She ate it up. This was not merely studying numbers. Her lessons went much, much further. She was granted an opportunity to *apply* her abilities. After mastering some particularly difficult lesson, she would lie awake for hours, imagining that she had been handed a sniper's weapon and told, go hunt.

Added to this was a very special connection she made on her own.

Soon after beginning her lessons with the dandruff prince, Eva entered the apartment building's gym to discover a man working his way through a complex series of combat movements. Eva began her own routine and observed. The man was quite old and on the small size, which made his silken yet deadly smoothness all the more enticing. When he paused, Eva approached and introduced herself and begged for him to teach her. The man reluctantly agreed, but only if she promised to give the absolute best she had to offer. Every day.

This new instructor was not kind so much as infinitely polite, chiding his new pupil in softly spoken terms, correcting her with utmost care, and reducing her to a sweaty puddle. He never offered his name. All she learned about her new teacher was that he had recently moved into their building. His near-daily instructions left Eva sore and bruised, limp and groaning. The man instructed Eva to call him sensei, or teacher. He was patient, so long as Eva gave her utmost. Which she did. After all, there was nothing else demanding her attention except her lessons in forensics.

Though he never said anything, the enigmatic teacher must have found some approval in her work. After six months together, the sensei no longer referred to what they were doing as self-defense. At some point they had become lessons in hand-to-hand combat. Eva loved hearing that word, *combat*. It suited how she felt, what she needed.

It did not make up for all she had lost. But still.

She read voraciously. Her grandmother helped with this as well, suggesting books that extended Eva's awareness back to Earth's earliest days. Eva became transported in place and time, so involved she often became blind to the passage of days and nights, devouring texts instead of food, or sleep.

Visits with her mother increasingly became little more than hours spent in the company of some distant relative. Salma demanded Eva meet with Maxine at least once every home-leave. Eva complained bitterly, but knew her grandmother was right to insist.

On days when she was freed from lessons, Eva and her grandmother walked. Together they explored all five inner wards, then went even farther, crossing the wasteland with a guide, out to the mines dominating the city-state's farthest region. Treaty possessed rare elements that were found nowhere else in the human Stellar Empire. Eva did not enjoy these treks out to study vast gouges in the earth, or observe men and machines labor at their seemingly impossible tasks. But her grandmother insisted. These mines were the source of Florian's wealth. Eva needed to witness, and seek to understand.

Sometimes during those months of waiting, Eva woke in the night, wondering at the silken ease with which she had adapted to solitude. As if she had gradually cast aside the attitudes of childhood, elements that had shaped her according to other people's expectations and demands. On the one hand, she despised this vacuum, on the other, she thrived. As if only within this enforced waiting could she become her true self. A woman destined to walk solitary ways.

Three days before her twenty-first birthday, Eva stood by her bedroom window and watched dawn spread over a different world. One where Eva had no place, no destiny. She overlooked the second city wall, each one extending the state's reach ever further into alien territory. The planetary treaty limited human habitation to one site on each of the planet's four continents, plus a fifth and much smaller island colony serving as both refinery and interstellar port. Though the spaceport and frontier lab were officially owned and operated by all four city-states, Florian was the closest. Unofficially, Florian's ruling Council held iron-clad authority over both.

Florian's mines were located far to her left, beyond the outer boroughs where most miners resided. Those boroughs were known to residents as the Stretch. Eva had no idea why—a very odd name by any standards. She had visited taverns and music halls in the Stretch several times, back in the era when she assumed the world was hers for the taking. Before all portals and opportunities became part of her very own forbidden zone. Back when she had her pick of friends, and men, and avenues for shaping her future.

The men had stopped calling months ago.

She had still not been assigned a gradient.

Eva survived by doing her best to ignore it all. That and how her grandmother continued to assure her in terse, mysterious yet definite terms that things were as they should be. Salma's response became a mantra. *In time all this will become clear. A purpose will be revealed. Your job now is to grow, learn, adapt.*

Eva's world remained tightly focused upon the avenues open to her. Her rage fueled the daily workouts with the enigmatic teacher, who had added knives and spears and batons to her repertoire.

And her studies with the smelly old man also continued to accelerate. So much, in fact, that the week before her invisible birthday, Eva sat the forensic accountancy exams, the youngest person in the hall by more than a decade.

She was dressing for her self-defense lesson when her grandmother knocked, entered, and declared, "Lessons are cancelled. We're going to celebrate. You passed your forensics exam with flying colors."

Eva's days all began by searching for the certificates that still had not arrived. "How do you know?"

"I know." Which was a typically enigmatic response. "How does the Crillon sound?"

"Isn't that, like, incredibly expensive?"

"Outrageously so," Salma agreed. She swept her gaze over Eva's form. "But first some shopping is in order."

Eva's grandmother rarely shopped for more than the necessary elements like food and the occasional wine. She never mentioned money. She had never offered Eva a regular stipend. Just the same, whenever Eva asked for something, Salma's usual response was to hand her a payment ring and the instruction to "hold yourself to what I might consider reasonable." They lived in a pleasant apartment in the upscale area known as Second Ward. And when she took Eva anywhere, like this morning, she was known by everyone and greeted like visiting royalty.

Dress, hair, makeup. Finally they entered an elegant store selling women's fashions. Salma told her granddaughter she was free to choose, so long as Eva remained within very firm boundaries. "You are graduating into adulthood. You need to look the part."

Eva selected an outfit that called to her from across the room. Jacket and slacks, navy in color, high collared, cloth buttons that angled their way up the jacket from waist to neck, with hand stitching on her right trouser-leg and right sleeve that fashioned a dragon from threads one shade paler than the outfit. She knew it would be outrageously expensive, and as she spun in front of the mirror Eva waited for her grandmother to demand she select something they could actually afford. Instead, Salma's only response was to say, "Now another outfit in grey, and one pastel, and shoes to match."

Salma instructed the salespeople to deliver all their purchases except the navy outfit, which she told Eva to wear. They left the shop and walked farther along the city-state's most exclusive shopping street, a place Eva had seldom visited, past the spa which had done her hair and nails and face, and settled into a café's outdoor table. Salma angled her chair to watch the fountain creating a liquid melody to this remarkable day.

Eva felt partially disembodied. A hard breeze, a loud noise, and she might become separated from her body and this place. Just float off into alien territory, which this most certainly was. For almost three years her world had shrunk further and further, down to where her daily existence was defined by two near-strangers. One granting an outlet to her rage, the other to her mind. And now this.

Her grandmother waited until their drinks were served, then said, "I want you to pay careful attention."

"All right."

"No, not like that." Salma wrapped her knuckles on the table. "Focus, young lady. This is important." She must have seen what she wanted, for she said, "We're going to meet a former associate."

"I thought we were having lunch."

"This is part of your celebration. If you want it to be."

"I don't understand."

"The gentleman's name is Tanner. He owes me. He . . ." Salma revealed a rare moment of indecision. "I can only take you so far. I have opened this door, but whether you actually enter depends on what happens. What you *make* happen."

Salma halted further discussion by catching the passing waiter and rising from her chair. "We don't want to be late."

They took city transport to the First Ward. Other than a

solitary museum to humanity's earliest days on Treaty, every original structure had been torn down and replaced by palaces and other grand structures. They got off just a couple of stops removed from the Regent's palace and entered a building whose doors were embossed with a shield Eva did not recognize.

Salma showed her ID and badge three times, at the door and to the receptionist and again when they entered the top floor's antechamber. A young man noted both their names, then led them directly into a large functional office with a spectacular view across the Royal Plaza.

If the man occupying the overly large desk was a friend of Salma's, he had a strange way of showing it. He was beak-nosed, tall even when seated, utterly bald, and possessed the coldest eyes Eva had ever seen. He waited until they were seated opposite him, then asked Salma, "What have you told her?"

"Nothing, as per your instructions," she replied. "Which I still think are ludicrous in the extreme."

It was like a pair of gun-barrels swiveling in her direction. "Young lady, your grandmother thinks you have what it takes to enter the federal service. I have counted Salma among my most trusted allies for over thirty years. She has never been known to make a grave error in judgment." His features tightened from forehead to collar. "I do hope you won't prove to be a blemish on this otherwise perfect record."

Eva had no idea how to respond.

He barked, "*Well?*"

His impatient ire shoved Eva out of her utterly futile existence. She marveled at this remarkable sense of distance. Freed from the glum helplessness, the rage, the terror of lost days, the futility, the loneliness. And *see.*

He opened his mouth to snap a second time, but Salma halted him with, "Give her a moment to assess."

Assess. Which was precisely what she felt happening. Eva's internal distancing granted her an opportunity to watch the swirl of events that had defined her life coalesce, reshape, tighten, and become . . .

She turned to her grandmother. "You arranged for the lessons in combat?"

Salma shook her head, smiled thinly, and pointed across the desk.

Eva met Tanner's gaze. His frigid hostility did not touch her. "Not just the combat. Everything comes down to you, doesn't it. All the horrid days of waiting. Because of you."

Salma said, "Tell us why."

"You wanted me to vanish in plain sight. My existence, my friends, my entire world has been stripped away. I didn't do anything, made no move that might draw attention. My friends, even my own mother, they all pulled away . . ." She stifled the rage that would have emerged with the words, *because of you*. What she had endured, the lonely pain; nothing good could have come from releasing her fury. When her momentary cold detachment was restored, she continued, "I can be inserted into whatever life you need, and no one will notice when I vanish."

The man's inspection required him to tilt his head, check her from a different perspective. All he said was, "Well, well."

"Told you," Salma said.

"Indeed." To Eva, he said, "Young lady, I am director of FSA, the Financial Services Authority. Have you ever heard of us?"

"Sorry. No."

"Which is precisely how we prefer to exist. It is the only way we can operate successfully. The FSA's investigative branch forms the smallest division within the city-state's police and Guards. We operate in the shadows. There are no accolades for a lifetime of service, no medals, no status."

Eva knew he waited for some sort of response. Probably some expression of gratitude, respect, whatever. But just then she was too busy reviewing what she had just learned to care. "Why the secrecy?"

Her question caught him off guard. "I beg your pardon?"

"What is it about this work that made it necessary for you to erase my place in society?" She shifted slightly, including Salma in her question. "You're saying these new duties require me to hunt the numbers trail and track down bad guys. Why couldn't I have done that as I was, gradient at eighteen, normal higher studies, friends, the life you denied me?"

Tanner shifted uncomfortably. "The answer to that is highly confidential. You must earn the right to such information."

Which was exactly the sort of response she might have expected from her mother. But before the bitterness could be shaped into words, Salma barked, "Stop with this nonsense! How many people have successfully made it through this *ridiculous* process of yours? One! And she deserves to know why this is happening!"

Now the man's anger was directed elsewhere. "I absolutely forbid you to speak of this!"

"Climb down off your ladder. You are not my superior and you never have been." Salma's chair could no longer hold her fury. She rose and towered over the man. "When you are ready to address my granddaughter in a proper manner, if that is even remotely possible, you may contact us."

He jerked to his feet, a marionette lifted by outrage. "I am waiting for her response!"

"What utter rubbish. You haven't even made her a formal offer." She stormed toward the door. "Come, Eva. This meeting is adjourned."

The First Ward building housing the Crillon hotel and restaurant was one of the city-state's tallest, with multiple floors given over to guests of the state. Uniformed guards served as doorkeepers. Eva had been in the park fronting the Crillon multiple times. She had always been fascinated by the solemn parade of wealthy and powerful, the limos and the servants and the glittering fashions on display. Never in her entire life did she imagine one day this would be her destination.

They walked. Down the long promenade, past the three fountains anchoring the central plaza, across the park, and over to where the doormen offered them a white-gloved salute. The receptionist checked their names on the penthouse register, then signaled to yet another guard, who escorted them into the elevator and accompanied them up, where they were handed over to the restaurant's maître d'. They were led to a table on the broad veranda, sheltered from the sun by square parasols larger than Salma's sitting room. Vents in the stone-tiled floor blew soft whispers of cool air.

Eva knew her grandmother waited for the outburst. As in, you and Tanner did this to me? Destroyed my life? Caged me for three years? Split me away from my friends, my world? How could you do such a thing to your own flesh and blood?

Eva remained silent mostly because she knew exactly how her grandmother would respond. If Eva had failed to make the grade at any point, all this masquerade would have vanished. Her gradient would be assigned, her life restored. The same could happen now. If she wanted. All she needed was to say the word, refuse the offer, and . . .

That was the crux. The real purpose behind this elegant, expensive outing. From the clothes she now wore to this very moment. Seated in one of the planet's finest restaurants, so high she could see the yellowish-ocher horizon where Florian ended and the alien world took hold. Her grandmother's intention was not merely to offer her a job. It was to show her a different life. If she was willing.

Eva had no idea what she wanted. Nor, interestingly enough, did she feel any pressure to decide.

Her grandmother and Tanner might think they could cage her again, only in a different arena.

Ha.

For the moment, though, what she mostly felt was thrilled beyond words.

Become a secret agent in an authority most people didn't even know existed? Go after bad guys by following the numbers trail? Live a double life?

This was a role she was made for. It suited her as well as the new outfit. Better.

Eva let her grandmother order for them both. She did not recognize most of the items, or the descriptions their waiter gave as to how the dishes would be prepared. But the lack of understanding did not disturb her. She felt a growing sense of calm, a genuine thrill with her view of the days ahead. The yellow-red cloud on the horizon beckoned to her, a haze of mysteries she might spend a lifetime getting to know and understand. Behind her, on the terrace's other side, was a different cloud, grey and rich with the smoke and debris rising from Florian's mines. All those tables were filled, while either side of where they sat the places remained empty. As if most of the restaurant's patrons were made uncomfortable by this glimpse of the world beyond humanity's control.

Late at night, when the cage's confines left Eva struggling to find her next breath, she would rise and read the news feeds. Drawing a feeble glimpse of the world that had been denied to her. It hurt more than it helped. But she could not look away. She couldn't.

She knew Florian was bursting at the seams. Every two hundred years or so, a new wall had been erected, each time almost doubling Florian's size. The work was enormously difficult and always cost lives. But it was going to happen again, and soon. The Regent had spoken. Population pressures created risks to Florian's stability. And yet, despite the royal decree now set in place, a group of Florian's most powerful citizens continued to object. And their spokesperson, the most vehement of the voices, was Maxine. Her mother.

When the waiter departed and they were alone, Eva asked without turning from the incredible view, "Why hasn't my mother ever invited me out to her lab?"

"That is an excellent question."

"I would really like to see the frontier zone for myself."

"Sometimes I wonder what your mother actually sees beyond her microscopes and lab equipment," Salma replied. "I asked her to let you make that journey. Many times."

"And?"

"She replied that you had to earn the privilege."

"Exactly what she told me as a child."

Salma shook her head. "Maxine baffles me almost as much as she infuriates."

"I've read about tours," Eva said. "Can I take one?"

"Of course."

"They're very expensive."

Salma smiled. "Something Tanner forgot to mention. Now that you've been officially accepted into the FSA ranks—"

"Have I really?"

Her smile grew broader still. "My dear, you are the prize Tanner has been hunting and hoping for. He just can't bring himself to say it. In any case, you will now receive a recruit's backpay covering the past three years of your . . ."

"Imprisonment."

"Transition," Salma corrected. "You have enough to take several such tours. And dress for the occasion."

Eva knew an electric desire to leap up, dance her way around the terrace, shriek her joy to the skies. But if her grandmother could remain placidly calm, then, OK. She asked, "Will you come with me?"

Salma's smile vanished. "Thank you, no. You are not the only one wounded by your mother's antics."

Eva thought that Salma had found an interesting way to describe her own daughter's behavior. Antics. Her grandmother's sorrow was briefly revealed.

Eva waited until Salma's placid calm was restored, then asked, "Do I have a gradient?"

"Most certainly. You are now a provisional One."

Eva mouthed a silent wow.

"You have earned it," Salma assured her. "But as far as the outside world is concerned, you have barely scraped by with a flat Two."

"The same as you."

"How did . . .The plaque. You sneak."

"You should have hidden it better," Eva said.

Their first course arrived. The food was delicious. But as she ate, Eva was jolted by a sudden realization, more an impression than something that formed itself into words. She had a momentary glimpse at how hard it was for her grandmother to smile. What Eva had herself endured over the past months became a portal through which she glimpsed the avenue up ahead. The danger. The risk. The mysteries and crimes and criminals she would now investigate.

Eva remained focused on her plate and the yellow-ocher cloud to her right until the food was gone. When she set down her utensils and looked across the table, her grandmother observed her with a deep and knowing gaze.

She said the first thing that came to mind. "Tell me about my father."

Salma nodded to the waiter when he returned to sweep away their empty plates. Silent.

Eva spoke again, wanting to emphasize her desire to have yet another mystery revealed. "You and I both know my mother will never tell me anything. If I'm old enough for you to insert me into some secret agency, I'm old enough to know who he is."

"Who he was," Salma replied. "Darin died soon after you were born."

"Your father was deputy director of our only frontier zone lab," Salma went on. "His duties involved maintaining and supporting their ranks of communicators."

"What exactly does that word mean?" Eva asked. "Communicators."

"It's a highly confidential part of the lab's functioning," Salma replied. "I probably should not know about it at all. May I continue?"

"Please."

"From the very start, your mother experienced an extremely difficult pregnancy. When she was three months along, the doctors insisted she return home, giving up all lab duties and her role as director."

"She must have hated that."

"You cannot imagine." Salma's expression turned grim. "I was still recovering from my wounds, and moved in. Maxine was going quietly berserk. She called it imprisonment for all the wrong reasons."

When her grandmother went silent, Eva realized, "Mother wanted to halt her pregnancy?"

"We will not discuss this again. Ever. Do you understand?"

She forced herself to lean back and resume a semblance of calm. "How long was she kept away from her lab?"

"Almost a full year." Salma stared out the restaurant's boundary wall, lost to hard memories. Far in the distance, the yellowish haze rose so high it blanketed the horizon completely. Eva knew the so-called humanization process cleansed the city-state's atmosphere of airborne alien life. But she had no real idea what that actually meant, other than how its study was more interesting to her mother than bearing and raising a child.

Finally, Salma turned back and said, "I'm sorry. Where was I?"

"I was born."

"Seven more months passed before the doctors allowed Maxine to resume her duties part-time. Only then did she discover that Darin had decided to leave both her and the child he had never met. Your father had fallen in love with another woman at the lab. The affair had been going on for some time—years apparently—but while Maxine was away Darin's lover had become pregnant. She was due to give birth any day. A girl." Salma resumed her study of the horizon. "When she told me, I could not decide whether Maxine was more distraught over Darin being unfaithful, or that he was leaving her for a lowly lab technician. I never felt more distant from your mother than at that very moment."

Eva silently shaped her late father's name. Another scientist, working in the frontier zone, his duties still confidential twenty-one years after his death. "So my mother kicked them out of her lab?"

"She did indeed. Maxine sent the two of them packing with the next supply convoy."

"And I have a half-sister?"

"You don't. No." Salma inspected her carefully. "Are you certain you want to hear the rest?"

"Tell me. Please."

"Darin's partner went into labor on the return journey. It is a full two-day trip from the lab to Florian's outermost ring. The woman's labor started well after they passed the first day's midway point. Do you understand what that means?"

"I . . . No."

"They could not go back. Not and make it before sunset, when by treaty all traffic must be off the highway. Nor could the woman apparently endure the horrid road conditions any longer. The convoy chief was a mother herself and ordered the vehicles to halt." Salma paused, studying her granddaughter with a cop's intensity. "That is expressly forbidden, actually written into the original treaty document. Whenever a vehicle has in the past broken down and been left on the wayside, the next convoy finds no sign it ever existed. No airborne transport is allowed beyond the city-state boundaries. Shipments by sea from the other city-states to the island spaceport must follow a precisely charted route. There can be no road traffic after dark. Our life on this planet is very strictly defined."

Eva forced herself to ask. She had to get this right. "Aliens killed my father and my sister?"

"Half-sister," Salma corrected. "You must understand. Humankind was originally granted permission to remain simply because our first visitors, your mother's scientific forebears, arrived during a pandemic that threatened all alien life. We saved them, and they allowed us to remain. But only within the strictures of this unbreakable code."

Eva searched through the mental tumult and extracted the first clear question that came to mind. "But the city-states keep expanding."

"The first ships landed because their planetary survey had already revealed these massive deposits of unknown minerals. Which also explained why they went against convention and made contact with the sentient race. When the treaty was drawn up, allowing us one city-state per continent plus the island spaceport, our forebears intentionally drew the boundaries very large, allowing us space to grow. Which we have, and continue to do so." Salma gestured toward the distant yellow cloud. "But beyond the outermost wall . . . we are held to our one road, one lab, one everything."

She breathed. Again. Salma waited with her. Finally, she had no choice but ask, "What happened?"

"When the convoy halted and night fell, they broke the treaty." Salma's expression had become stonelike. Revealing the cop she once was and would always remain. "According to the few survivors, Treaty's original inhabitants attacked less than an hour after sunset. Of the convoy's eleven vehicles, only one managed to escape. Your father, his lover, their daughter, gone. The next day, rescue vehicles returned to the site. There was no sign the convoy had ever existed."

THREE
Kirra Barret

Quinn spoke softly into his commlink as he drove from the depot. The vehicle held a quiet safety, an assurance as gentle as the surrounding night. The loudest sounds were Kirra's own gasping breaths and her occasional moan. Quinn made five calls, quick conversations that Kirra tried to follow, since they were all most definitely about her. But every time she almost managed to focus, some fractured image drew her back to what had just taken place. Then it all fell apart.

He was still involved in the fifth conversation when the vehicle halted. The first words Kirra understood clearly were, "We're here."

She heard the sound of a metal gate grinding open. When Quinn started forward, Kirra moaned, all the sound she could manage. Then her terror abated, and she accepted this was not the depot, and she was safe, because an assassin was looking after her.

By this point all the liquid she had been doused by and then fell into had dried into a viscous goo that encased her entire body. Her eyes were gummed shut. Her limbs resisted every move, every breath. She was beyond uncomfortable. She needed to shift around, try and find a position to ease the pain in her chest. Her head throbbed.

She came fully awake as the metal door rumbled shut and the vehicle's rear side door opened. Kirra heard a woman say, "Oh no."

Quinn replied, "Far as I can tell, none of it is her blood."

"What a mess. How many were there?"

"Hard to say," Quinn replied. His voice was flat, calm. Untouched by what he had witnessed. "My guess, about a dozen. But it could have been more."

A long silence as the woman's weight caused the vehicle to shift slightly. "Let's get her inside."

As hands touched her, Kirra forced her lips apart and moaned, "Ribs."

The woman asked, "Did you understand that?"

"I think she's cracked some ribs. And she said something about her head."

"There's a gurney just inside the doorway." When it was just the two of them, the woman leaned in close and asked, "Your injuries are on the left or right side?"

"Left."

"Your head. Where does it hurt?"

"Back. Left."

A hand probed gently as wheels rattled over the concrete flooring. "Shifting you is going to hurt worse than anything. Can't be helped. Scream if you have to, but it will only amplify the pain." The hands felt around Kirra's neck and shoulders. Something about their assured probing actually helped. Not a lot. But some. When the gurney's wheels rattled on approach, the woman said, "Quinn, grab her ankles. Press them together. Good. When I say lift, we're going to ease her up and move her out and settle her on the gurney. One fluid motion. You ready?"

"Yes. Where is Arno?"

"Coming."

"Have you heard from Elder Barret?"

"No idea who that is. Here we go. Grab tight. One, two, three, lift."

Maybe it was good, how Kirra could not find the breath to scream. And even better how she then passed out.

Kirra woke to the sound of gurney wheels rattling over another hard floor. The sound echoed off a large empty chamber. She lay with eyes glued shut, feeling a languid ease along with the pain. The gurney halted and the woman said, "Three doors down on your right is the supply room. Bring me a cart with a pair of surgical scissors, a tube of antiseptic, gauze bandages, hospital gown, drawstring trousers, and an armload of towels. Got all that?"

"Yes," Quinn replied. "Need help with her?"

"Hmmm. Let me think. This lady somehow managed to escape a gang rape. Now a strange man wants to help strip and bathe her. How does that sound?"

"I'll go get the supplies."

"Leave them in the corridor." When the footsteps retreated and a door sighed shut, the woman said, "He may be the most dangerous man I've ever met, but he clearly cares for you. That has to count for something."

It should not have cost her that much to shed a single tear.

"This looks like a four-stage process to me. First, I'll shower you down to reliquefy this coating of goo. And it's a good thing you can't open your eyes, because it looks like you've been painted with somebody's entrails. No, don't you dare get sick on me. Here we go." The woman raised her voice to be heard over the shower. "That too hot? Good. Once we're done with that, I'll cut away your clothes. Which means shifting you again. I'll be as gentle as I can. Then I'll towel you down, and after that I'll do a more complete wash."

The warm water cascaded over Kirra's head and face, then played slowly over her body. The sensation was so exquisite Kirra wept. She could not remember the last time she let herself cry. But she was safe now, and the woman was very kind.

They kept her hidden for a day and part of the next night. Kirra wished it could have been longer. But Arno grew increasingly insistent, and gradually Elder Barret was brought around to his way of thinking.

Beyond the safety of this semi-secret clinic, the Black Watch swarmed.

The nurse's name was Elyria, a professional who had been allied to Arno for many years. She was matter of fact and very knowledgeable. She moved Kirra slowly through exercises, probing gently as Kirra moved, loosening and adjusting the injured ribs in the process. All the while Elyria described how Arno had raised her from the lifetime drudgery of a Five's existence. He had paid for her training, financed the clinic, kept the books, handled collection of payment, and used her services when necessary. Arno never mentioned the nurse's lifetime debt. Kirra watched the two together and saw how Arno was respectful, polite, almost gracious in his manner. Before departing he backed up his gratitude with cash. Elyria tried hard to refuse, but Arno would have none of that. Kirra liked the form of their relationship. She sensed Arno wanted Kirra to witness it for herself. Understand what it meant to forge such a lifetime bond.

The two conversations with Arno and Elder Barret took place in Kirra's chamber. It was a simple windowless room, whitewashed concrete walls, tiled floor, industrial lighting. But it was utterly clean, and the air was filtered so well the antiseptic odors remained very faint. The first meeting was brief and focused upon what Kirra remembered about the depot. What happened, how was she saved, who was behind the rescue. Kirra responded to every question with a simple truth: Everything was a total blur.

The second time, all five of them gathered in Kirra's room. Elder Barret was seated close to Kirra's head, there to offer the occasional assuring touch. Arno was further back, his metal chair angled so he faced Kirra directly. Elyria and Dell stood on the bed's opposite side. Quinn took up his normal position in the room's farthest corner, partially hidden behind the bathroom's open door. They formed a unifying presence, one that included Kirra. For the very first time she felt fully part of it all. Come what may.

Arno was saying, "The camera system in both the transit and the depot were disabled. They clearly wanted no record of your coming and then disappearing."

Quinn offered, "They've done this before."

"No question," Arno said.

"Those vile, despicable scum," Dell offered.

Arno addressed Kirra. "As far as the outside world is concerned, you traveled safely home from your job. Only then were you taken ill. The Fifth Ward clinic's records show you being brought in, examined, and sent home. They're not certain what exactly is wrong, but you've shown a fever and stomach cramps. Blood has been taken to ensure it's not an alien infection."

"That is rare, but it happens," Elyria said.

"Indeed." Arno gestured toward the nurse. "The clan is keeping you in isolation until the bloodwork comes back. Elder Barret is supposedly paying one of the clinic's professionals to visit you. All this gives us time to think things through and utterly separates you from what happened."

Elder Barret said, "She's not going back to work until you've found her a residency near the company."

Arno's features seemed to pinch together in very real pain. "We're trying."

"Try harder."

It was Dell who said, "It could take a year. The waiting lists are so full they're not accepting more names. We can't simply bribe her way further up the food chain. The authorities would be alerted."

"We can't wait that long." Elder Barret remained unmoved. "And I was not making a request."

"Think of what you're asking," Arno continued. "We must find a single-occupancy residence. We can't have her comings and goings noticed by others. Her hours don't mesh with a low-level employee."

"Rents anywhere near that company are incredibly high," Dell added.

Elder Barret settled a hand on Kirra's shoulder, then looked straight at Arno. "You'll work something out because you have to."

"Madame—"

"The matter is closed."

Arno was not so easily silenced. "Putting off her return means erasing all our work and planning."

But the clan leader was already up and moving. "Let's get my young lady home."

They took her back to her apartment two hours before daybreak, when the stars were mostly erased by the rising second moon.

Only one of the clan's night watch was on duty, and that woman had been forewarned. Kirra was transferred to the central building's top floor by a seldom-used lift and granted sole use of the apartment normally reserved for visiting dignitaries—meaning those who offered the clan money or opportunities or both.

Once they were alone in the spacious bedroom, Barret said, "Arno won't wait as long as you or I want."

Kirra rose slowly from the wheelchair, shed her blouse, and took her time unstrapping her ribs. Elyria had urged her to sleep without the brace, saying it would speed up the healing process.

Barret went on, "Arno is doing his best. And I'm using all my contacts. But there just isn't a suitable place. Nothing a single young professional could possibly afford."

Kirra began the slow-motion exercises that Elyria had claimed would keep her muscles loosened. She had also said they would hurt. Which they did. A lot. "How long do I have?"

"The revised schedule is focused upon a transport cycle in eight days. Arno insists you need to be back in place at least two days before then."

So. Six days. "I'll be ready."

"We'll set you up a ride," Barret said. "They can drop you off somewhere unseen, same for the pickup."

"Going is not a problem," Kirra protested.

"They will take you both ways until you're fully healed," Barret insisted. "It's the least Arno can do."

Kirra offered the older woman her good arm. "Help me into bed."

"Do you want a pain pill?"

"Maybe later."

Once she was settled, Barret asked, "Lass, how are you really?"

Kirra closed her eyes. "Tomorrow."

Kirra granted herself a couple of hours of much needed rest. Long before she was ready, she rose and shuffled into the kitchen and brewed tea. She was as tired as she was sore. Every part of her body ached to a greater or lesser degree.

Just the same, she had work to do. And there wasn't much time.

Kirra settled on the small balcony jutting from the living room. She was high enough to see over the Fifth Ring. For once the wastelands stretching between her perch and the distant mine-heads appeared almost beautiful. The smaller moon cut a narrow swath from the planet's rising sun. This created a gleaming crescent over the moon's upper-left edge, like it wore a lopsided crown. The mix of sunrise and shadow blanketed the wasteland in a mystical glow.

By the time Kirra finished her tea, she was ready.

There was a secret element to her memories of that horrid night. But with so much crammed into that short span of time, she was tempted to think it had been shaped by her trauma and thus was not part of reality. Just the same, if her fractured memory actually represented what she thought might have happened, well, that promised something she did not dare name.

Every waking hour inside the clinic had been spent inspecting this memory. Gradually the events had come into focus. With this came an idea. Despite the horrors of what might have happened, her concept represented a new sense of potential.

Kirra closed her eyes, scrunching down as much as her damaged ribs allowed, and called.

That very instant, even before she relaxed enough to open her eyes, the flutter of leathery wings announced that the diddybirds had arrived.

The trio's appearance was so swift, Kirra's first thought was that they had merely popped into reality. Then she lifted her gaze and saw how dozens of the alien beasts now rimmed the roof. She felt so completely overwhelmed by this presence she struggled to say, "Thank you."

The trio gave no response. They remained still, watchful. It took Kirra a long moment to realize the words held no meaning because the birds waited for two things.

A connection. And following that, a command.

Kirra's breath caught in her throat. Frightened both by what she proposed doing, and because of something she could not yet identify, a dark whisper that filtered around the edges of her brain.

She had to see. And time was not her ally.

She closed her eyes once more, then spoke the first word aloud. Giving the order verbal form helped a great deal. Not them. Her. "One of you fly."

They all left. Whoosh and gone. She knew they had taken flight, and opened her eyes to the realization that her sense of number or identity meant nothing. Which only added to her fears over what she was about to do.

She clenched her teeth, her shoulders, her fists. Crouched in the chair. Closed her eyes. Whispered, "Show me."

The experience was so overwhelming Kirra crashed from her chair. She crawled off the balcony and sprawled on the parlor floor. She did not have the strength to go further. Now that she was prostrate and breathing more easily, she shifted a fraction so as to observe the cloudless sky through the open balcony doors. This was Florian's dry season. It would not rain for another twenty or thirty days. The mid-morning air was crisp and dry and hot and odorless. The empty void made a useful backdrop upon which she might reach some form of clarity.

Kirra dared not shut her eyes again. Not yet. Not until she was absolutely certain the bond was severed.

Back in the depot, when the diddybirds attacked, Kirra had joined with them. As she lay there on the carpet, she was forced to accept the entirety of what she had experienced. She had no choice. The exact same thing had happened again in the here and now. On her balcony. The immensity of what just took place sent tremors from her hairline to her heels.

The birds were separate entities only so long as she was not engaged. In the instant of joining, back in the depot when the barrier shattered and again now, they joined. With her, with each other.

She did not see through one set of eyes. All their eyes were hers. Their wings, strength, abilities. And far more besides.

The beasts did not respond with thoughts of their own. As far as Kirra could tell, in those instances of bonding, they were utterly blank. Mere extensions of *her thoughts* and *her will.*

She heard the front door open. Heavy steps along the corridor announced Elder Barret's arrival. She was unable to move as the woman entered the parlor and cried, "Kirra, lass, what's happened?"

She closed her eyes in a futile attempt to shut out the reality that screamed inside her brain. And failed.

"Look at you, you're trembling like a leaf. Here, wait, I brought you a hot meal." Footsteps retreated to the kitchen.

The momentary solitude only heightened her internal clarity. The fury and the terror Kirra had felt in that first moment of joining, the havoc that had resulted . . .

Kirra had murdered eleven men.

The next morning, they all gathered in Kirra's temporary apartment. After asking about her health and progress, Arno announced, "The Regent's minions are inspecting the company's books."

Despite his evident concern over Kirra's health, Arno sounded almost jolly. Even Dell was smiling. She explained, "It happens every five years."

"They swoop in unannounced, put everything through a microscopic inspection, and off they go on their merry way." Arno blew on fingers that opened to his breath. "Poof. Gone."

Elder Barret studied their smug expressions and realized, "There's nothing for them to find."

"I hate to even suggest such a thing," Dell said. "But the attack on Kirra might actually have saved us."

"Perhaps, perhaps not." Arno's head bobbed from side to side. "Boaz and I are both certain their inspectors would have found nothing."

Quinn had settled in a corner away from the balcony and daylight. "Unless there's a spy."

"We've been through that," Arno said. "An agent counting the Regent's fruits and vegetables? Please."

"They're a year early in their inspection," Quinn pointed out.

"Four years, five," Dell said. "Boaz says they've always varied their timing."

"Not by this much," Quinn said. "I've checked. I still say you should let me search for a mole in the Council's pay."

Arno hesitated. He glanced at his assistant. Dell shrugged and replied, "Can't hurt."

Arno surprised everyone by asking Kirra, "What say you, young lady?"

"I have a voice?"

"At least on this point we are all in agreement," Arno replied. "From now on, you are fully one of us."

Kirra looked at the normally silent man. "If Quinn thinks this spy is worth pursuing, so be it."

"Then it's settled," Arno said. "Though I for one suspect nothing will come of it." To Quinn, "Use outsiders. Do not under any circumstances show yourself."

"As you say."

Elder Barret asked, "Any word on the housing?"

"No, no, we're getting nowhere."

"In that case, she needs transport," Elder Barret said.

"Not going," Kirra said. "But coming back. I can meet them on the park's far side."

Arno sighed. "Dell?"

"I'll arrange it."

Arno asked Kirra, "You still can't recall who saved you?"

"No, nothing. Everything about that night remains a blur."

"You must let us know the very instant you remember." He looked at Elder Barret. "You're certain the clan weren't involved?"

"We've been through all that. The answer is the same." When she was certain Arno would not press further, she asked, "When does Kirra go back to work?"

"Nothing's changed there either," Dell said.

Kirra said, "I need more time."

"You have five more days," Arno replied, regretful but firm. "We cannot put it off any longer."

"We've spoken with Boaz," Dell said. "He'll make sure you stay on light duty."

"People need to see you," Arno said. "Your absence came down to an illness. They will observe your present state and any suspicions will fade."

When Kirra did not respond, Elder Barret replied for her. "The lady will be ready."

"She has to be," Arno replied. "She has no choice."

The next four days passed in a sweep of stress and exhaustion and guilt. Kirra labored until her weary brain threatened to split in two. She ate when Elder Barret arrived and stood over her until the plate was nearly empty. She slept when forced by exhaustion.

The impressions that assaulted her with every joining nearly blinded her. Progress beyond that initial stage remained impossible.

Kirra woke most nights and sat on her balcony, worrying that she might never reach a point where she could handle the full potential this bonding represented. The immense cloud of incoming images remained just that. Hundreds of alien creatures emptied of all thought except a wholehearted desire to serve. Thousands of eyes. All vying for her to see through them.

Impossible.

On the fourth and final night, sitting on her stubby balcony, Kirra watched the moons tread their silent path across the starlit sky. The next day, she and Elder Barret would return to Arno's office. The old man would set out parameters for her reinsertion into the corporate offices. Her fate would be more or less sealed.

Kirra lifted her right hand and used her thumb and two fingers to form a W, so that each moon became separated. It was an act drawn from her earliest memories, back when she imagined the moons as a clan all their very own, casting the world in palest silver as they made their nightly promenade . . .

She sat up. Called the birds. Connected.

They had no names or identity. Even when bonded like this, she could not tell them apart. Which was where all her previous attempts had failed. Kirra sought to identify and track a single beast, holding fast to one set of eyes, one pair of wings, forging an alliance.

And failing.

This time, she began a mental dance.

One set of eyes. Two wings. One bird.

Then another.

She no longer fought their tumultuous demand. Every one of them pulled at her, an insistence that did not actually seem to come from any one animal, but rather was developed through her joining. *One* urge shared by *all*. Kirra resigned herself to the necessity.

And shifted to another bird.

Three breaths, four, then the next shift.

Kirra was setting the cadence. She readied herself in advance of each transition.

And now another.

And another.

It was hard, the strain wrapped her head in a vise, but it worked. One viewpoint could remain stable through several breaths, then before the field extended to multiple birds, she shifted. Again. Over and over until she was certain.

Then Kirra halted her winged dance, returned to the apartment kitchen, brewed tea, ate food she knew she needed. The realization she had seized upon earlier was now more clearly defined.

When they joined with her, they became a single entity.

To insist upon a single bird, a unique viewpoint, threatened this reality.

Their reality. Not hers. And she had no choice but to adapt.

It was an hour before midnight when Kirra began her first hunt.

She would have preferred to wait until daybreak. But time's passage was too strong a pressure. That same morning, she and Elder Barret would journey into the Fourth Ward, meet with Arno, and then Kirra would enter the corporate cage. She had never considered it that before. But now she was in possession of a new option. Her life might, just might, take flight if she could make the most of the opportunity this deeper connection with the diddybirds presented. If she could make this work.

She had a concept. Nothing more. Kirra feared the need to refine, redraft, explore, search again, would push her into days she did not have. Not if this truly represented a genuine chance at success. On her terms.

Her heart fluttered like diddybird wings as she called her allies, bonded, and sent them aloft.

Flying with the diddybirds at night was enormously disconcerting. Their night vision was excellent, but it sheared away elements of color and shading. The result was a jagged-edged clarity that made Kirra's head ache.

They flew high and fast. Their destination was the string of palaces at the heart of First Ward. She had never been there. Fifth Ward IDs effectively barred her from the inner two rings. And since obtaining her illegal Third Ward identity, Kirra had been too busy. But she had viewed numerous images of these bastions of wealth and power. The prospect of breaching their supposedly impenetrable barriers carried an exquisite thrill.

Splitting the birds into teams was easy enough, so long as she did not try the absurdity of counting. A clutch or cluster or flock found perches by each of the nine palaces she identified in her first sweep. One group at a time rose and circled and searched. Kirra hunted with each in turn.

She had no clear idea what she was looking for. Only that she hoped she would know when it appeared. Which she did almost immediately upon arriving above the sixth palace.

The manor held a pearlescent glow in the birds' manner of seeing, neither white nor silver, and gleamed brightly. A high stone wall surrounded the estate, rimming a pristine garden large as their Fifth Ward block and the playground. Security patrolled the perimeter, while a crowd of elegant people chattered and shouted and drank and danced and strolled. The diddybirds' hearing was acutely refined. Kirra heard music and conversation and whispered secrets and chiming crystal. Life was so easy for these people, so fine. Kirra struggled to suppress the sudden rage. It would be altogether too easy for the diddy-birds to sense it as a signal to attack.

She did her best to limit their numbers by asking for a trio of birds, similar to what always approached her. Just three, while the others hovered.

Her restricted crew closed in, hunting the higher floor for an open window. She found several.

One in particular excited her. Grand double doors opened onto a large veranda. The chamber was masked by gauze curtains that puffed and shifted in the night wind.

The bedroom was the largest chamber she had ever seen or imagined.

She shifted more easily between birds now. These glimpses formed quick flashes as the birds rushed about the room, the adjoining pair of dressing rooms and baths, revealing everything she had hoped for and more.

The woman's dressing room held a central island where treasure spilled in careless abandon. Jewels not selected for the night glittered in the birds' acute vision. A tray of earrings. A mound of bracelets. A scattering of necklaces.

The man's compartment revealed an open cabinet holding shelves of antique timepieces. As if the gentleman took pride in mechanically controlling time's passage, rather than the other way around.

Kirra called in more allies. She was sorely tempted to take everything. The desire was as strong as rage, as her hunger for a better existence.

In the end, she ordered the birds to take only a few items.

The night vision made selection a difficult, exhausting process. Kirra knew she risked choosing less valuable pieces. From the woman's hoard she took a bracelet, necklace, choker, three rings, and a heart-shaped gemstone twice the size of her thumbnail. Taking items from the man's closet proved far more difficult. In the end she stole just three treasures—a ring, a bejeweled pendant, and one timepiece which sparkled when the bird nudged it, suggesting a face covered in gemstones.

The birds handled these items with delicate ease. If the additional weight proved burdensome, Kirra could not tell.

They arrived back soon enough and deposited their loads at her feet. Kirra tried to thank them, stroking their wings, back, and heads. But she received a distinct impression they only tolerated the touch because it was her. In the end, she gave up and sent them away.

She gathered up her new possessions, so exhausted from the events her body trembled. Kirra felt nothing at all, no triumph, no pleasure, no relief. She carried her hoard into the bedroom and dumped them into the drawer holding her clothes. She collapsed into bed, but she did not sleep.

Kirra marveled at how these alien beasts cared for nothing save the link. Not how they were used, nor the risk, nor her own motives. For them, the bond was everything. It made them whole.

After a moment of weary wonder, she pushed the thoughts away. She only had until daybreak to prepare.

Kirra was seated in the parlor, dressed and as ready as she could possibly make herself, when Elder Barret came to collect her. The older woman declared, “You don’t look at all well.”

“I’m OK.” Which was both true and not true.

“We can put this off.”

She levered herself up, favoring her undamaged side. “You know that’s not possible.”

“Kirra—”

“No.” Firmer now. She started for the door. “You heard them same as me. I’m due back at the office. This is our last chance to plan.”

Thankfully a private hire transport awaited them by the interior playground. They rode to Arno’s office in silence, not even speaking when the Black Watch patrol halted them at the Fourth Ring and demanded to know their business. Elder Barret offered a stony gaze and their two IDs. The man finally snorted and retreated and waved them through.

When the transport let them off, Kirra waited for the driver to pull away. Then she told Elder Barret, “I meant what I said.” When the older woman turned back, Kirra continued, “I owe you everything. And I always will.”

Barret pressed the entry button, allowed herself to be scanned, waited for the steel inner portal to slide back, then entered. "Lass, if I had ten like you, I could rule the world."

The grand office hidden behind the building's grimy façade had never been more welcoming. Arno rose and rounded his desk and personally ushered them into chairs. He expressed concern over Kirra's fragile state, apologized for the need to follow time's strictures, assured her of every precaution they were taking—

"I'm not going back."

Arno took his time settling into the high-backed chair. He waited while Dell served them all rough-hewn mugs of tea. Then, "I'm so sorry for what you've endured. We all are. But I give you my word, the rewards will prove well worth your reinserting yourself into our project."

"I've come up with a new project. One that promises a far greater return for much less risk."

Arno probably did not mean for his smile to be so condescending. Kirra did not think scorn was part of his nature. "Young lady, I am sure that in time you will produce any number of mutually rewarding ideas. But right now, we must focus upon what is already set in place."

"How much do you intend to make from our current project?"

He lost his smile. Arno asked the older woman, "What is this?"

"I have no idea what she's on about," Elder Barret replied. "But I tell you one thing for certain. We'll all be better off if you treat her seriously."

Kirra continued, "I'm asking about your personal take. After all the bribes and payoffs and the share to Boaz. How much will you and the Barret clan be gaining?"

Arno frowned, studied Kirra a long moment, then, "We won't know for certain until we've completed two full passes."

"Just a basic idea will do."

He nodded at Dell. "Go ahead."

His assistant said, "Somewhere around half a million credits."

Arno said, "This figure is not something you can bandy about."

"I don't intend to," Kirra replied. "Half a million every three to four months. What if I can promise you three times that? Minimum?"

Dell was the one who said, "You *promise* this."

"I do. Yes." Kirra extracted the cloth bundle from her pocket and set it on Arno's desk.

"What have you brought me?"

"My alternative," Kirra replied.

"Why . . ." Arno leaned forward. "Is this a dishrag?"

"It's all I could find in the apartment." She waved her hand. "Open it, please."

Slowly, with almost gentle motions, he untied her bulky knot.

And gasped.

Dell leaned over and cried aloud.

Quinn left his shadowed corner and approached. "What is it?"

From Elder Barret there was no sound at all. Kirra met the older woman's watchful gaze as she said, "This is the first of many."

Arno lifted the large emerald, heart-shaped gemstone, the pendant still attached to its gold chain. "Where did you get these?"

"I don't know."

"You don't . . ."

"Even if I did, I wouldn't tell you."

"Use the analyzer," Dell said. "Check the quality."

"I don't need to." Arno dropped the pendant and told his normally silent aide, "You were right."

Barret asked, "About what?"

"Rumors," Quinn replied.

"A thief," Arno said. "Last night someone invaded the Baron's private residence."

"Baron Knowles?" Dell was aghast.

"None other." Quinn appeared mildly amused. "They suspect the thief was one of his guests."

Arno added, “The reception was to mark the construction launch of our Seventh Ring.” Arno swept his hand over the glittering treasures. “These treasures belonged to Knowles and his wife.”

Elder Barret asked, “How can you be certain?”

Arno lifted the timepiece. The face and golden frame were encrusted with diamonds. “The Baron has a thing for antiques like these.”

Elder Barret asked, “What’s the value of these items?”

“Incalculable.” Arno unlocked and opened his middle drawer and swept it all inside. “Which makes it impossible to safely dispose of them as they currently are. In time the gems can be sold, but this largest emerald must be divided and reshaped.”

“The gold can be melted and sold as bullion,” Dell added.

Arno closed the drawer and settled his hands upon the desk. He told Kirra, “All right, I’m listening.”

Thanks to her sleepless night, Kirra was ready. “First and foremost, I’m not demanding. I’m asking.”

Arno glanced at his aide.

Dell acknowledged, “This is new.”

“Indeed.” To Kirra, Arno said, “Go on.”

“A third for you. A third for the clan. A third for me. Our shares come now. Me and the clan both. Not everything. A low estimate. You hold the things as long as you want or need. Once every year, we have a reckoning.”

Dell said, “That’s steep.”

Kirra replied, “It’s fair.”

Dell said, “The going rate is fifty-fifty.”

She was ready for that as well. “If you supply the target, you get half.”

It was Quinn who asked, “You can steal to order?”

She directed her response to the man seated across from her. “Not me.”

“Your crew, then.”

“I can’t guarantee a specific item unless you show me a picture. No safes or locked drawers. The items have to be out in the open. Speed is everything.”

Arno asked, “What about paintings? Treasures on display?”

"Maybe. Perhaps even probably. We'll see."

Quinn persisted, "Can you control your crew? We can't risk carnage."

Dell nodded. "Especially if your targets are inside private residences like the Baron's."

"I can control them, and it doesn't have to be a house. Any place that's empty and has an open window." She focused on Arno. "Something else. I want a home for myself. It doesn't have to be in Third Ward. But it has to be nice, and it has to be mine. It must also have a balcony that's completely private." She swept her hand around Arno's office. "I'd be more than happy with something like this. On the outside, nothing. But the interior is new and elegant." She hesitated, then said it a second time, "And mine."

Elder Barret asked, "You're leaving the clan?"

"Not now, not ever." Another part of her nighttime deliberations. "But for this to work, I have to effectively disappear. Until my home is ready, can I keep the top floor apartment?"

Elder Barret pondered, decided, "It's yours."

"Thank you." Kirra started to rise. "Are we in agreement?"

"Just a moment." Arno waited for her to settle, then demanded, "What are you holding back?"

Kirra felt no need to deny. "I trust you with my life. What I can't decide is whether to trust you with my tomorrow."

Arno laughed. He liked that very much. "You can indeed. My word on that."

She slipped the final item from her pocket. The choker was meant to encircle a royal neck snug as a collar. It was broad as Kirra's thumbnail, a design of woven gold framing sapphires and diamonds.

Arno inspected it briefly, then slid it into the drawer with the other pieces. He stood and reached one hand across the desk. "A pleasure doing business."

FOUR
Eva Fourier

The fifty-five days of basic training were dreadful, of course. Eva's fellow recruits were all police or Guards trainees. She was the only one from the FSA. The staff officer responsible for training let it be known that Eva was expected to fail. And Tanner, that cold fish of a director, actually told her she could leave at any time. All FSA recruits were required to enter basic, but none had passed. Or rather, none that mattered. Tanner actually suggested she would be doing them a favor to walk out. He was impatient to have her start on the real work. All this said without looking directly at her. Dismissing her with his attitude, and long before the conversation was over.

Which of course was all she needed to hold fast.

The initial ten days were grim. Brutal. Her fellow recruits called her Numbers and treated her like a wasted bunk. But the neighbor who had patiently trained her in combat techniques had also insisted Eva include a daily regimen of running and calisthenics and free-weights. And that helped. Not as much as Eva might have wanted. But it made enough of a difference that their training officers stopped using Eva as the example of how to do things wrong.

On the eleventh day, everything changed.

That morning they began hand-to-hand training. And to Eva's immense surprise, her very own neighborhood sensei stepped onto the training mat and introduced himself as Kim. While Eva was still recovering, Kim ordered her to step forward. "Using this trainee I will now demonstrate the basic stances and strikes that will form the foundation for everything that follows. By correctly applying these first lessons, you will remain safe and in control when under attack."

The class grinned. Not quite all of them. But close. The two instructors standing behind the recruits crossed their arms and shared a look. Here we go.

Kim asked, "Your name?"

"Eva, sensei."

"Very well, Eva. Do you know the zenkutsu dachi? Yes? Please show me." Kim examined her position, made two unnecessary corrections to her hip and elbow. "The front stance is a core component of all that is to come. From this position you enter into blocks, lunges, and forward strikes." He stepped back. "Now demonstrate for us the musubi dachi. Good. And the hachiji dachi. No, do that again, and this time flow from one to the other. And now the kiba dachi. Flow, yes. You are water. You move effortlessly. One simply grows into the next."

The words were enough to take her back to the basement gym, the calm manner Kim had always spoken, almost chanting the words. Gradually Eva shifted away from the day and the training grounds and all the observers. It became just the two of them, him instructing, her doing her best to follow the quiet commands.

The other recruits and their instructors lost their smiles as she followed Kim's instructions. Kansetsu geri, stomping side kick. Chudan tsuki, stomach level punch. Jodan tsuki, head level strike. Ura uchi, forward back fist. Yoko ura uchi, side back fist.

She was sweating and breathing hard now. Eva had shifted into the calm mental state required to perform as Kim wished. Her sensei noticed that as well, for he asked, "You have combat training?"

At some peripheral distance, Eva noticed a number of the recruits rise to their feet. The two instructors uncrossed their arms and shared another look. She replied, "Some, sensei. Not enough."

Kim took two paces away from her, stripped off his instructor's sweatshirt, and said, "Please to show."

Eva bowed slowly, another of Kim's regular demands. Taking her time to draw down to her most essential elements. In extreme cases, this of course would not be possible. But in formal combat situations, the bow was essential. It split the fighter from everything except the battle to come.

When she straightened, the diminutive man did not actually smile. Rather, a tight glint of humor shone from his dark gaze. As if he spoke to her and her alone. *Now we show.*

Almost instantaneous responses were necessary. Knowing at the level beyond conscious thought what her attacker was going to do. There was simply no time to think things through. Kim's impossible command, repeated before every such period of controlled violence, was the same. Read the enemy and know their next move before they do. Impossible, of course. But still.

The recruits were shouting now. Yelling and bouncing up and down. The instructors had shifted to the front, mouths open, uncertain what to do or say.

Too soon it was over. Much too soon.

"Yame! Enough!" Kim stepped back, waited for Eva to catch her breath and straighten from the combat stance. Then, "Your technique needs much work, yes? Years and years. For today, we stop."

"Thank you, sensei." She bowed to him, then at a gesture from Kim she turned to the recruits and bowed a second time. The message in their astonished gazes was clear enough.

Her training had entered a different phase.

Eva graduated with thirty-two others, not the top of her class, but close enough for Tanner's bitter impatience to become temporarily silenced. She had made one genuine friend, a woman older than Eva and drawn from hard beginnings. Despite excellent records in school, Ven had been unfairly graded a Four Minus because of her family, who ran to thieves and brigands. Ven had fought her way into the Guards, only to be assigned a dead-end administrative job and told she should count herself fortunate. Her only way out was to apply for agent status and enter basic. After Eva's performance on the training mat, Ven had offered a guarded welcome.

Three days after graduation, her grandmother invited Eva back to the Crillon to celebrate.

Tanner had of course demanded they meet the day following her graduation ceremony. Salma had served as Eva's official buffer and refused with such cold indifference the man had been temporarily silenced. Which was good, because Eva had spent the previous afternoon, evening, and most of the night with her fellow graduates. Eva had finally stumbled home when a bleary sunrise had forced her to retreat inside. The next two days were Salma's gift, a chance for Eva to enjoy slow-motion promenades along the realm's premier shopping streets, taking in the rhythms of transition. Readying herself for whatever mysteries their coming lunch might reveal.

They took the same table as before, only now it was set with four places. Eva did not complain at the prospect of Tanner joining them because she knew it would do no good. Instead, she listened with genuine pleasure while Salma described the director's furious tirade at being forced to meet here and not in his office. As if eating a five-star meal caused him genuine pain.

The day's first surprise came when her sensei arrived. Eva started to rise and bow, except her instructor showed her an open palm and said, "Today we shake hands, greeting one another as new friends." He kissed Salma's cheek and said, "Our honorable director is downstairs talking on his commlink and chopping the air."

Salma smiled at her granddaughter. "Maybe he'll run out of ire before he shows up."

Kim took the chair next to Eva. "We can always hope."

Tanner arrived soon after, stern and irritated and impatient. He said in greeting, "I'm here. Now what."

Kim apparently found the director's irritation as humorous as Salma, for he insisted on the waiter describing two of the starters in minute detail.

When he and Salma began debating the wine selection, Tanner reached a boil. "Give me that." He plucked the leather-bound list from Kim's hand and stabbed at something Eva suspected he didn't actually see. "We'll take this one. Now go away!" He reddened at how Salma and Kim smiled in response. "Baron Knowles isn't breathing fire down your necks."

Salma replied, "The good baron can't possibly object to a celebratory meal."

"We're wasting time, and you know it."

Kim said, "Nonsense. You finally have exactly what you've

been after. A young individual who is both gifted and capable of disappearing without anyone noticing. A ghost of your own making."

Salma added, "Not to mention how she's been expertly trained by a former director and the realm's premier expert in close combat."

Kim offered a combined smirk and bow. "You are most kind."

Tanner snapped, "I dislike being told the obvious."

Kim and Salma exchanged a look, then her grandmother said, "Now is the time you answer Eva's question."

"What on earth are you talking about?" Tanner said. "This one has not spoken a word. Which is hardly a surprise, with you two having such fun at my expense."

"The question," Salma replied, "you refused to answer when we last met."

"What utter rubbish." Tanner's fury was a radiating force. "Just because she's finished one initial phase of her training . . . *What!*"

Kim said, "Actually, Director, we must insist. Eva learns today."

Tanner's features looked par-boiled. "I am FSA director. She is now an agent assigned to my department."

"That is true and not true." Kim's features held the same placid calm as when he prepared the killing strike. "She remains on your books. But she is now officially assigned to *my* case."

Salma offered, "Eva learns when Kim says. Not you."

"Indeed."

Tanner's chair slammed into the neighboring table as he leapt to his feet. Two crystal goblets smashed on the floor. Eva doubted the director even noticed. "The Baron will hear about this!"

"The Baron already has," Kim replied. "He agrees with my assessment."

Tanner's hands formed fists, but he maintained enough good sense to refrain from striking the most dangerous man Eva knew.

Kim merely smiled.

The entire restaurant watched the FSA director storm away.

Salma turned to where their waiter stood frozen in place. "It's safe for you to approach now."

Kim waited until their wine had been poured to ask Salma, "How did you describe Tanner?"

"Petty tyrant."

"Quite so." Kim stared at the restaurant's empty lobby. "I'm astonished you backed his promotion to director."

"In his own way, Tanner is a brilliant man," Salma replied. "And was by far the most qualified of the candidates." When Kim frowned in response, her grandmother added, "You work with what you have, no?"

"Indeed. Which brings us to the matter at hand." Kim lifted his glass. "Here's to the arrival of our new graduate and crucial asset."

Eva spoke for the first time since Tanner's arrival and hasty departure. "I don't have to work with that man?"

"The question," Salma replied, "is whether you will ever be directly under Tanner's control."

"So long as you are successful in your coming role, which I have no doubt you will be," Kim offered, "the good director will have no choice but pretend this exchange never happened."

Eva lifted her glass. "I'll drink to that."

Their meal then took on a heady, happy air. Eva found herself weightless, a tight bundle of pure potential.

Over their first course Salma explained, "You are officially an FSA agent. Which means that on paper Tanner is responsible for your career."

"Only on paper," Kim emphasized. "Certain events have rearranged your orbit. And mine, for that matter. So long as you succeed, you will enjoy a rare amount of freedom."

Kim shifted to the table's other side, so that Eva was now seated across from them. They shared what to Eva looked like a weightless moment of their own.

"Then why did we meet with him at all today?"

"Some confrontations are best handled in person," Salma replied. "Recent unexpected events have resulted in changes the good Tanner is finding hard to digest."

"Which explains the hand-waving outside the Crillon," Kim said. "Losing control of your good self is only part of a much larger series of issues."

"Such as?"

Salma said, "To understand this, you first need to know that Kim was formerly the director of my investigative branch."

"After your dear husband was lost to us." He turned to Eva and added, "One of the finest men it has ever been my honor to serve."

"Kim retired when the agency was placed under the supervision of a second-rate son of a minor royal," Salma continued. "Who then proved to be a spectacular failure at almost everything except taking bribes."

"Such news should not be bandied about," Kim warned.

"Piffle. It's true and everyone who's anybody already knows." To Eva, "Kim was offered the top job and refused. So the Council appointed Baroness Ricard."

"The right person at the right time," Kim said.

"Indeed. She was a decorated officer, served as deputy director of my former division for ten years, then her father died and she resigned to take his position on the ruling Council. I like her. What's more, I trust her."

Eva looked from one to the other, "So now Kim is what, an instructor?"

"Hardly. He took that on because of you."

Kim offered a happy shrug. "Nonsense. I merely needed something to keep myself occupied while the wheels of state slowly ground away."

"Like teaching an ungraded teen in her building's gym," Eva said.

Another shrug. "I was between things when Salma asked. I've always had difficulty refusing your grandmother anything."

Salma continued, "Kim told the Council he would only return to active duty if or when they assigned him to a specific case, one so important that he would answer to the Baroness herself." She smiled at Kim. "Unfortunately, during his first day on the job, a new crisis erupted in our faces. And now Director Kim is handling both cases."

"Lucky me," Kim said. He paused as a waiter refilled their glasses, then said, "And that, my dear, brings us to you."

"Two different cases," Eva said.

"Tanner only knows of one," Kim said. "The initial crisis for which you were trained. And which now has been put on hold."

"So, what we are about to tell you," Salma explained, "has to do with what you won't be doing."

"Not yet, but soon," Kim said. "First, the crisis you were trained for. You are aware of how the treaty governs humanity's city-states?"

"Of course."

"This has functioned most successfully for centuries," Salma told her. "The wealth and power shared by Treaty's city-states were maintained by working mines. The off-world demand for our minerals stayed steady. And the prices kept rising. The question no one ever wanted to consider was what happened when a city-state's mines ran out."

"Our spies insist this is about to happen in our neighbor to the south," Kim said.

"Corinth was formerly our closest ally," Salma said. "Now the Council members speak the name with genuine concern. Even fear."

Eva could read the danger in their expressions. "They want to take us over."

"An actual invasion of Florian is nigh on impossible," Salma declared. "Move an army along the designated routes and in secret? Impossible."

Kim remained grimly silent.

"What they intend is much more subtle," Salma continued. "That is, if the rumors are correct."

"They are far more than rumors," Kim stated. "We have indirect proof that Corinth is using its considerable wealth to acquire controlling interests in Florian's essential industries."

"We think they are working by proxy," Salma said. "Someone here is serving as their secret representative. The plan would be for this individual or group to become so powerful as to sway our ruling Council."

Eva asked, "To what end?"

Kim nodded. "The crucial question. We have no idea."

"We know enough," Salma insisted. "They want to reach a point where they can demand a shared ownership of our mines."

Kim told Eva, "And now you are privy to our gravest secret."

Salma nodded agreement. "Our plan was to insert you into Corinth and see if you might identify precisely in what form this financial invasion is taking place. And who is serving as their secret power broker here in Florian."

Eva took a long moment to digest what she was learning. The pair seated across from her clearly were willing to grant her as much time as she required. Finally, she said, "I don't understand. There is another crisis even worse than this?"

"Not worse. Only more pressing," Kim replied. "Unfortunately there is a growing certainty that the corruption within Florian's ruling elite extends much further than our wayward princeling."

"We are forbidden to speak more about this just yet," Salma told her. "I only know the tiniest hints myself."

"Be glad for this absence of knowledge," Kim said. "I only know a bit more than you, and I haven't enjoyed a single decent night's sleep since this arose."

"Which brings us to the reason why we've just had this public confrontation with Tanner," Salma continued. "He needs to understand that his hold on you is tenuous at best."

"For your next step, you will be inserted into the FSA system," Kim said. "All new agents must serve their duty at the desk."

"Let Tanner have his way," Salma said. "Or so he thinks."

Eva agreed because she had no choice. "When do I start?"

Two days later, Eva arrived at the main FSA operations system located in the Second Ward's administrative district. She entered the faceless building with a very real sense of dread. She had no choice in what was about to happen. Her allies, Kim and her grandmother, were barred from entry. Despite their assurances over lunch, Eva feared her isolated state meant Tanner would take his vengeance and grind her down to nothing.

Tanner's division was mainly responsible for all the province's taxation and auditing. Every license, every new construction project, the financial oversight of mines and other corporations owned by the royal clans, all this fell under Tanner's supervision. The prospect of entering into a vast bureaucratic system after her many years of solitude terrified her.

As a foyer guard checked her name on his system and wrote out a temporary pass to the fifth floor, Eva watched a faceless, uncaring tide of bureaucrats sweep past.

"What Tanner really wants," Kim had told her, "is to make sure you are well and truly under his thumb."

The words had drawn an unwelcome chill into her otherwise wonderful second visit to the Crillon. Eva had asked, "Am I?"

"Only if you fail," Salma had replied. "Which you won't."

Eva joined the elevator's crush and endured the silent ride. The confidence Kim and Salma had shown belonged to a different time and space. As she entered the fifth floor's lobby, Eva was surrounded by a leaden sense of permanence.

A receptionist with an expression of the condemned made note of Eva's name and said, "You're in eight-nineteen."

"What . . ." She left her question unformed, as the receptionist's attention had already shifted to an incoming call.

She followed other arrivals around the lobby's rear wall and stopped. One look was enough to know that this place was where hope came to die.

Even without guidance, her cubicle was easy enough to locate. Nine rows of cubicles stretched out beneath the industrial-strength lighting. The question, of course, was how to count and from which direction. Eva decided to try from the left, counted her way down the eighth lane, and discovered she was correct.

Her cubicle was a pastel cage with a desk the same color as the walls. Five binders bearing the Regent's seal were stacked on the otherwise empty surface. A computer tablet and palm-sized box holding a commlink were the only occupants of shelves lining the opposite wall. She drew out her chair and discovered a sixth binder resting on the seat. This one was the thickest of all, and its cover bore the words, *FSA Rules and Regulations*.

Eva sighed, sat down, and began.

She completed the rulebook in less than an hour. The passcodes for her tablet and commlink were taped to the book's internal cover. She coded in both and scrolled through the tablet's directory. As she debated next steps, her commlink chimed. When she fit the device to her left ear and answered, Kim said in greeting, "You must assume everything you say will be recorded. The same goes for anything you save on your computer."

She swung her chair in a slow circle. She searched the high ceiling and her cubicle, found nothing. "You're watching me?"

Her boss might have laughed. "I have better ways to occupy my time. As does Tanner. He will have some minion check your electronic progress, you understand?"

"Yes."

"If you have any hint of trouble, what will you do?"

Eva knew he spoke for all the invisible listeners. They had been through this twice during lunch. "Contact you."

"The first sign. No hesitation. Otherwise, be in touch when you are ready." Kim signed off.

Eva reached for the first binder. Sighed as she opened the cover. Somehow the conversation had rendered her feeling even more isolated than before.

Even Kim assumed the duty was little more than make-work.

All properties and corporations where one or more of the royals held a stake were audited by the FSA every five years. This particular corporation controlled a number of hydroponic farms, food processing facilities, distilleries, and one pharmaceutical factory. The most recent audit had just been completed and came up clean.

And yet.

Because of the company's interests in booze and drugs, a mole had been enlisted by the FSA among the mid-level employees. This too was common practice. Over time, the information generated had become increasingly trivial. Personal grievances and baseless accusations mostly, tidbits the mole used to maintain his secret payments.

And yet.

The audit had been shifted forward because of a new item. Something so far outside the mole's normal complaints, the authorities wondered if perhaps it contained a kernel of truth. So, a memo had been sent from the surveillance division to Tanner's office: Probably nothing, but the mole reports a plan to steal truckloads of food and booze and drugs every quarter; these corporate thieves will redesign the system so these products did not simply vanish; instead, they never existed.

Tanner's reaction was there with the memo, supplied by Kim and stamped *Top Secret*. The level of corporate maneuverings and subterfuge this theft would have required, Tanner insisted, was mind-boggling. Not to mention the number of people they would need to pay off. And the complete reworking of the corporate books from the production line to the transport; who could arrange such a thing?

Kim's response was written there below Tanner's objections: *A senior director and one highly skilled employee could make this work*. Tanner had rejected the notion out of hand.

And yet.

Over their lunch at the Crillon, Kim had described his and Tanner's recent meeting with Baron Knowles, minority shareholder of the company. Kim had presented the Baron with a simple enough option. Why not have their new recruit, this young lady who graduated top of her class in forensics, give it another look? Tanner had insisted Eva spend time at ground level, Kim explained, so why not give this initial period at FSA a real purpose?

Tanner, of course, had some other minion-style duties in mind. But the Baron had approved the idea, so here she was. Trapped in a pastel cage, staring at all the documents generated from a thorough audit, knowing in her heart there was nothing for her to find.

* * *

The hours and days spun into a web so tenacious Eva only noticed time's passage when she exited the building—which was late—or when she clocked in well before daybreak. At some deep and secret level, Eva grew increasingly unconcerned whether a crime had actually been committed. This was her first opportunity to see just how far she could delve into the complexities of a real-world situation, using nothing but numbers on a page.

And the answer was very far indeed.

Thirty-five days later, Eva felt ready to make the call. Kim responded with mild irritation. "I expected to hear from you long before now."

"I wasn't ready."

"You do realize this was never intended to be your primary investigation."

"I may have found something."

"Thirty days and you still don't know?"

"Thirty-five. And no. I'm not certain. But I think . . ."

"What?"

"It's better if I lay it out. You can shoot it down. Or not. Your choice."

"Is it urgent, this possible discovery?"

"I have no idea."

"Well. I have always found honesty to be a refreshing approach. Until tomorrow, then."

In the end, both of her erstwhile bosses arrived together.

Multiple heads rose from other cubicles up and down the nine rows as the FSA's supreme boss and the mysterious Kim slowly marched down the aisle, taking aim at one of their own. When Eva rose to greet the two directors, other minions smirked in her direction. Then the heads slowly descended, their gazes sparked with anticipation for the fireworks to come.

They were not disappointed. Kim stopped in the cubicle's entryway and exclaimed, "Great heavens above!"

Tanner, for once, was speechless.

Kim's dark gaze made a slow sweep of the three walls, all of which now were blanketed by the largest sheets of graph paper Eva had managed to locate. They were linked together by multicolored twine, their edges covered by layers of small sticky notes.

"Eva, what . . ."

"I needed to develop a timeline."

"But why . . ." He included the entire cubicle in his gesture.

"I wanted to view the timeline as a fluid system." The explanation sounded feeble to her own ears, so she added, "Not broken into calendar days."

Kim disappeared and swiftly returned, drawing two chairs with him. He shoved the first into the cubicle and told Tanner, "Sit." Once the FSA director had done so, Kim positioned his own chair by the entryway, as there was not room for both inside the cubicle. Kim said, "All right. Explain."

"The auditors looked for pilfering." Eva pointed to the Rules and Regulation binder propped open on her top shelf. "There is a specific pattern they are meant to follow. Identify any attempt to steal items from inventory."

"Which they did," Tanner said, speaking for the first time. "Extensively."

"Right. But let's go back to what the mole said."

Tanner glared at his fellow director. "Really, Kim? Really?"

Kim waved it aside. "Go on, Eva."

"Their task was to see if huge amounts of produce were being stolen on a regular basis. This theft was supposedly hidden by falsifying accounts."

"We know this already," Tanner said. "They found nothing."

"Right." She pointed to the center of the wall directly behind her desk. The point from which everything started. "Their books are clean. Totally free of any wrongdoing."

Tanner's ire began to emerge. "Then what on earth is all this?"

Eva found herself shielded from the director's anger. It bounced off, leaving her unscathed. "I asked myself, what if the would-be thieves discovered the mole and stopped before the theft actually happened? What if this is a momentary pause, and they'll soon be back in business—"

"That's enough." Tanner started to rise, but was halted from leaving by Kim blocking the exit. "This is a complete and utter waste—"

"You will sit down."

Tanner looked genuinely shocked. "How *dare* you speak to me like I was one of my own minions."

"Either you cease, desist, and shut up, or I will personally explain to the Baron why you are not present when we show him this woman's remarkable work. Now sit down, Tanner. That is an order." Once the outraged director resumed his seat, Kim said, "Proceed, Eva, with your fascinating report." He met Tanner's glare and repeated, "Fascinating."

Eva continued, "If I was right, nothing would have been uncovered by the audit."

"Because nothing untoward had been done," Kim said, nodding. "Yet."

"Correct." It was just the two of them now. Tanner's boiling presence was a mere sidebar. Of no importance whatsoever. "So, I went back to the company's original books."

"How far back?"

"Two years. Eight quarters. But I didn't need to, I just wanted to be certain."

Another glance at Tanner, then "Because you found . . ."

"This." She tapped nine of the sheets in turn. "Over the previous two cycles, a distinct shadow operation starts to take shape. These represent transit calculations that never happened."

Silence.

Eva was too excited to remain seated. And with the two men crowding her cubicle there was no room to pace. So, she made do with bouncing up and down, heel to toe, toe to heel, in time to her words. "The official records, what they gave to the auditors, show everything is normal. But their cloud accounts revealed a different story. Soon as I accessed the FSA records, the pattern began taking shape." Eva tapped one page after another. "Nine times over a fifty-day period, eleven truckloads appear and vanish, appear and vanish, over and over."

Somehow Kim managed to squeeze his way to where he stood beside her. "The same pattern?"

"Minor shifts. Like they're correcting weak spots. But yes. The primary elements remain the same."

"If discovered," Kim mused, "they could claim they sought improvements to their internal system."

"Most likely." She loved how they were now moving in synch. "And it could be just that."

"Which explains your hesitation and delay."

"Right. But this pattern, watch." Now she followed the navy-blue string. "This was the first run. Trucks leave the depots. These from food packaging, one from the distillery warehouse, and this from the pharma factory. And here, see?"

Kim's nose almost touched the cord as he shifted position. "The records vanish."

Tanner protested, "But their records are clean. Spotless."

"Because the actual theft never happened." Eva continued to follow the route laid out by her twine. "These are dry runs. They planned the theft. Which is brilliant, by the way. Great work. Really first rate. Without your mole it's unlikely we would ever have known."

Kim swung around and asked the other director, "Is the mole still in place?"

"I'll have to check." Tanner was nervous now. His world canted slightly on its very firm axis. "But I've heard nothing to the contrary."

Kim turned back. His smile was for Eva alone. "What are our next steps?"

Both of Treaty's moons were skybound when Eva arrived at the Fourth Ward market. She had never been here before, and twice became utterly confounded by the sprawling mass of unnamed passageways. The directions she had been offered were clearly intended for someone who knew the place and thus were of little use to her.

When Eva finally arrived, the woman was already closing for the night. She offered Eva a sour look and said, "You're two hours late."

"I couldn't have been any more lost if I'd gone to the wrong market," Eva replied.

Ven was the singular friend Eva had made during basic FSA training. She was hard-faced, tanned, and tonight wore clothes that made her look a decade older than her twenty-nine years. Pale eyes blended with the headscarf, her gaze as unwelcome as early snow. She nodded to a trio of departing stallholders and pitched her voice loud enough to carry. "You have money?"

Eva slipped one hand into her pocket and drew out silver coins.

"It's too late for timewasters, dearie."

Eva replied just as loudly, "I came to buy."

"Well, I suppose you can have five minutes. No more, mind." She unlocked her portal, shoved the security gate aside, and gestured for Eva to enter.

Ven's birth-name was Lavender, something she described as a hated brand. The name had been part of her brigand family's legacy since the early days. The first Lavender had been hanged for murdering a royal, a crime she had not committed. But this first Lavender had done almost everything else deemed illegal by the hated Black Watch.

When her clan learned Ven had joined the Guards, they gathered at midnight and spoke words for the dead over an open grave. Which was precisely why Ven had told them of her intentions. She was Agent Ven now, and Eva was one of the very few who knew of the woman's hard beginnings.

Ven relocked the door and drew thick drapes over the portal, then turned on the interior lights. What Eva saw took her breath away. Ven smiled at Eva's astonishment and asked, "You like to read?"

"It saved me in my own dark time."

"You and I have that in common as well."

Eva felt a sudden lance of pure shame. "What I went through is nothing compared to your early days."

Ven would have none of that. "At the time, what happened to you was hard, and reading helped?"

"So very much." Eva made a slow circle. The stall was smaller than her grandmother's kitchen and lined with floor to ceiling shelves. Crates littered the floor. Every inch of space was crammed with . . .

Books.

Ven said, "Some people never find true satisfaction, reading electronic words." She pulled out a book at random and stroked the spine with two fingers. Until that moment, Eva would never have thought Ven capable of such tenderness, not in touch nor expression nor voice. "When I faced my early trials, these simple pages of ink and paper and bygone dreams became my dearest friends." Ven brought the book closer and breathed in deep. "I clung to them for dear life."

Eva had no idea what to say.

"Have you read Dickens?"

"Over and over."

"Your favorite?"

That required no thought. "David Copperfield."

Ven replaced the book, stepped to her right, searched, and selected a different title. She handed it over with, "Tell me if you think this reads the same way."

"Ven, thank you . . . I really must pay for this."

"Yes, you must." She offered Eva a jagged smile. "Treasures like these don't come cheap. The stallholder's name—do you need it?"

"Not really."

"She's been a friend through the hardest days of all. Tough as nails, bitter and cynical and even more passionate about books than me. She also loves money. The Guards are paying her dearly for the privilege of my giving her a few days off." Ven accepted the payment, waited while Eva slipped the Dickens into her backpack, then led her into a storage loft by way of a ladder with wheels. The reason crates now littered the shop floor was because of the monitoring equipment that filled the cramped attic. Ven opened the west-facing shutters a fraction and gave the surroundings a careful inspection. Satisfied, she settled back on cushions and said, "I assume you didn't stop by to see how your old pal was doing."

"No." Eva joined her on paddings spread over the floor, because the ceiling was too low to permit chairs. She described her hunt through numbers, her suspicions, the meeting with Kim and Tanner. When she reached the point where Tanner poured vitriolic scorn over her suspicions that a company's senior director was involved, Ven shifted to a small stove and brewed tea.

She handed Eva a rough-hewn mug and said, "I've met Tanner's counterparts in my travels."

"Kim considers him a petty tyrant."

"Sounds about right." She blew, sipped, grinned. "That's some turn of events, our combat instructor being a director."

"I'm not sure Kim wants that to become common knowledge."

"I have a lot of practice at keeping secrets." Ven eyed her over the mug's rim. "You like him."

"He's the best there is."

"The best, does it include a romantic angle?"

"Ha. No."

"Just checking." Another sip. "So, you put a tail on all of this company's senior executives—"

"Not me. Kim did. I was still stuck inside my cubicle."

"And one of them shows up here."

"The director's name is Boaz. Corporate board member and executive director." Eva pointed out the open shutter. "He traveled to an address flagged by the Guards, one that's being monitored by their investigative branch." Eva spread out her arms. "Which brings me here. Buying books."

Ven set her mug to one side. "My remit is top secret."

"You're not the only one good at holding things in confidence," Eva replied. "And Kim answers directly to Baroness Ricard."

"You don't say."

"What Kim wants, Kim gets."

"Including you, I take it."

"Not in the way your grin is suggesting."

Ven shifted closer to the open window. "Come look."

Music drifted up from some unseen tavern. The rising second moon painted the roofs in a pewter glow. The lanes were mostly lost to shadows and a rising ground fog. Eva asked, "What should I be seeing?"

"The man your suspect visited." She pointed across the thoroughfare to a featureless building with darkened windows. "That was his destination."

Eva knew a brief shimmer of accomplishment, having arrived where a professional agent on surveillance acknowledged her own search as real. "Your report stated that Boaz visited a man named Arno Held."

"I'm still having difficulty accepting you and our combat instructor gained access to that file," Ven replied. "There can't be more than half a dozen of the senior Guards who even know I'm on this job."

Which was good for another shimmering thrill. "Imagine my surprise when I discovered there might be a genuine importance to this meeting between the director we've only now identified and a Fourth Ward merchant named Arno Held, all because of an investigation where my pal Ven is head of surveillance."

"Again, highly confidential. There are a lot of questions I can't answer. Mostly because I don't have a clue."

"Understood." Eva decided it was worth adding, "I probably don't know enough to ask anyway."

Ven liked that. She resumed her inspection of the featureless building. "Arno has a known associate by the name of Quinn. If you spot a man shaped from shadows who looks like a blade with legs, you run."

It probably should not have thrilled Eva like it did, hearing of danger's proximity. "So, who exactly is Arno Held, and why are you perched in the attic of a treasure trove?"

Ven spotted a night watchman strolling the lane directly beneath their perch. She motioned for Eva to slip back. The watchman's lamp cast a soft glow over their aerie, carving Ven's features in stone. When he passed and they shifted back into position, Ven said, "On paper, Arno Held is totally clean. We know he's involved in unlawful acts. There are too many rumors. Dozens of unsubstantiated reports going back years. Decades. But the Guards have never managed to pin anything concrete on the man."

"How long has he been under surveillance?"

"Not long. The request for surveillance came soon after we finished Basic. They needed someone who could go unnoticed in the Fourth Ward market. I volunteered." She swept her gaze around the loft. "Lucky me."

"But if suspicions about this Arno go back years, why did they start an investigation now?"

"Hard to say."

"I don't understand. Are you sure this isn't just some punishment detail?"

"Not with how high up the food chain my reports are going." Ven swung around and rested her back on the window frame. "A few days before I was assigned this duty, Baron Knowles was robbed."

"I heard about that. A party celebrating the launch of the Seventh Ring construction project."

"We investigated the guests. A totally futile move. You don't just pull in royals and grill them. We filed it as unsolved. Then an emerald from the Baroness's favorite necklace showed up. We traced it here. Sort of. Nothing definite. A whisper. A dozen hands that might or might not have originated with Arno."

Eva waited. "That's it?"

Ven shook her head. "It raised flags, sure enough. But there is something else at work. A problem or concern that has Ricard and Knowles and others on the Council demanding any intel I can deliver."

When Ven went quiet, motionless, Eva pressed, "Some secret issue has the royals buzzing? About a Fourth Ward merchant who may or may not be tied to a stolen gem?"

"Round the clock, totally confidential. When I'm off duty the cameras are monitored from Fourth Ward HQ. Answering directly to the Guards Chief. No one else to even know what we're doing." Ven directed her words to the attic's opposite wall. "All I can tell you is something's got the top brass in a boil. Three times in the past twelve days I've been called into headquarters. I spend an hour or so with three top deputies, same people each time, trying to answer questions they don't actually state outright." Ven pointed a thumb out the window behind her. "Arno's gotten himself involved in something more than a missing necklace and your company director, that's for certain."

A low mist had gathered in the lanes leading from the bookstore back to the thoroughfare and her transport. Eva emerged from the shop carrying the precious book in her pack. Eva never used a purse or shoulder-bag. Kim's combat lessons remained too deeply imbedded for her to feel comfortable being unbalanced or encumbered. Plus her mother detested the pack and complained about it every time they met. Eva assumed it was Maxine's way of registering yet another protest regarding her daughter's profession. Which was a perfect reason for Eva to carry it everywhere.

The fog condensed as she proceeded, and the tavern had gone silent. A faint hum of voices sounded from somewhere distant. Otherwise, the lane was so quiet she could hear droplets falling from the eaves.

Then she caught a harsher sound. Down the side lane opening to her right, a boot scraped upon stone.

What Eva noticed most clearly was how she instantly became aware of the night's tiniest elements. The parchment glow of moonlit droplets, the drifting ribbons of mist up ahead, the softest whisper of traffic along the distant thoroughfare. Her rapid-fire heart's drumming, the soft cymbals of each breath—both accelerated as a second set of boots joined the first. Then, softer still, a third scraping of feet. Only the mist and surrounding structures made determining its location very difficult. Eva decided two people walked together along the lane directly behind her, and now the third approached from up ahead and to her left.

Eva's pack was not a regulation Guards piece of equipment, but it might as well have been—so many agents not in uniform used them. The material was ultra lightweight, almost indestructible, and most importantly was the pack Kim used. Beside the book, it held a pepper spray and electric-shock defense weapon—both of which were useless in this fog unless she was inches from an assailant. She also had a Guards-grade torch, also no help. Her commlink was no good, since by the time help arrived she would be chewed up and spit out, if indeed these were assailants on the prowl. Her Guards' hand weapon would certainly stop them, but firing it when not under direct attack was a criminal offense.

The final item in her pack, however, was made for just such a situation as this.

Ditto for Kim's training.

Eva slowed and adopted a more hesitant pace, as if the encircling fog had made finding her way even more difficult. Quiet as possible, she unslung her pack and unzipped the right-side pocket.

She drew out the first weapon Kim had included in her training, all those many eons ago.

She repositioned her pack, tightened the shoulder straps, then reached around with both hands and pulled together the extra components that gave this pack its singular value. Normally this third strap appeared to be little more than thumb-size appendages extending just below the side pouches. Eva pulled them around and fastened them tight against her lower ribs. The pack was almost part of her now.

She reached a juncture where five lanes came together, forming a space almost as large as the academy's training ground. Eva had been aiming for just such a point ever since hearing the first bootsteps. And here she was.

Eva turned in a slow circle, as if wondering which way to go. The motion helped clarify the assailants' positions—two now approached from her right, one from straight ahead.

As she turned, Eva kept her hands tight to her body, masking her actions. There was a chance one or more of them would be wearing night-goggles, and if indeed they were bent on attack, her survival required secrecy. She quietly extended the collapsible baton, locked it in place, then dropped her hand down to her side, molding the weapon to her pants-leg.

In that single instant beyond time's normal hold, she wondered if this was how warriors felt before battle. The entirety of her life and world condensed to this one tight instant. Every breath was an adrenaline rush, so precious and heady she might have been breathing some intoxicating elixir.

A single shadow took form within the mist directly ahead. She called, "Can I help you?" The exact words were unimportant. What Eva wanted was to show them weakness. The rapid heartrate made her voice unsteady. As if she were afraid.

The pair now visible to her right were so large they filled the lane, one solid mass of flesh possessing four legs. The third man appeared to drift in the mist. His voice was high as a young boy's. "What you got there in your bag, Missy?"

"The lady sells books. I bought one."

"We'll take that book. And everything else you've got in that bag, plus your money, and if you're very cooperative you might just—"

Eva struck.

The trio had such contempt for her they had not even bothered to coordinate their attack. This was evident the instant her baton whirred through the mist, an angry buzz, the hiss of pure menace. She struck the right-side brawler on his temple.

The man dropped in a heap.

"Armed! She's got—"

The second man choked then, breath and words both trapped where her baton stabbed his throat.

This was the secret to baton fighting. The temptation was to swing wide and hard, especially when under attack. Kim's constant refrain was to move quick, strike quick, shift quick, strike again. The baton was equally effective in stabbing, perhaps more so. When the man reached up and gripped his throat, Eva stabbed a second time, now at the groin. A third strike, this time to his forehead. The second brawler joined his mate on the ground.

Then she heard the unmistakable whisper of a blaster powering up.

Eva dropped to the stone pavement alongside the groaning, choking pair. As she hoped, the shooter hesitated, both because her dark clothing masked her in the fog, and because he risked firing on his own men.

She rolled.

Kim's directives were so engrained she did not need to think, which was good, because there wasn't time. Not if she wanted to survive.

Her motions were so fast she bounced across the paving stones, bringing her within baton-reach of the armed third assailant. She stabbed upward with all her might, aiming for the gun-side of his body. He moved to shield himself, which brought his weapon-hand into range of Eva's strike.

The man shrilled a high note and dropped the weapon. Or rather, his fingers were no longer able to keep hold.

Again, Kim's directives saved her life. She did not rise, did not spend precious moments getting to her feet. Which was a vital move, because the man's other hand now held a blade. She caught the flicker of light-on-steel, but she was faster, stabbing a second time, not aiming so much as gouging with all her might for the center of his body.

She heard a rib crack.

The man was unable to emit more than a soft whimper.

Eva struck again from the prone position, this time swinging for his closer knee. Then a fourth strike to his face.

The knife-hand was now joined with his other in seeking to shield both his injured chest and his head as he dropped.

Eva sprang to her feet, kicked both weapons out of reach, and swung down on the man. All the force she had in her body went into hammering him. Again. With both downward strikes she screamed, top of her lungs, a raw bellow of everything that now demanded release. "*Alert! Guards! Alert! Guards!*"

FIVE
Kirra Barret

Kirra strolled along the city-state's most elegant shopping promenade. Treaty's larger moon formed a ghostly presence in the late afternoon sky. These days she visited the elegant Second Ward shopping district after every new theft. It was not so much a reward as her attempt to make the high linger. Opening her eyes after a joined flight, watching the diddybirds land on her Fifth Ward balcony with all their treasures, was a thrill so intense she often wept. Walking along Florian's center of elegance and style formed a pleasant follow-on, like dessert after an exquisite meal.

There was no official law or barrier halting passage between the rings. But the closer a visitor came to Florian's heart, the tighter and more cautious the inspections grew. Of course, none of that was her concern. Not any longer.

It had been fifty-two days since her first theft. When she paused like now, seated in the park closest to the First Ring's main gates, dining on a cup of flavored ice, the speed of her personal transformation left Kirra breathless. Her initial plan had been to take a long pause between every theft. But this had proven impossible to maintain for a multitude of reasons, the largest being how the diddybirds implored and begged for her to fly and hunt. The bond was growing stronger by the day. They did not care what the reason was to her linking with them. Only that it happened. And that there was a *purpose*.

Together they had made fourteen forays. In fifty-two days.

Every time Kirra arrived at Arno's with another collection of stolen treasures, the old man was ready with her next target. She did not ask how he identified them. Nor did she care. Kirra liked how he partitioned his work. It left her certain Arno did not share her role with anyone beyond his inner circle—Dell and Quinn.

She rose and wiped her hands and mouth clear of the sticky residue, and decided to give the First Ward a visit.

The books and stories of Kirra's childhood had showed Florian's six rings as tidy circles. The suggestion these books made, the way they were written, intimated that a good citizen's world began and ended within Florian's walls. And for most people, that was all they needed to know or see. Anyone with greater ambitions or a more adventurous spirit had few options. They could study and compete for one of the very limited places inside Treaty's lone outpost frontier lab. Or they could study and compete for placement within the city-state's embassies. If they possessed certain skills, they could apply to emigrate and live in the spaceport or even another city-state.

Unless, of course, they were very rich. In which case there were two additional options. They could leave Treaty altogether and start life on another planet. Which happened very rarely indeed.

Or they could travel to Treaty's frontier lab as a tourist. Something Kirra intended. Very soon now.

Arno had requested another theft, a high-value item that carried a special challenge. Stealing from the embassy of Corinth, their closest neighbor. Corinth also happened to be Florian's primary rival. Kirra had no idea why, nor did she much care. This theft would be a magnificent conquest, if she could pull it off. Once she had completed this fifteenth sortie, she was going to visit the place where her parents had worked, the lab from which they had been expelled, the reason Kirra had been orphaned at birth.

The First Ring was almost a thousand years old, and rose like a bastion of some bygone era. The inner two rings each possessed four gates, set equidistant around the points of a city-size compass. After that, the rings became too large for such imaginary restrictions. Gates were placed according to need. The Fifth Ring held eleven gates, six of which were designed for traffic to and from the Sixth Ward mines. The Sixth Ring was shaped like a great bulbous extension that pushed Florian's northern boundaries so far it almost doubled the city-state's total size. The Fifth Ward was in fact built upon the original mines, a fact that added to the bitter hatred most inhabitants felt toward the royals and their minions, the Black Watch. Any number of diseases and afflictions, both real and imagined, were caused by the detritus upon which the Fifth Ward housing stood.

By the time the Third Ring was constructed, Florian's rulers no longer felt any need to erect barriers against some alien invasion. The simple fact was that the aliens never approached human habitation. In the previous thousand years, contact between humans and the planet's original species had remained restricted to the lab. Other than the diddybirds, no alien had ever been sighted near a city-state's outer wall.

As a result, the outer rings were little more than boundary markers. The danger inherent in extending Florian's reach did not arise from the aliens. The construction risks, which were huge, came from Treaty itself. The land was mostly swamp. Veins of hard earth formed a lattice within all four continents. Beyond these, however, nothing was stable. Draining away the viscous liquid and fashioning a solid base for the city-state's expansion was hard and dangerous work. But Florian's rulers had no choice. The city-state's population had grown to such a point that anger among those who could not find proper housing had reached a fever pitch. Murmurs of revolt against the Council and the entire ruling class were growing. Those in power had almost left it too late.

The great First Ring was a massive structure, almost twenty meters in height. Guard-towers rose every half kilometer, most of them crumbling structures, none of which had been manned for centuries. Stone used in the ring's construction had been formed from compressed earth cemented into manageably sized blocks. Time and countless rainy seasons had weathered and polished the surface. The First Ring glowed with a honeyed warmth in the late afternoon light. To Kirra's right, blooming vines climbed the wall and encircled the nearest guard-tower. The scene was a smug declaration of humankind's claim to permanence on Treaty.

The gates might have been ceremonial, but the Black Watch guards were extremely vigilant. Kirra carried two bags from different boutiques. A new purse was slung over one shoulder. She took the same attitude she'd perfected when dealing with those honey-badgers in the Third Ward corporate offices. The guards and their stone gazes did not even register. Soon as their ID monitor chirped, Kirra walked into First Ward.

Let them look.

Her destination was midway between the ring and the Regent's palace. Corinth's embassy was a single-story palace spread over a vast acreage. The result was a confusing array of interior courtyards and covered walks and outdoor plazas all hidden behind the façade she now studied. Arno had somehow managed to obtain a detailed plan of the structure, which was vital if she was to succeed. Her objective was a painting hung inside a royal audience hall deep within these confusing recesses. Supposedly the artwork had originated on Earth itself. The value was incalculable. Arno had named a figure, his payout for a successful venture, which would almost double her secret hoard.

There were very special moments these days, when her entire world came into such joyful clarity Kirra wanted to dance; skip down some sunlit avenue, sing to the sky above. Returning to her Fifth Ward balcony and watching the diddybirds swoop in and wait for her to link. Checking the incredible sums now resting safely in her secret accounts. Arno held controlling interests in the two main banks operating through the Third and Fourth Wards, and had shown her how these new numbered accounts could only be accessed through her fingerprint and retina scan. Otherwise, no one would ever know the hidden sums even existed. Stepping through the bank's narrow side entryway, accessible only to the richest of clients, seeing the sums on display, adding money to her wrist-chip, carrying a new wallet filled with cash, all that formed an exquisite joy. Knowing she would soon move into a new apartment Arno was busy fashioning, safe behind a façade as bland and featureless as his offices, that too was incredibly beautiful. A genuine step toward true freedom.

But nothing compared to this.

She seated herself in the park fronting the embassy. There was no need to be here; she knew how to enter; she knew when the theft would take place. Everything was arranged. Twenty minutes before midnight two days from now, the embassy's power would be cut off, and all the security cameras would go down. She had memorized the compound's layout. Kirra was not here to prepare. She was here to become filled with the electric thrill, the anticipation of another blow against all the powers that had done their best to hold her down.

After a time, Kirra rose and walked, pretending to take in other neighboring palaces. She moved just fast enough to blend in. She studied other young women, saw how they strolled and talked and proclaimed with every action and breath who they were. They did not simply belong here. They owned this world. It existed for their pleasure.

As she entered the First Ward's largest plaza, her commlink chimed. She lifted her wrist and saw an accompanying text replace the time on her wristband. Arno. Urgent.

She touched the contact-point. "I'm here."

"Where is that, exactly?"

"First Ward. Central Plaza."

A pause, then, "Wait right there."

Kirra settled by the central fountain. The old man had never been one for casual conversation. Yet she detected a new level of tension, one that threatened the moment's pleasure.

Four minutes later, he called again. "You know the Crillon."

"Arno, my crew stole a brooch and crown from there ten days ago, of course I know."

"Dell is in the process of securing a suite. It's to be registered under her name, but you will appear as a second guest. Give her five minutes more . . . Never mind. It's done. Go now."

She rose and walked by the central fountain. "What's the matter?"

"This is something we must discuss in person. Go straight to your suite. Don't leave. I'll join you soon as I can."

Kirra moved forward in slow motion, a gradual process that granted her time to process what just happened. Whatever Arno needed to tell her represented more than some new risk. A monumental change was in the wind. Another threat to her new life and independence. A new attempt by all those unseen forces arrayed against her to hold her down.

The hotel was built to resemble the grand private residences sharing the Regent's Plaza. Three Black Watch guards stood sentry outside the main entrance. A single glance was enough for Kirra to know this was not some honor guard for an official guest. The Watch was on high alert. As if their sole duty was to reinforce Arno's worrying conversation.

The lobby was, in a word, palatial. Two waterfalls adorned the foyer, masking all sound from beyond the front doors. The welcome desk appeared to have been shaped by blocks of ancient stone, as if stolen from one of the collapsing First Ring guard-towers. A trio in matching uniforms stood in formal attentiveness, all of them smiling at Kirra's approach. She strived to ignore the dark-suited hotel security, four of them, flanking the welcome desk and scattered about the vast lobby.

A young woman with hair oiled tightly in place and makeup that rendered her face into a polished mask asked, "Can I help you, madame?"

Kirra had mentally practiced the words on her approach. "An associate has booked us a room."

The lady took Kirra's name, then processed her fingerprints and did a retina scan. All the while, security strolled in somber dark-suited alertness. The woman asked, "Shall I show you to your suite?"

A suite, no less. "Actually, I'm quite hungry."

The woman displayed professional regret. "Unfortunately, the veranda restaurant is fully booked. I know because my associate just checked for another guest. Shall I ask your butler to serve you in your parlor?"

As the woman escorted Kirra across the lobby and into the lift, she reflected on how simply Arno could have made this entire relationship into something far different. As it was, she had a boss who was both a partner and a friend. Someone she could genuinely trust. A man whose motives meant Kirra waited in a Crillon suite simply because Arno wanted to keep her safe.

Lunch on her private balcony held such a dreamlike quality Kirra never wanted it to end. Her suite was one floor below the veranda restaurant, so close she could hear the occasional clink of cutlery, a crystal chime, the soft bray of laughter. Her view was out toward the alien cloud. Somewhere beyond that yellow-ocher horizon was the lab where her parents had worked, been expelled by the dragon lady, and perished. But not even such thoughts could break this meal's idyllic wonder. Kirra was served by a white-gloved woman who came and went in a silent and respectful ballet. Everything was perfect, the setting and cutlery, linen tablecloth, wine and food. If the server thought anything amiss in how Kirra lingered almost an hour over her first course, the woman gave no sign.

Arno arrived just as the server brought in two covered dishes holding her main course. He observed her, the balcony, the vista, and asked, "What are you having?"

"I forget. But it's all delicious. Want some?"

"Please." The old man's movements were in keeping with this place, as if Arno was accustomed to a young woman holding his chair, settling a cloth napkin across his lap, bringing plate and cutlery and glasses, serving them both. He accepted bits of Kirra's various dishes but seemed uninterested in what he ate. Arno was not a heavy eater. His shapeless and overweight bearing did not originate from diet so much as an absolute indifference toward exercise. He viewed the concept of a physical fitness regime as ludicrous, which Kirra found mildly hilarious, since Arno owned the six finest gyms in the Third and Fourth Wards. They even bore his name, Arno's Studios, the only components of his empire that were not a carefully guarded secret.

Kirra knew whatever brought Arno here would probably fracture her happy state. She minded, but not nearly so much as she might have expected. The old man's grim presence was merely part of this transition. Settling into this new definition of life did not mean an end to bad tidings. She was too much a realist to hold such hopes. Instead, Kirra was immensely grateful for his patience. Despite whatever pressed Arno to rush over and ask her to hide in such luxury, he granted her time and space to savor the meal, the lingering afternoon light, the second moonrise.

When she finished and the server had swept away the dishes and brought them coffee and little cakes, Arno set a device on the table. It was something she had never seen before, a stubby item the size of a jewelry case. Two antennae did a series of circular sweeps, then a red blinking light on its surface went green and Arno said, "We're in the process of forming another new identity for you. It's as close to perfect as anything I might have personally designed."

"The way you rushed me in here," Kirra replied, "I was expecting something, I don't know, funereal."

"This first. Some time back, a young girl aged four and a half succumbed to the alien pox. Her father was a mine director. According to hospital records the child had found the digs fascinating and visited the mine-heads every chance she got. She must have caught the alien virus there. Soon after her death, the family relocated to the spaceport and from there to a more completely terraformed planet. The deceased child would now be three years older than you, but close enough . . . What?"

She shook her head, banishing the queasy thought of stealing a dead child's identity. "Nothing. Go on."

"The ID and related history are being redesigned as we speak. You will soon have a new wrist chip confirming you to be the daughter who refused to go to space with her family. All this will grant us a perfect reason for your growing wealth." Arno offered a very satisfied smile. "And of course coming from a family with this level of wealth you were naturally assigned to the highest possible gradient."

Kirra gave that news the moment it deserved. A new life, offered without the hint of strings because Arno trusted her as she did him. She breathed deep, taking it in, then released a solemn, "Thank you, Arno. So much."

"You are most welcome, my young friend and partner." His smile gradually faded. "And now we must insert the bitter in with the sweet."

"Someone is hunting you," Arno told her. "Someone good. And highly connected."

Kirra had no idea how to respond. On the one hand, being the object of a search could hardly be a surprise. She had stolen from some of the city-state's wealthiest and most powerful citizens. Yet she could not dismiss the news out of hand. Not with Arno appearing so deeply worried. Almost frightened.

"We only discovered her by sheer chance." He fiddled with a button on his shirt cuff until it finally came loose. Arno tossed it over the balcony railing, his sleeve now flopping about his forearm. "A couple of thieves I know from the Hawkins clan recently teamed up with a fellow who might resemble Quinn if he was not somewhat lacking in the brains department. They targeted a late-night visitor to the Fourth Ward market's bookseller. Apparently, she came in by way of private transport. It happens from time to time, wealthy patrons in love with words on paper." He mulled that over, frowning at the thought of someone willing to waste money on such trivia. Then, "Where was I?"

"Arno, I have no idea."

"Books. Yes. The attack was apparently all stitched together while they were seated outside the main tavern. A bad idea to begin with. They intended to use the empty late-night market as a chance to rob, accost, take their pleasure. Totally unacceptable."

"Arno, I'm sorry, I don't understand." She searched the whirling jumble of thoughts for a coherent question, came up with, "I thought the market was off limits."

"It is." He shrugged. "I am personally responsible for the market's security. The lady saved us the bother of doling out punishments."

"This customer fended them off?"

"She wasn't just a customer. And she destroyed them. Armed with nothing but a collapsible baton, she rendered them unable to walk or feed themselves. This would-be customer would have done permanent damage if she hadn't yelled for a Guards agent, who then intervened."

"An agent?" Kirra said. "Not a Black Watch on patrol?"

"Correct."

"At night. In the Fourth Ward market."

He nodded. "Absurd as that may sound."

She read his expression clear as written script. "You checked."

"Thoroughly."

"They have you under surveillance."

Another nod. "I suppose that should have been anticipated."

"Why? What have you done?"

He hesitated, then decided, "Best we leave that for another day. We risk muddying the already murky waters. Agents have occasionally been assigned such duties. Anyone with my financial reach is bound to come under scrutiny."

"But now is different?"

"Very." His gaze was bottomless. "It is crucial that I go unnoticed."

She did not feel so much disappointed as resigned. The all-too familiar sensation of being stymied threatened to smother her. She managed, "You want me to stop?"

"No, my dear." His voice no longer matched his gaze. The words were almost gentle now. "I need you to disappear."

"The two agents from the market," Dell told her. "They're part of a new team of investigators. We don't know much about them. Yet. But what Arno has managed to uncover is troubling in the extreme."

Kirra and Dell rode along the Second Ward's main avenue in the Crillon's own private transport. The driverless vehicle was whisper-quiet. Their chairs, hers and Dell's, were incredibly comfortable and swiveled about, granting them a circular vision through darkened windows. The world swept casually, comfortably past. Far beyond her reach. Kirra might as well have been offering the city-state a silent farewell. "I don't understand." Nor, in truth, was Kirra certain she wanted to know. Her only clear thought was she was being expelled. Deported. Her fate lay elsewhere.

And worst of all, the unanswerable question that filled her with a genuine terror, was whether her bond to the diddybirds was about to be severed.

"They're hunting Arno," Dell said. She glanced down at the device resting on her chair-arm, the same one Arno had used on Kirra's balcony. The light blinked green. Dell continued, "Their resources are effectively limitless."

"But what does that have to do with me?"

"It's a valid question. But Arno has ordered me not to discuss certain activities. He's not shutting you out. He's just doing what has kept him safe for years."

"Compartmentalizing," Kirra said. "But I need to know." When Dell grimaced, she insisted, "*I need this.*"

"We have allies on the Council. One of them is privy to this investigation. Your thefts have become part of their search. Which on the surface makes no sense. But apparently a jewel Arno released into the market through intermediaries has been traced back."

Kirra could almost hear the portal slamming shut. Sealing her from any hope of remaining in Florian. "One jewel."

"One small portion of that gorgeous emerald from your first foray," Dell agreed. "It's not much, I agree. But it came from the manor of Baron Knowles. Arno's opponents have seized on this as their one and only chance to put him down." A flush of anger reddened her features. "Like a dog. That's how they see him. Someone to eliminate by whatever means possible."

"I don't understand." The words had almost become a litany.

"And I can't tell you more. What's important here is this. They're hunting you. They think or they hope that you may prove to be the link they require to arrest and charge and exclude him."

"Exclude him from what?"

"Wrong question. Listen to what I'm saying. In time they will find you. They would eliminate you along with Arno. And we can't let that happen." Dell's voice resumed its normal brisk tone. "The new identity we're fashioning should be ready in four or five days. Perhaps less. Certainly not more. We're also in the process of erasing you from their system. By this time tomorrow, Kirra of clan Barret, Gradient Five citizen of Florian, will effectively cease to exist. In her place you will rise up and resume your new identity." Dell gave her a chance to object, then passed over a manila envelope. "In the meantime, you'll be traveling under the identity we fashioned for your insertion into Boaz's group."

Kirra accepted the documents and wondered at her absence of any emotional response. But it was all coming too shockingly fast. In time, perhaps. But now, all she could think to ask was, "What is my new name?"

"You will soon become Blythe Breigh," Dell replied.

"You have got to be joking."

"When all this is behind us, you're more than welcome to change your name back to Kirra. Tell anyone who asks you're making a total separation from the family who left you an orphan, while they flew off to another planet, never to return." Dell shrugged. "Certainly works for me."

Their destination was a small shop at the far end of the Second Ward's exclusive shopping district. The front window was as opaque as their transport's. Gold-colored letters above the entryway declared it to sell luxury travel.

"Making this trip to the frontier lab is a brilliant idea," Dell said. "Though I'd much rather hide away inside the Crillon for the next few days."

"This trip is something I've always wanted."

"Personally, I can't see why anyone would bother," Dell mused. "Spend two days getting to a lab where you're not welcome, surrounded by alien life that would probably eat you given half a chance. Two days there, two back, for the cost of an ocean cruise and ten days in Corinth's premier hotel?"

The reservations had been remarkably easy to put in place. From her sofa in the Crillon lobby, Dell had contacted the lone agency handling trips to the frontier lab while Arno and Kirra remained seated on the suite's balcony. Arno had been enormously pleased with the concept. Get Kirra safely out of the city-state, stowed away where no one could possibly hunt her down, and more importantly give the techies a firm do-or-die timeline for completing her new identity. When Dell confirmed a convoy departed the next morning, Arno beamed.

She told Dell, "I'd rather not sit around and wait for a knock on the door. Do these hunters have my photograph?"

"We don't know. I personally think it's only a matter of time."

"My original name?"

"Not yet."

"You think or you know?" When Dell's only response was to stare at the shop's blank window, Kirra said, "This is a much better idea, and Arno agrees."

Dell offered a minute shrug. "Arno wants me to ask if you're positive you can control your crew."

"Yes."

"You're absolutely certain? A great deal more than your own survival is at stake."

Kirra disliked how Dell stressed that word: *Survival.* She was certain Dell would only have said it because Arno had emphasized the need. The man was very precise in his usage of terms, and Dell was equally good at exactly following instructions. "As far as you're concerned, they are smoke in the wind."

Dell must have found what she needed in Kirra's expression, for she nodded and reached for her door panel. "Let's get you on that convoy."

Kirra left for the frontier lab's main supply depot more than three hours before sunrise. The hotel's transport swept her through unfamiliar streets, almost all of them empty. The guards by the First and Second and Third Rings saluted them through, the car's AI driver scarcely slowing. She had never been in this region before. The Fourth Ward was divided into carefully defined segments—market and manufacturing and housing and this, the laboratory depot, situated not far from the Fourth Ring's southern entry point. The moons were both high and brilliant in the cloudless sky when they swept onto the avenue paralleling the depot's exterior fence.

The depot's lone entry-point was manned by four Black Watch on high alert. The tall gates were embossed with the Regent's own seal, and above that illuminated letters read 'Treaty Frontier Lab, Authorized Personnel Only.'

Purchasing Kirra's ticket had proven to be a tedious process requiring almost four hours. Once Dell had paid the enormous sum, the agent had settled Kirra in a side alcove where a technician had appeared on a screen and spent ninety minutes running her through a questionnaire in a bored voice. Following that, they had returned to the Crillon and encountered a medical technician waiting to give her a full physical. The physician's assistant had been pressed for time, as Kirra was one of nine would-be travelers he was required to test, all on the day before traveling. Five of them were waiting in other Crillon guestrooms, visitors from Treaty's other city-state, there to view the planet's lone frontier lab for themselves.

While she waited for entry into the lab's Fourth Ward depot, five other vehicles appeared and fit themselves into line. The guards kept the gate in place while moving along the line of transports. Inside the gates rose two structures, a vast warehouse and a smaller windowless building rimmed by a second fence with guards on foot patrol. Eleven vehicles were positioned along a wide loading bay, while workers sped around, all of them moving at a near-run. An officer in full regalia and two young people, a man and woman, stood with electronic manifests, observing everything. Kirra watched the young man speak to the officer, who barked at a forklift operator. Instantly the loader swung around to the next transport.

The vehicles themselves were curious indeed, each possessing eight giant tires and bulbous front windscreens and roofs crowned by vents and air-filtration systems the size of coffins. Their coloring was a mottled khaki-grey, as if the designers did all they could to make them appear both alien and ugly.

When the exterior guards finally raised the barrier, the female technician was the first to notice their approach. She nudged her companion, who glanced over and made a face. The woman smirked and went back to checking items off her tablet.

The young man waited until they had all disembarked to say, "Follow the yellow markers to the changing room. Leave everything electronic in your assigned locker. You are required to cycle through the chemical shower, then change into the coveralls which are—"

"Just a minute." The woman was narrow and tall and angry. "I've purchased a very fine set of traveling clothes, and I demand to wear what I like. The very idea of being ordered to spend six days in your garments is absurd! And something more, young man. After the outrageous amount we've paid, I expect you to speak to us with respect!"

The male technician glanced at his associate, who rolled her eyes and resumed ticking items on her tablet. The officer paid them no mind whatsoever. The young man replied, "These were not requests, and I am not here to play servant. My name is Dr. Marcel Obon, and I am a microbiologist on my sixth year at the frontier lab." He pointed to the vehicles which had not yet been allowed to pass back through the exterior gates. "If you are unable or unwilling to follow orders, your transport is waiting. Leave now. The rest of you, the convoy departs in eight minutes."

Kirra and the eight other travelers followed yellow arrows planted on raw concrete walls into a pair of unadorned changing facilities. The medical examiner had taken Kirra's measurements, and waiting for her were four identical grey coveralls in plastic wrapping, with another hanging from the door of her assigned locker. She thought the outfit was as ugly as their convoy's vehicles. The tall narrow woman complained loudly as they all proceeded into the shower stalls and were sprayed with a foul-smelling chemical wash, then water, then a second chemical dousing, and water again. Then they went back into the locker room, where Kirra donned the coverall and a pair of canvas slip-on shoes. On the locker's lone shelf was a satchel made from the same material as her clothing. A notice taped to her locker door repeated the instructions the medical examiner had offered—three kilos of personal items max, no electronics or any cosmetic that contained fragrance.

The eldest woman among the travelers looked ready to weep. "None of this makes any sense."

The tall woman's shape was made worse by the coverall. "What possible good can come from forcing us to dress like, like *miners*."

"And this three-kilo restriction," the elder said. "Sheer madness."

Kirra spoke aloud what she had been suspecting since completing the two-hour questionnaire. "They don't want us here."

All four women turned her way. "What?"

"The lab scientists and technicians," Kirra said. "They resent our presence. They think we're invading their space."

The fourth woman assigned the locker next to Kirra was aged in her late forties and possessed a keenly intelligent face. "That actually makes perfect sense."

The larger woman sniffed. "Well, I for one see nothing whatsoever *sensible* about this entire process."

The male changing area lay behind a separate door, but the space above the lockers was open. A man's voice demanded, "What makes you say that?"

The woman next to Kirra said, "It seems the most logical answer to this series of insults." She smiled. "I'm Adeline."

"Kirra."

The man said, "Tell us why. Please. I want to understand."

Kirra directed her words to the woman sharing her bench. "The ridiculous cost, that questionnaire, the contract we were forced to sign."

Adeline added, "How the medical inspection was held at the last possible moment, and was preceded by the warning that if we failed, our payments were forfeit. It was utterly unnecessary to wait until the night before departure."

Kirra demanded, "You think, or you know?"

"I'm a pediatric surgeon," the woman replied. "There is no good reason on earth why the exam couldn't have been done days in advance."

Kirra said, "I suspect the frontier lab is required to make room for visitors. But they hate it. We interrupt their work and take up space."

"Not to mention the supplies we consume," Adeline added. "They have every reason to despise our invasion."

"But they have to do it," Kirra repeated. "So, they design a process as unpleasant—"

The lab technician called from the changing area's entryway, "Three minutes!"

Marcel waited for them on the loading platform. He pointed to the transport closest to him and said, "You are traveling in T7. Find a berth and have your carryall ready for inspection." He indicated a woman standing by the entryway. "Clarissa will ensure you are correctly settled."

The bossy woman demanded, "What does that mean exactly, settled?"

But the young man had already turned away. "We depart in two minutes."

One by one they stepped forward and Clarissa checked their wrist-chips and gave their canvas sacks a perfunctory inspection and pointed them inside, all without meeting anyone's gaze. She was determinedly removed from them, a waifish woman in her early thirties, slender as Kirra's little finger. As Kirra climbed the transport's stairs, Adeline muttered, "I've seen more personality on cadavers."

"My guess is, they're both on some form of punishment detail." Kirra followed the surgeon along the central aisle. She had not expected to find anyone among the wealthy and powerful she actually liked. Yet here she was, waiting as Adeline stowed her goods in the overhead compartment, settled by the left-hand window. Kirra then took the seat opposite. "You're from Florian?"

"I was originally." Adeline paused as the young scientist and Clarissa slipped down the aisle, entered the forward compartment, and told the driver to get underway. "I moved to Corinth after my training. They were in desperate need of pediatric surgeons and offered me a top position."

Several travelers were still settling as their transport pulled into line and the convoy wheeled out. When the lady complained over being rushed, Marcel told them, "We have to make the midway hostel before sunset. No exceptions."

Kirra heard herself ask, "What happens if we're late?"

"No one knows. No convoy that left the route or was delayed en route has ever been found or heard from again."

When he faced forward, the portly gentleman seated behind Adeline asked, "Was he joking?"

After they passed through the periphery gates, Kirra became

enveloped by a heady sense of disconnect. She observed the world beyond her windows as if seeing everything for the very first time. Simultaneously observing herself, this new-old Kirra in the midst of total transformation, and the world seen through the lens of change. She was leaving not just the city-state, but the single plane of existence that had defined her. Until now.

As they approached the Fourth Ring, Adeline whispered, "And here we go."

Every now and then Marcel swiveled partway around and offered a comment, bland and functional, like he was checking points off a mental list. Such as, "Restrictions laid out in the original treaty are both precise and non-negotiable. One such point is, no flights of any kind at any altitude are permitted outside the human habitation zones."

"I came back by sea," Adeline told her. "Nine days each way."

Once Marcel swung about, Kirra replied, "I've never been anywhere."

"You should come visit us in Corinth," Adeline said. "See what else our planet has to offer."

"You're traveling alone?"

"My husband and children are waiting for me back at the hotel. They think I'm insane, making this trip. You?"

"No one to travel with."

"I've wanted to do this since forever. I begged my husband to come. If not for the trip itself, then so we could share the memories."

"I can't imagine what that might be like," Kirra replied. "Wanting to share memories with someone."

Adeline gave her a slow inspection, then said, "The men in your life have not been so kind, I take it."

Kirra heard herself reply, "More like, life in general hasn't held much in the way of kindness."

"Well, well." A genuine smile. "And here we are. Solitary companions and potential friends."

Kirra's need to respond was cut off by Marcel rising from his seat and standing in the doorway of a partition that divided the drivers' cabin from the travelers. He waited as the Fourth Ring's shadow slipped past their windows, then offered, "As most of you know, we are now entering the Fifth Ward by way of the southernmost gates. For those of you who are not from Florian, the Sixth Ring is relatively close, just six kilometers ahead. The main Fifth Ward developments lie well to our north, where it encompasses all residences occupied by our mining community."

Kirra waited for the bitter wash, a natural response to this casual dismissal of her clan and upbringing. She stared out the side window, watching the pre-dawn shadows of hydroponic farms, row after endless row of odd bulbous-shaped structures. To her mild astonishment, she felt nothing at all.

Marcel pointed to a video screen imbedded in the overhead panel, now displaying a map of Florian. Only this one was unlike any Kirra had ever seen. Across the aisle, Adeline frowned and leaned forward. The city-state itself was mostly blank. The only internal illustrations were a compass placed where the Regent's palace should have been, and the unevenly shaped six Rings.

Beyond this was a dotted line indicating where the Seventh Ring was to go. Much further still, shrinking the city-state itself down to a palm-size imprint, was a broad indentation that formed a nearly perfect circle and trebled Florian's size. Within this outer boundary were eleven illuminated markers. Just inside the Sixth Ring, a fourth point that bore the notation, *Convoy 4X477*, moved slowly south.

"The final perimeter marks the dimensions established by the planetary treaty," Marcel told them. "Those illuminated points denote as-yet untapped mineral deposits. Florian's full size is two hundred and fifty kilometers north to south, three hundred west to east."

Adeline asked, "Where is the lab?"

"I'll address that later." He pointed out the side windows. "First, you need to observe what happens when we pass through the Sixth Ring and enter unclaimed territory, deeded to the city-state but as-yet untouched."

As they passed through the gates, all heads craned and searched, and saw . . .

Nothing.

The scene beyond their windows was utterly blank. The earth was a bland grey, so void in shape and color it was hard for Kirra's gaze to fasten and take hold. In its own way, the flat, featureless void was both hostile and frightening. They did not belong. Life did not exist in this grey expanse.

Marcel continued, "Within days of our treaty becoming finalized, all alien life disappeared from the four regions assigned to humans. What you see here was repeated on all four continents and the spaceport's island. No shred of alien lifeform remained, right down to the microscopic level." Once again he swept a languid hand toward their windows. "This region has remained precisely as you see for over a thousand years."

Adeline said, "I thought the city-states are responsible for keeping our atmosphere safe."

Marcel and Clarissa exchanged a look. Their male guide replied, "That is a myth propagated by people who should know better. Ten centuries ago, in the time of the First Ring, we had our own purification system. But as our city-states grew, we realized there was no need to maintain what the aliens did for us."

Kirra asked, "What about the diddybirds?"

This time, both technicians and the relief driver all turned toward her. Marcel's voice lost its disinterested tone. "They first appeared in Florian twenty years ago. And just here, in this one city-state. Nowhere else. Not then, not now. That same day, as far as we've been able to establish, we were ordered to have nothing to do with them. We may not study them. We may not speak of them. Contact of any kind is strictly forbidden."

His tone and the manner which all three watched the travelers captured everyone's attention. Adeline asked, "But why?"

"We have no idea."

"Who could possibly order such a thing?"

"The master aliens."

Adeline looked at Kirra, as if seeking permission to keep questioning. "Who or what are they?"

"We don't know."

"But . . . You're the *lab*. You're *supposed* to know. It's your *duty*."

"Our tasks and responsibilities are as carefully defined as Florian's boundaries," Marcel replied. "What we can study, what we are permitted to ask, the limits to our examinations are . . ."

Clarissa spoke for the first time. "Hampered. Confined." Another shared look, then, "Restricted by the treaty."

"A word of advice," Marcel told them. "Once we pass the city-state's treaty boundary, do not mention the birds or our lab's restrictions."

"Especially at the lab," Clarissa added. "If word ever reached the director, you would be confined to this transport for the duration of your stay."

Marcel said, "We arrive at the midway station in . . ."

"Ten and a half hours," Clarissa supplied.

"Enjoy the ride." Marcel pointed down the central corridor. "Freshers are available behind the rear seats. Beyond that is a fairly well-stocked kitchen." He glared at the complaining woman, as if daring her to protest the lack of service. Wisely she chose to remain silent. Marcel then retreated and closed the door.

The convoy gradually sped up, faster and faster, until all Kirra could make out beyond their side windows was a grey blur. This went on for almost an hour, the massive wheels creating a high-pitched whine. The empty desolation silenced them all.

The yellow cloud grew slowly until it dominated the forward horizon. Kirra rose from her seat and started forward. When she knocked on the partition's paneled door, the tall woman asked, "Can she do that?"

When no one responded, Kirra tested the knob and found it unlocked. She opened the door and asked, "Can I please watch? Just for a moment? I feel like I've waited my entire life to see this."

The only sound came from the tires' high-pitched whine. Then the waifish woman snorted, as if she found something comic in how Marcel and the relief driver stared. Even their pilot cast Kirra the occasional glance, despite his high-speed pursuit of the transport directly in front of them.

Clarissa occupied the front passenger seat. Marcel and the

relief driver had seats positioned behind and elevated slightly above the front pair. Behind these were two fold-down seats fastened to the side walls. At a nod from the pilot, Marcel said, "Make yourself comfortable."

"Thank you." As she settled, Kirra looked back through the open doorway and motioned for Adeline to join her. Adeline smirked and rolled her eyes in response.

Clarissa snorted a second time.

The relief driver's pale-blue coverall held the same insignia on his shoulder as their pilot. He gave her the lingering sort of inspection she had learned early to detest. "What's your name, pretty lady?"

Kirra had a lifetime's practice at ignoring unwanted comments and looks and questions and invitations. Yet in this case, she had asked to be included. Politeness required her to answer. But in that instant, a woman's deep voice came over the forward speakers, "Chief here. Slow for passage through the veil. Drivers sound off."

"That's what you call it?" Kirra asked. "The veil? It suits."

The mountainous golden-ocher cloud dominated the world ahead. Its face was a slow-moving myriad of currents, multiple rivers in conflicting tidal surges.

One by one the convoy became swallowed and vanished from sight. Each time, another voice sounded through the speakers, saying the same words—the transport's number, then *Holding steady*. A few moments, then four words more. *Pilot confirms safe passage.*

They were moving slow enough for Kirra to watch the cloud's approach and observe the tension on those four faces. She was glad to see how, despite their years of experience, this first contact with the alien powers still unnerved them.

They entered full darkness. Their pilot touched a button imbedded in his wheel and spoke the words, "Transport seven holding steady."

The exterior world was obliterated. The transport's interior lighting shone on taut expressions.

Soon as they emerged into sunlight, their driver reported, "Pilot confirms safe passage."

The instant they were fully beyond the veil, Kirra cried aloud. A great gasping shout as . . .

They entered a different world.

The transition was instantaneous. Before the veil, all was grey, swampy nothingness, utterly void of life and color and movement. But in the split second they emerged from the dark passage, they experienced a visual explosion.

Kirra felt as if she had been physically assaulted. The scene defied her ability to interpret, much less understand. The earth to either side of the road *pulsed*. Great rippling waves launched and flowed out to the horizon. Each massive undulation caused currents of illumination that grew ever more brilliant with each oscillation.

As the convoy gradually accelerated away from the veil, trees appeared on the road's right side. Within the space of a few tight breaths, these grew from little saplings into a forest. The trunks twisted and writhed into massive vine-like growths that rose in pulses timed to the earth's vibrations, expanding until they towered high above the passing transports. Then they sprouted great bulbous tops that ballooned out to join with the neighboring trees, not so much flowering as exploding in colors that shone in the same rhythmic pattern as the earth.

Then the trees began to move.

This forest walked or rode or careened, Kirra could not be certain. The trees were so tightly bunched their colorful growths now formed a single unit that flowed and writhed and marched. Try as she might, Kirra could not see how they moved, only that somehow the forest kept up with the speeding convoy.

The driver said, "The natives are restless today."

Marcel leaned forward, frowning at the forest.

Their radio clicked on, and the deep-voiced woman said, "Chief here, calling for technicians traveling in the transport. Are these trees a concern?"

When neither technician responded, the relief driver poked Marcel's shoulder. "Answer the chief. Are we in danger?"

Marcel reached for the commlink. "Marcel here, Chief. We witness this in the regions beyond our lab."

"Never in the dry season," Clarissa added. "Never on this route."

Marcel nodded and told the chief, "It's out of synch with normal annual cycles, no question."

The chief hesitated, then said, "Keep me aware of anything that suggests a higher degree of risk."

"Roger that."

"Chief out."

Only then did Kirra realize how the other travelers had become so noisy it sounded like they let out a single massive yell. Marcel rose, walked back, and slammed the divider. "They always do that."

Clarissa said, "I hate the racket more than anything."

The relief driver pointed to the pilot and told Kirra, "You should have heard this one scream his first time out."

"I did not," the pilot replied. "And even if I did, you weren't there."

"I heard," he said, grinning at Kirra. "Two years on, they're still talking about it. High as a little girl, this one."

The tires were literally singing now, yet their speed remained matched by the undulating currents on their left and the forest to their right. Kirra thought the trees most resembled a graceful ballet. As far as she could tell, these alien beings did not possess limbs of any kind. Yet they held to the transport's passage with liquid ease.

Then they vanished.

The forest halted so swiftly it seemed as though they became swallowed by the earth. But when she flung open the partition doorway and craned out the rear windows, there they were, an undulating mass heading back toward the veil.

Clarissa asked, "Should we alert the director?"

Marcel did not respond.

The travelers were all massed by the rear windows now, chattering and gesticulating and frightened.

Clarissa took the empty undulating vista as her cue to tell Kirra, "Why don't you go join the others."

But as Kirra started to rise, the pilot said, "Oh, let her stay."

"Brightens my day, this one," the relief driver agreed.

Clarissa looked ready to object, but Marcel cut her off with a soft, "Oh no, no, no, no."

As if in response, the transport chief came back on. "Chief here. Marcel, alert the lab."

Marcel grabbed the commlink and replied, "Ma'am, the director is back in Florian. Supposedly on leave, but she hasn't left the warehouse lab for days. She's the one—"

Clarissa interrupted with, "This can't be happening!"

The chief was yelling now. "Alert the director *immediately.*"

Clarissa protested, "This is totally off cycle!"

"Let's hope we have a signal." Marcel leaned between the two front seats and fiddled with the commlink's controls.

Abruptly the pilot snapped, "Let me do that." A few swift adjustments, then, "Go ahead."

"This is Dr. Marcel, traveling in transport six—"

"Seven," the pilot corrected.

"Seven. Is the director available?"

The response was broken and static filled. "She's left orders not to be disturbed."

"This is urgent," Marcel replied. "Tell the director we have hills rising to our right."

In fact, both sides of the road were undergoing transitions that Kirra found utterly fascinating, despite how the forward compartment's other four occupants now shared an expression close to panic.

Marcel said, "Yes, I know it's out of phase and I'm telling you it's happening."

The pilot said, "They're growing. Fast."

"Did you hear that?" When the only response was a windrush of static, Marcel lowered the commlink and said, "Try another frequency."

The pilot made further adjustments, then said, "Use the earpiece. Sometimes that helps."

Marcus fit the device into place, listened, then replied, "Of course I'll wait." He told the others, "As if I have any choice."

Kirra thought the road's left side was almost as interesting as the low hills rising to her right. The undulating fields had developed a very distinct rhythm now, a color-coded rise and fall that were bounded on all sides by what appeared to be illuminated dikes. Great pearl-white streaks ran to the horizon, which she assumed were lines of hard earth, with these rainbow swamps writhing in unison.

"Hello," Marcel called. Then more loudly, "*Hello?*"

To her right, where the trees had formerly made their racing ballet, now rose steep-sided golden hills. They grew steadily in size and shape, extending in a line parallel to the road, growing fast as the convoy traveled.

Gradually the hills became modest mountains. As they did so, their color deepened to a rich copper and their façades appeared to harden. Solidify. Something. Kirra thought it was like watching these new facets of the alien world ripen and mature at an astonishing pace. Ahead of the convoy they emerged small in size, a brilliant shimmering gold, then rose and steepened and hardened and darkened, all in a matter of seconds.

She asked, "Are they alive?"

As if in response, Clarissa jammed a finger at the side window and yelled, "Caves! I see caves!"

Marcel, however, spoke in a voice that was almost bland. "Yes, Director. I confirm what Clarissa said. There are definitely . . . How many?" He squinted out the side window. "Dozens. More."

Their relief driver confirmed, "Too many to count."

"*Eyes!*" Clarissa shrieked now. "*I see eyes!*"

There were indeed eyes opening along the ridgeline, huge and globular in shape, a slightly greenish alteration to the mountains' coloring. Each as large as their transport. Bigger. They swiveled and observed as the convoy sped onward.

The pilot touched his own earpiece and said, "I've got the chief." He played with the controls. "OK, she's coming through our intercom."

The deep-voiced woman demanded, "Marcel, are you in contact with the director?"

"Barely, Chief. The link comes and goes."

"Tell her I suggest we reverse course."

Marcel shouted the information a second time. Then, "Chief, the director confirms."

When the chief did not immediately respond, their driver hit the intercom button and said, "T7 pilot here, Chief. Do we reverse course?"

Clarissa's terror was now given a concrete form. She screamed so loud Kirra felt the words strike with physical force. "*TURN YES CONFIRMED TURN NOW!*"

As if in response, the chief came on with, "Chief to all transports. We have official confirmation of possible danger en route. We are ordered back to Florian."

Kirra assumed the instructions had been anticipated, for the other transports were already slowing.

The tall woman jammed herself into the portal and yelled, "I demand to know what is happening!"

"One moment, Director." Marcel rose and shoved the woman back down the aisle. "Everybody sit down, strap in, and shut up!" He slammed the door shut and declared, "I've wanted to do that since forever."

"No, leave it open," the pilot said. "I need a clear view out back."

Starting from the rearmost vehicle, the convoy began a squeaky-tight sequence of maneuvers. The entire convoy completed a hundred-and-eighty-degree turn, in synch, all without a single tire leaving the road.

Kirra said, "It's like you've just performed metal gymnastics."

"We practice it," the relief driver said. "Boring days on end."

The pilot fit their transport into proper position and accelerated back in the direction from which they had come. "Not so boring now, though, is it?" When Clarissa restarted her wordless keen, he asked, "What's her story?"

Marcel did not even glance at his associate. "Remember the convoy we lost two years ago? Her best friend was on it." The central commlink chimed. "Yes, Director?" To the driver, "She wants to know if you're filming."

"Since passing through the veil. As always."

"She wants you to try and link her into the live camera feed. Clarissa?" When the woman remained frozen in place, her gaze steady and unblinking on the fast-growing hills, he leaned forward and fit himself between the two front seats. A long pause as he worked the controls, then, "Director, if the signal is strong enough you should be . . . OK, Good."

They accelerated back in the direction of the veil. Kirra thought they were now moving even faster than on their way out. She found herself breathing somewhat easier now, as if the earthbound cloud dominating the horizon offered hope.

"Beasts!" Clarissa pointed beyond the pilot, who angrily swiped her arm away from his field of vision. *"I see beasts!"*

Marcel said, "Yes, Director." He leaned forward and took the pilot's commlink from its station. "Transport six to convoy chief."

The pilot and relief driver spoke together. "Transport Seven."

Marcel swatted it away. "Director Maxine requests confirmation no one left the road."

The chief's voice came on. "Pilots sound off in order."

As the transport drivers responded one by one, a rainbow tide poured from the cliffside caverns and spilled down those very steep slopes. Kirra's first impression was of a collection of alien beasts melting and flowing at incredible speed. As they reached level ground, Kirra saw legs sprouting. Great muscular pistons hammered the earth as these cavern beasts flowed into tight lines, following the veins of solid earth.

The beasts were so crammed together Kirra could not make out actual shapes. Here and there she saw heads, eyes, predatory mouths open and roaring. But no complete shape. There were so many, so tightly packed. All of them aimed at the convoy.

The transport's rear compartment was filled with noise. The other travelers shrieked and yelled, their voices melding together tight as the alien beasts. She heard Marcel say in a resigned voice, "Yes, Director." He rose and stepped into the open portal and motioned for silence. When the noise reduced to whimpers and more softly spoken protests, he said, "Obviously we can't go forward."

The large woman demanded, "What is *happening*?"

"We have no idea." He pointed to the tidal surge of beasts, who had now traversed almost half the plain. "We witness this from time to time, but normally in cycles so regular we can avoid any such contact."

"But what do we *do*?"

"We run." Marcel lifted both hands and shook his head to the unison of protests and queries. "Listen up. I don't have time for this. We are heading back as fast as possible. Stay strapped in. We'll do our very best to keep you safe—"

Clarissa leapt to her feet and pointed out the front windscreen. *"Trees! The trees are going on the attack!"*

Marcel's entire body tensed, a rigor tension so tight he actually silenced the rear compartment. He whipped about, leapt into his seat, fumbled with his straps, said, "Yes, Director. The reports are confirmed." He reached for the pilot's commlink. "Chief, the director says all restrictions on speed are lifted. Redline the vehicles."

In response, their convoy sped up faster and faster. The engine's noise was audible now, a tight electric whine louder than the spinning wheels. The pilot struggled and fought to keep them on the road.

The beasts were close enough now to see the heads and enraged faces of the lead animals. Another minute, less, and they would strike.

The relief driver fumbled with his personal commlink, said, "Darling, if you can hear me I love you more than life—" The transport hit a bump and he lost his hold and dropped the commlink. It rattled across the compartment's floor and vanished under Clarissa's seat.

Marcel shouted now. "Director, the trees are lining both sides of the road between the convoy and the veil! It's true! It's true! The entire forest is leaning back, ready to strike!"

All the while, the ferocious tide of beasts grew closer.

Kirra shut her eyes.

She joined with a first bird. Hissed the words, speaking so quietly she scarcely heard herself. Which of course did not matter. *Come. Help. Attack. Now.*

Despite the transport's soundproofing, she thought she heard the diddybirds' arrival. Or perhaps it was a sensation carried by the visual link.

So many, many wings.

In her mind they sounded like a waterfall, a great liquid rush, almost a roar. Until that moment she had never heard any sound when bonded, and perhaps did not now. Maybe it was all in her mind, linking to this huge and growing cloud of alien birds. The largest number she had ever experienced. More diddybirds than she even thought existed.

With each transfer, linking with one bird and then swiftly moving to the next, Kirra's ability to shift between beasts became more fluid. Which was crucial now, because the cloud grew ever larger and denser. It seemed as if every diddybird on Treaty had been waiting for this very moment. Hundreds of them were with her now. Thousands. And still more came.

For the first time ever, she sensed an emotion or response or *something* that flowed back from the birds to her. Not so much a communication as a resonance. It bound them more tightly still, until she was able to catch fleeting moments, tighter than the space between breaths, when her link expanded and she joined with *all* of them.

She and the diddybirds were united by what she could only describe as a lust for the coming battle.

When she looked back on this, from the safety of her haven inside Florian, she marveled at the instant when *they* communicated with *her*. She glimpsed the way these alien birds had somehow been excluded from the ability to link with other aliens. They were set apart from all the other life forms on this world. They yearned for the unification, the bond all the other beasts knew as an intimate component of their existence. They lived in an isolation that tore at them.

And now these other beasts, who lived in a visceral union denied to the birds, sought to destroy the convoy holding Kirra. Which meant their unifying link was threatened.

The diddybirds, Kirra's friends and allies, would not let this destruction happen.

To call their assault on the marauding beasts savage did not

Kim greeted her with, "You can never mention this to Tanner."

"If I never see that man again, it will be too soon," Eva replied. She asked Ven, "What are you doing here?"

"Excellent question," Ven replied.

"She is part of what you may never discuss." Kim steered her around. "It's a lovely day. Let's walk."

"As long as it's away from that dreadful man, gladly."

Ven asked the man striding along between them, "What's got her stewing?"

"A certain Director Tanner," Kim replied.

Eva pointed back behind them. "Inside that building are several thousand poor souls who are trapped and enduring a slow demise. Mental agony doled out by the hour."

Kim did not even slow. "You are no longer counted among them." He gestured. "Hurry now. Baron Knowles wants to meet you."

"What? No!" When the two continued on, Eva hurried to catch up. "I don't have anything to report!"

"Which is exactly what Ricard and I told him. But the Baron insisted."

Ven asked, "And my job is . . ."

"Baron Knowles and Baroness Ricard both wish to interview you."

"What about?"

"We will all know soon enough."

"You know, you're just not telling," Eva challenged.

He showed them an irritated scowl. "Can you two young women possibly walk any slower?"

Eva told Ven, "He gets like this. As if offering a decent response would cost him."

"Baron Knowles and Baroness Ricard are friends," Kim said. "A rarity in their circles. They have decided it's time to hear from you personally. Now the both of you hush with this futile fretting and accelerate!"

Where the central plaza fronted the Regent's palace, a broad avenue ran in both directions, flanked by trees so vast they draped the lane in a green veil. Grand estates rose beyond tall stone walls. Burnished metal gates bore royal seals, many of which Eva could not identify. Eva and her grandmother had often walked this Royal Promenade, savoring the quiet peace, the sense that here was perhaps a taste of what life might have once been like, back on humanity's home world. Florian's wealth was on full display; saplings flown the incalculable distance from Earth, tended and pampered by generations of arborists, gently forced to grow in alien soil. On the city-state's holidays, the Promenade became a favorite gathering point for citizens of the inner wards. People flocked, fun rides sprouted for the children, spaces between trees were filled with carts selling sweets and savories and toys. Today the lane held a quiet solemnity.

Kim halted on the avenue's shaded promenade. Opposite them rose the Knowles manor's open gates, flanked by a pair of private guards. He told Ven, "Eva thinks highly of you. I believe you should know something in advance. Baroness Ricard intends to ask that you find someone within your Hawkins clan—"

"I have no clan." Ven's response was quiet and swift and cold. "No family. My file must tell you this is precisely the response I would give to any such comment."

In such rare moments when Ven revealed a tiny fragment of her inner world, Eva felt awe for who she was and where she had come from. The strength this must have required, the determination, were on brief display. Her own trials felt reduced to mere shadows. Her grandmother had always been there to shield and challenge. A luxury Ven had never known. And yet here they were, almost friends.

Kim asked, "May I continue?"

Eva could see Ven wanted desperately to refuse. She actually chewed on the words before emitting them with a bitter edge. "Go on, then."

"I don't know why the Baroness wishes to make such a proposal. Despite everything you have endured to arrive here. Standing outside the Knowles manor gates. Talking with a near stranger. About your hated past." Kim stared across the lane, through the open gates and past the guards, at the unseen manor within. "Baron Knowles has recently become chairman of the ruling Council. Perhaps you already knew this. No? It changes on a rotating basis among the royals. It is his turn to reside on the dais. This is an honor he neither wanted nor is suited to hold in such a time as this."

Despite herself, Ven was fully engaged now. "You think or you know?"

"What I know, Agent Ven, is that if you agree to this impossible request, I am to serve as paymaster."

Eva found herself taking a mental step back. The same reaction she often needed in order to fully understand Kim's instructions on the training mat. She tried hard to delve beneath the surface, discover the hidden meaning behind his gentle tone. He was a slender man with skin the color of old parchment, and wore clothes that heightened a false sense of fragility. Just as his calm manner masked the order he was passing on, granting Ven a much-needed chance to come to terms with the inevitable. Find her balance once more. Despite everything.

Ven protested, "I have no interest in taking the Council's money."

"These funds," Kim replied, "are not intended for you."

Ven's gaze widened, "I'm supposed to find someone to bribe?"

"You are to find, Agent Ven, someone to make rich. Baroness Ricard is making me responsible for quite a large amount of gold."

"Why?"

Kim's smile carried him into a slight bow, as if genuinely moved by the question. "I asked the very same thing. All I can say for certain is their interest is not directly aimed at any criminal activities. But they are desperate to learn more about Arno Held."

"I don't understand." Ven glanced across the avenue and through the open gates. "Have they hinted at flaws in our investigation?"

"No. Of that I am certain."

"Because there wasn't anything for us to find," Ven continued.

"Whatever Arno Held is involved in, legal or otherwise, he hides it well."

"Which is why, I suspect, they are looking for someone to bribe." When Ven did not respond, Kim went on, "I have no idea what they want. Or why we are called to report on this specific day. I can only tell you that the level of resources they have put at our disposal means the entire Council is involved. Something about Arno Held has them very worried. Perhaps, Agent Ven, even afraid."

Florian's governing Council held nineteen members. The nine baronial families were supposedly descendants of the original space-going settlers. This had been drilled into Eva's early years and remained part of Florian's annual celebration. Eva had long suspected it was merely some yarn intended to pacify the city-state and grant authenticity to the people and clans in power. Likewise, the Regent was supposedly the direct descendant of that first ship's captain, who of course had negotiated their treaty with the ruling alien race. As a young child, Eva had voiced her suspicions to Salma. Her grandmother had patted Eva on the head and replied that even if it were true, even if the tale was merely time-worn propaganda, nothing good could come from speaking of it again.

Senior members of the nine baronial clans were joined on Florian's Council by a representative of each ward, elected every three years, plus three more representing the entire city-state and chosen on the basis of merit. In rare occasions where there was a tie vote between those eighteen, the Regent cast the determining ballot.

They entered the Baron's estate and walked a lane of mosaic paving stones. This private avenue swept around a central fountain before depositing them at the home's main entry. They climbed the broad steps, up to where a white-gloved gentleman stood flanked by stone columns. He offered them a formal welcome and ushered them inside.

They were led into a salon larger than Salma's home. The high ceiling was painted with a skyscape, or so Eva assumed. Then Treaty's smaller moon rose into the placid sky, and a songbird chirped its greeting to the serene impossibility of a chamber possessing its own celestial realm.

The Baron was a slender and foppish man whose scarlet foulard was tucked inside his open-necked shirt. He sprawled in a chair with crimson padding, one leg slung over the arm. "You're here. Excellent. Join me for tea." He asked the servant, "Where has Ricard wandered off to?"

"I believe the Baroness is in the conservatory."

"Probably best to interrupt her musings."

When the servant had departed, Kim said, "I wasn't certain the Baroness would be able to join us."

"Yes, well, that's typical of the woman, declaring she's too busy to involve herself in the mundane, then popping up at the last moment, disturbing whatever peace we've managed to formulate."

A woman snapped, "What utter drivel you spout."

"And here she is at last." He waved them into seats, then told the Baroness, "I suppose you'll be wanting tea as well."

Baroness Ricard could not have been more different from Knowles if she were drawn from the alien race. Blade lean, hard edged, tall and fit and possessing a predator's gaze. "Are you quite through wasting everyone's time?"

"That is your bailiwick, not mine." Knowles waited as the white-gloved butler and two other servants wheeled in a pair of carts and served tea. When they departed, the Baron went on, "Since you're here, I suppose you might as well go ahead and dominate the proceedings."

If anything, Baroness Ricard's gaze was even more frigid and intensely focused than Tanner's. And yet on her Eva thought the force was magnetic. She felt genuinely drawn to the woman. There was an instinctive harmony at work, a desire for this severe woman to offer her approval. The Baroness addressed Ven, "I have read your report summarizing your analysis of Arno Held's influence over the Fourth Ward market. Good work, by the way. Excellent."

The federal agent managed to remain seated and yet appear to be at attention. "Thank you, Baroness."

"Now tell me what the report does not include." When Ven

hesitated, Ricard pressed, "Come, come. Your gut response. You've been observing this man for eleven days. I want your suspicions."

Ven was ready. "There's nothing for us to find, Baroness. The surveillance was a waste of everyone's time."

"From your tone, I assume you do not think the man is innocent."

"How can a man born in the Fifth Ward rise to control the Fourth Ward market?"

"And much else besides," Ricard agreed. "Go on."

"He is a professional at remaining hidden. The way he dresses, the utter absence of airs, he is determined to mask himself and his power."

Baron Knowles was no longer slouching. He sat fully upright, his gaze steady, his voice intent. "He knew we had him under surveillance?"

"Wrong question," Ricard said.

"Probably, my lord Baron," Ven replied. "But it made no difference."

Ricard glanced at Baron Knowles, who lifted his eyebrows in response. The Baroness turned to Eva and said, "You have completed your analysis of the corporations where Arno Held holds a significant interest?"

Kim answered for her. "Several days ago, Baroness."

"And?"

"She found nothing of significance. So she extended her search to include all businesses where we either know or suspect Arno Held is involved. Same result."

Ricard's gaze had not shifted from her examination of Eva. "Why am I not hearing this directly from her?"

"Because she loathes Director Tanner is the simple answer. If your questions shifted in that direction, I feared she might inject some unnecessary acid into her response," Kim said. "Not the initial impression I hoped she might make."

Knowles laughed.

"Let her speak for herself." Ricard demanded, "You are certain the records are clean?"

"Ma'am, Baroness, that is not the issue."

"Explain." When Eva cast Kim a worried glance, Ricard added, "Assume we are already in agreement, young lady. Tell me what you think."

"For my analysis to make sense, I need to give a preview of my original suspicions."

"Very well."

"Take your time," Knowles added. "Assume we are fascinated by everything you have to say."

Eva's telling took long enough for sunlight to begin tracing across the central carpet, turning the colors into a molten weave. The two Council members' unbroken intensity, the fact that she remained the focal point, granted Eva a unique ability to observe herself as she spoke.

When she had emerged from her years of enforced isolation, Eva had felt as though her life formed a house of nearly empty rooms. There were a few items of interest—her forensics and reading and combat skills. But those were amorphous, without true shape. As she addressed Florian's leaders, Eva found the entire life's structure becoming reshaped. Even though she could neither identify nor name this new objective, simply acknowledging its existence was enough. She felt emboldened, electrified.

When she finally went silent, Baron Knowles told Ricard, "You should tell them everything."

"That would be impossible," Ricard said. "Since we hardly know anything for certain."

"Everything we suspect," Knowles replied. "Everything we fear."

Ricard stood and walked to the tall central window. The direct sunlight cast her features into blades and crevices. "Arno intends to become a Council member representing the Fourth Ward."

"We suspect he already controls two other Council members' votes," Knowles said. "The current representatives of the Fifth Ward and the mines."

"And possibly the Third Ward representative as well," Ricard added. "If true, Arno's election to the Council would leave him in effective control of our city-state."

"The most powerful figure in Florian," Ricard said.

"The pressure he has brought to bear on the entire vetting process is so intense, the rest of us are left virtually powerless," Knowles said.

"As a result of Arno's unseen presence," Ricard told the window before her face, "all other candidates have removed themselves from the ballot."

"Including those who had the Council's official backing," Knowles said. He lifted one hand and blew on his fingers. "Poof. Gone."

Ricard swung around. "Baron, with your permission?"

"By all means," Knowles replied.

"Are you coming?"

"Thank you, no." He resumed his languid pose. "That is one nightmare I have no interest in reliving."

They climbed to the second floor and passed through what appeared to be an upstairs lounge with a balcony railing overlooking the domed foyer. From there they entered a chamber almost as large as the main salon. To her astonishment, Eva realized the baroness was leading them into the master bedchamber. Ven froze in the doorway until Kim stepped back, touched her arm, and led the agent forward. They followed Ricard down a stubby side corridor and entered a vast dressing room lined by doors and shelves. Everything was so neat, the shoes all polished, the scarves folded so beautifully, they might have entered an expensive shop on the Second Ward promenade.

Baroness Ricard stepped to the central island, touched a button recessed in the side, and a top panel slid back. Tray after tray of jewelry rose and unfolded. "I assume you've heard about the theft."

"Indeed so," Kim replied. "They have not made an arrest?"

"We do not even have a suspect." Ricard gave them a moment to gape at the wealth on display, then touched the button a second time, and the trays slid silently away. "This was the first of a series of impossible robberies."

Kim appeared genuinely shocked. "What?"

"Knowles and three other Council members are the only others who are aware," Ricard replied. "They know because they too have been victims in precisely the same way."

Eva found it interesting to study her boss and friend, how he was captivated now by the news. "Impossible thefts, you say."

"There is no realistic explanation. And this impossibility is all we have to tie the victims together." Ricard led them back into the bedchamber, across the thick hand-loomed carpet, over to tall double doors. The Baroness unlocked them and motioned for the others to join her on the balcony. They looked out over immaculate gardens and two ornamental pools. "The Baron was hosting a party that night. We initially assumed one of the guests managed to slip past the guards and make their way upstairs."

"Or one of the guards?" Ven suggested.

"All seven on house duty that night have been on either the Baron's staff or members of my own personal guard for years," Ricard replied. "Just the same, they all went through the vetting process yet again."

Eva asked, "Was Arno a guest that night?"

"An interesting question," Ricard said. "And the answer is no. Arno Held has never been invited to any First Ward event."

Kim surveyed the room, crossed back to the balcony, peered out, returned. "Any unexpected guest? A last-minute stand-in, perhaps?"

"Nothing of the sort."

"Baroness, I confess to be at a loss."

"As are we all."

"Then the other thefts began," Kim said.

"The count now stands at fourteen," Ricard confirmed. "Three private residences of Council members. Two other wealthy families. Five of Florian's most expensive jewelers. Two art galleries. And two guests at the Crillon hotel."

"And all you have to tie this to anyone is a single gemstone," Kim said.

"Actually, it was just part of one. The jeweler who purchased the item knew of the first theft, and the emerald brought to him was both large and not set. Which made no sense. How could a valuable stone like that not be part of a pendant or necklace—something that matched its value? So he passed the word to associates, who agreed with his assessment that the stone they held had been recut from an even larger stone. The jeweler is a friend of the Baron's wife, and knew of the robbery. That brought the stone to us."

"And the seller?"

"Sellers. Five in total. One less than savory individual after another. A chain of empty voices, all claiming to have purchased the item so cheaply they knew it could be resold for a profit."

"And Arno?"

Ricard shook her head. "None of those five individuals claimed to even know him. No, Arno's name was whispered to one of our Third Ward informants. An individual with a grudge." Ricard showed them open palms. "It's very little to go on. But the slightest hint that Arno might truly be the individual we fear him to be . . ."

"He could use the Council as a means to leverage his power, and do so without scruples to keep him in check," Kim said. "A despot in the making."

"And now you share our nightmares." Ricard turned to Ven. "Has the director told you of our need to locate a source inside your clan's upper echelon?"

"Former clan," Ven softly countered.

Ricard continued, "We have one slender thread that might help us unravel Arno's web. One of the men who attacked Eva in the Third Ward market is a Hawkins lieutenant."

Ven asked, "His name?"

"Caspian."

She frowned, shook her head. "That doesn't register."

"Apparently your clan has recently absorbed a smaller one. Caspian was its leader's nephew. Some of these new Hawkins members are less than pleased with the arrangement."

Ven breathed. Nodded. Remained silent. Finally, she turned to the garden and clenched the balcony railing with clawlike intensity.

Ricard waited, the unspoken request there in the sunlight.

Eva decided it was time to help her friend out. If she was indeed reading the situation correctly. "A senior member of the dissolved clan might work. Someone young and ambitious. With his or her clan now gone, their chances of making it to the very top are gone. Erased. Caspian can't go higher than lieutenant."

Ven straightened, turned, and offered, "The Hawkins clan have never followed an outsider and never will."

Ricard and Kim exchanged a glance. "How would you see this happening?"

"A straight arrest won't work. Same goes for the clumsy sort of Guards assault usually used on any Fifth Ward suspect."

They waited.

Eva suggested, "We could make a targeted series of grabs. Bring in all the senior Hawkins clan members. Nine, ten, eleven, it needs to be a major sweep of the Hawkins power structure, including Caspian and his uncle."

Ricard offered Kim a tight nod of approval. "Go on."

"All of those targeted are held separately from the moment they are taken off the street," Eva continued. "They are brought in and questioned by senior officers. All of them asked the same questions."

"The gemstone," Ricard said.

"No, Baroness," Ven said. "We ask them about Arno Held."

"Yes," Kim murmured. "We send the man a warning. All eyes are upon him."

"The sort of concerted effort that justifies the sweep," Eva agreed.

Ricard told Kim, "Director, I want you to put this in place immediately. We move tonight. Before any hint of this slips out."

Kim replied, "Baroness, I think it's time to recognize the vital roles these young women are playing."

"What do you suggest?"

"As of this meeting, they be granted provisional status as officers," Kim replied. "To be made official and permanent at the successful conclusion of this operation."

"Very well. As of this time, you are both now lieutenants—"

"Captains," Kim urged. "That would grant them enough clout to make things happen."

"Captains, then. Provisionally." Ricard might have smiled as she told Kim, "I assume you are willing to inform Director Tanner that this officer is now released from his control."

"It will be my deep and abiding pleasure," Kim agreed.

"Back to the key element of your investigation. We have no hard evidence to halt Arno's gaining a seat on the Council. We have nothing of any substance to tie Arno to any illegal activity. And that is now your primary target. We are certain there is something we are not seeing, evidence that will strip away his years of subterfuge. Your job is to find it."

Nine hours later, they met with Ricard and Knowles again. Only this time they traveled in the Baron's private transport to the Fourth Ward market. The pearlescent globe on wheels had a small forward cubby for the driver-guard. The main compartment was roomy even with the five of them, and was kitted out with the softest faux-leather Eva had ever felt. The carpets were black and shimmered in the late afternoon sunlight. There was a fold-down desk, a bar holding cross-hatched crystal bottles and goblets, and a sterling silver picnic hamper.

They were parked in a small rectangular area set aside for transports supplying the market. The area was littered with packing and detritus. Even inside the baron's sealed compartment, Eva smelled overripe fruit. They had been parked there for ten minutes, more, and no one had even looked their way.

Across the busy thoroughfare was Arno's office building. There was very little to distinguish the structure from its neighbors, just another featureless property that had seen many hard seasons. The filthy windows gave nothing away. Eva knew the entry possessed a hidden second portal, one fashioned from solid steel and controlled by Arno himself.

Baroness Ricard said, "Explain to us again what you've discovered."

Eva was coming to know the Guards director, how she used such repetitions to delve ever deeper into strategy. Baron

Knowles, however, protested, "Do all senior agents repeat questions like this?"

Kim was the one who replied, "Only the good ones."

"I'm only asking because this is the fourth time we've been through all this."

"I count only three," Kim said.

"Three, four, I was growing concerned this might signify a mental slowdown." He pretended to inspect Ricard. "Do hold off your retirement until we've dealt with this crisis, will you?"

The three of them, Ricard and Kim and Knowles, seemed so calm, so detached. On the other hand, Ven sat nervously by the opposite window, studying the scene and tapping softly on the armrest. A drumbeat of tension that Eva felt in her gut. Even so, she knew a genuine pleasure in playing such a role in her first major investigation, and doing so in the company of people she was starting to both know and like. It made for quite a nice way to pass a hard hour, while waiting to go on the attack.

Kim said, "Why don't you go back to the origins of your search."

Knowles rolled his eyes and slid further down in his seat. But when Ricard glared at him, he straightened like a schoolboy and pretended to be at full alert. Ricard said, "Excellent idea."

"I started with the assumption that Boaz, the company director, was indeed planning a heist. Which required two things. First, tactics that were being missed by the FSA auditors. And someone who served as the primary fulcrum, a skilled administrator, someone very close to Director Boaz. I asked if perhaps the reason why the first heist never occurred was because that individual was plucked away at the very last minute. I'm fairly certain the fake thefts I uncovered show the how." Eva stopped then, uncertain whether she should continue.

Kim spoke quietly. "You are among friends."

"Director Tanner accused me of failing at my duties." Eva took mild comfort in how her voice sounded bland to her own ears. "I tried to tell him what I thought should happen, and he refused to let me finish. He threatened me with dismissal. So I decided if I was going to be let go anyway—"

"Not happening." This time, it was Ricard who spoke.

Eva went on, "I decided I might as well try and find the who."

Baron Knowles told Ricard, "I am liking this young woman more and more."

Eva found herself thinking back to the third evening after Tanner's tirade, when she had told her grandmother about her investigation. It was the first time they had ever spoken as colleagues, as equals. Eva had felt utterly defeated by Tanner's resentment and his wrath. She dreaded entering the FSA building each morning, yet wanted nothing more than to continue with the job she had already come to love.

Her grandmother had not responded when Eva described Tanner's invective and threats. Nor did she condemn her granddaughter for starting an investigation that broke a dozen regulations. Even so, the years and divides had melted away. Salma had listened with unblinking intensity and, once Eva went silent, merely asked why she had not alerted Kim. The answer to that had been simple enough. Because she had nothing to show. On that point, at least, Tanner had been correct. Eva had failed utterly at her assigned task.

Until two days later, when her investigation finally offered Eva a reason to hope.

Knowles chose that moment to lean forward and look past Ven at the building opposite their station. "Are we sure he's even there?"

"He's there," Ricard replied.

"We've not seen movement of any kind since we arrived."

"Precisely the point." Ricard waved a finger at Eva. "Continue."

"Employees in Boaz's company are paid every ten days," Eva told them. "It took some digging, but I managed to locate a regular payment, made every ten days to the director's office, that ended immediately after the final trial run."

Ven straightened, clenched both hands in her lap, and spoke in a toneless drone. Like she was addressing administrators questioning her abilities. "Our source within the company confirmed that Director Boaz had an administrative assistant who was taken mysteriously ill around that same point in time. She hasn't returned to the office."

Ricard said, "What alerted our source to this missing individual's role?"

"He has no idea what she did, Baroness," Ven replied. "Only that the individual in question was, in his words, a heartstopper."

"She was, or is, attractive, this woman?"

Ven passed over an enlarged copy of the corporate ID.

"Oh. Well."

Knowles took the picture. Hmphed softly. Was reluctant to hand it back. "Her name?"

"Kirra Eblon."

"And?"

"No such person exists," Eva said.

Kim took up the telling. "FSA auditors interviewed Boaz yesterday. Ven accompanied them. Boaz confirmed everything. The auditors described him as calm and willing to answer all their questions. Kirra Eblon was hired to assist in a transition to their new accounting system. She was employed on a temporary basis, which explains the accounting methods regarding her payments."

"Boaz insists they would have kept her on," Ven said. "Except she became ill and was forced to resign."

"The documentation regarding her background is perfect," Eva said. "On paper, Kirra Eblon is a highly trained individual and ideal for her position as assistant to the company director. The problem is none of it is real."

Kim said, "Earlier today my staff completed a confidential search. This represents the most complete corruption ever of our city-state's administrative system."

The compartment was so silent Eva heard the soft rumble of passing transports. Then Ricard asked, "What happened to this woman?"

"Another mystery," Kim replied. "One of several, in fact."

"Fifth Ward clinical records show Kirra Eblon as having been treated for an unidentified illness," Ven said. "But no one on duty remembers seeing this woman."

Knowles demanded, "How is that even possible?"

"Wait," Kim said.

"Earlier that same night, eleven drivers and mechanics at the Fourth Ward transport depot were attacked," Eva said.

"What attack?" Kim protested. "They were murdered. Dismembered. Their bodies spread all over the repair warehouse. Inside and out."

Ricard asked, "You're suggesting a woman did this?"

"How could she," Kim replied. "Since the individual in question does not exist."

Ven said, "We have run the photograph through AI data searches."

"Twice," Kim added. "And turned up nothing."

"I don't understand," Knowles said. "How does any of this tie to our current investigation?"

Kim said, "What if all this is connected? What if it's not a collection of multiple mysteries, but rather a series of events that all are tied to the man in question—Arno Held?" He indicated Eva. "This is what my young colleague suspects, and what I am increasingly inclined to believe. The coincidence of timing, the number of seemingly impossible events, the complete absence of leads or suspects. The murders, the corporate heists that did not happen, the impossible thefts that did."

"That is a stretch," Ricard said. "I'm not objecting, mind, so much as demanding more evidence than one single emerald that might have been cut from the Baroness's pendant."

"But what if all this does lead us to Arno?" Eva persisted. "What if we lack one item, a link that explains these mysteries, and explains how Arno sits at the center of it all?"

Knowles had lost every hint of lethargy. "We have been searching for a reason to deny this man—"

"Deny?" Ricard said. "Arrest and incarcerate. Permanently."

"—for over five years."

"Longer," Ricard said. "What are your next steps?"

"First, identify a source inside the Hawkins clan who might supply us with the information we require to begin forming a case against Arno Held," Kim said. "Second, identify this invisible woman and determine if she and Held are operating together."

"Very well." Ricard lifted an eyebrow and Knowles nodded in response. "Whatever you require, we approve in advance. But remember at all times your primary objective. Bring clarity to this enigma and determine precisely what role Arno Held is playing. And above all else, give us specifics on any and all illegal activities Arno Held is involved in."

Knowles added, "And if he's as bad as we fear, you must supply us with the necessary evidence to cage this beast once and for all."

The three of them, Ven and Kim and Eva, traveled to a diner near the Guards' local headquarters. The head office was a huge structure, as it was responsible for policing both Fourth and Fifth Wards and shared some responsibility for the mines. From their outdoor table Kim could see the building's exterior lights already illuminated against the gathering dusk. The diner was just one of a multitude of bars and other restaurants and shops that extended in every dusty direction. Eva marveled at how so many small businesses managed to survive. The odors were thick and dense. As the sunset faded, she studied her two companions and wondered if her own features were cast in the same shadows and craven lines.

At a chime from her commlink, Ven connected and said, "Go ahead." A moment, then she offered the others a thumbs-up and said, "We're on our way."

They rose as one and started back in the direction they had come. Eva did her best to match their easy stride, the calm way they approached danger. If only she could ease the electric tension, slow her frantic heart, stop the urgent desire to shriek her fear to the night.

By contrast, Ven might as well have been out for an evening stroll, the way she calmly asked Kim, "Have I thanked you for including me? Granting me the chance to lead my own raid?"

"Of course you have."

"Not in so many words."

Kim shrugged. "What value do such vague elements hold among friends of good bones?"

Ven showed her ID to the duty officer at the headquarters'

main gates. When the others followed suit and were waved through, she said, "Thank you, Kim. So very much."

They gathered in the rear lot by nine black transports, fierce and heavily reinforced vehicles with the Regent's shield embossed on both sides. Each of the convoy's vehicles carried six agents, two drivers, and at the rear a windowless cage. Everyone save Eva and Kim and Ven already wore the Guards' version of battle gear. Ven introduced herself and Kim, then pointed to Eva, gave her name, and said, "We are acting on intel supplied by this lady. Your first duty in tonight's ops is to ensure this agent remains intact and makes it home safe. Tell me you understand."

Eva had no idea how to respond to the verbal salutes, so she remained silent. Still. Holding tight to her nerves. Or at least trying.

Ven seemed to grow in stature her indrawn breath was that strong. "Some of you already know I was born and raised a Fifth Warder. I still have nightmares of Black Watch raids. The way they bulled through, crashing and breaking, as if we all deserved punishment for the crime of being alive. Your second duty, now and every Fifth Ward entry you make from this point going forward is this: Treat them as the citizens they are. Tell me you understand."

This time the response was more muted. The expressions Eva saw were varied. Some surprise, others sullen. A few were stoney with anger. But they all responded in the affirmative.

Ven met each gaze in turn, then said, "Let's roll."

Eva and Kim and Ven together entered the command transport. Behind the stubby pilot's cabin stretched the mobile unit with its array of electronic equipment and stations, and two weapons caches. As Ven led Eva down the central aisle she asked, "What's our sit-rep?"

"Green across the board." The voice belonged to a whippet-lean blonde woman, all sharp angles and edges. On the wall above her station was an illuminated number one. "We are waiting on the final target confirmation."

"Let's roll." She pointed to where Kim leaned against the

wall dividing the unit from the pilot's station. "Everyone, meet Director Kim."

"Former Director," he corrected. "Now merely an advisor."

"Who still carries enough clout to pull this mission together."

The sharp-featured woman asked Kim, "Should I relinquish my station, sir?"

"Certainly not to me," Kim replied. "I'm about to make myself comfortable in some empty space and disappear for the duration." He pointed to Ven. "The captain is running tonight's show."

"Stay where you are," Ven ordered. "Otherwise people might think I actually know what I'm doing. Where's my gear?"

The blonde woman had clearly been designated spokesperson for the crew. "Rear cage, ma'am."

Ven pointed to Eva and added, "If anything goes wrong tonight, you are hereby ordered to blame it on this one."

The narrow chamber at the back was windowless and painted a matte black. Eva settled on a narrow bench attached to one wall and watched Ven slip into the Guards armored black suit. "Every time I tried to put that on in training, I grew ten thumbs."

"It wasn't the suit, it was what came after," Ven replied. "Nerves will do that." She adjusted her chest straps, settled a crease down her right hip, then fit on the weapons belt. "You OK?"

"Yes." She could feel the transport's vibrations through the bench as they headed out. The motion only amplified her nerves. "Maybe I should come."

As if response, there was a knock on the door. Kim opened it and said, "May I?"

Ven stepped back far enough to allow him entry. "Eva has second thoughts."

"About what?"

"Tonight. She wants to come."

Kim sealed the portal and leaned against the metal surface. He told Eva, "Ven has spent countless hours training with this crew. So long as everything goes smoothly, your presence would be welcome. But if there is trouble, they can act as one."

"I understand. My coming might hinder things," Eva said. "So this is me, feeling relief and guilt in equal measure."

Ven's features were not made for an easy smile. Which made this one special indeed. She told Eva, "Do you know, I actually think we might become friends."

Kim cleared his throat. "I respectfully ask to be included here."

Ven did not fully lose her smile as she checked her sidearm's charge. "Never thought I'd consider applying that word to an agency director. Retired or otherwise. Not in a million years." She picked up her helmet with its mirror-black visor and reached for the door-lever. "Let's go snag some bad guys."

The female officer serving as coordinator in the unit was named Senna. She seemed more than happy to remain behind as Ven and four others slipped into the night. At a request from Kim, she unlatched two of the other chairs and drew them into position behind her station. When Eva and Kim were seated, she told them, "The red dots are our targets. Nine in all. Accessing the suspects' IDs, tracking their movements, and prepping our teams make up ninety-nine percent of a successful Fifth Ward insert." She held up a finger, then spoke into her mike confirming the target's position to another team, then gave the green light to apprehend. Senna cut the communication and told her observers, "Happens I agree with the captain's orders regarding making this a clean move. Too many of the Fifth Ward officers deserve the name these people give us."

"Black Watch," Kim said. "I've despised that tag since my earliest days on the force."

The voices coming through the system's loudspeakers formed a series of barked signals, most of which Eva did not understand. She felt a total outsider, and a coward. Her distance from the action was too great. She wished she had insisted on being out there, on the front line where she belonged.

"Here goes our crew," Senna said.

Five yellow dots spread into a semi-circle and waited. The red dot, Ven's target, made very slow going of the street. Senna demanded, "Is that guy drunk? Stoned? Catatonic?"

"Regards the first two, hard to say," Kim replied. "As for

number three, definitely not. He's walking an almost straight line, see, which is a considerable feat given the damage our lady of the hour recently inflicted on him."

Senna glanced around, saw Kim pointing at Eva, then went back to scanning her screens. "I heard something about a greenie taking out three assailants with a baton. That was you?"

Eva asked, "Everybody knows?"

Senna held up the finger, acknowledged another team's successful sweep, then came back with, "There might be a blind and deaf retired agent out there somewhere, maybe they didn't hear. But for the rest of us, it made a happy tale."

Together they observed as one target after another was apprehended and brought back and successfully incarcerated. Nine targets, nine teams, nine transports. From the moment of contact until the time they were to be released, each suspect was to remain utterly isolated. Without any knowledge that others had been taken as well. Except for the one man, their reason for all this. He had to be informed.

Baroness Ricard chose to join them.

The leader of all Florian's security greeted the colonel responsible for the Fourth Ward headquarters, then allowed herself to be ushered into the control room. Wall monitors showed the nine individuals who had been brought in and sequestered. They remained hooded in separate interview rooms, their wrists cuffed to the metal desks. "I want biometric feeds attached to each of these suspects."

The colonel hesitated. "Baroness, they are not actually accused of any wrongdoing."

"Not tonight, they're not." She inspected the senior officer long enough for him to grow uncomfortable. "Is there a problem?"

"No, Baroness. Of course not."

"Use equipment that requires they be aware the feed is happening. If they object, shackle them." Another intense inspection, then, "That will be all, Colonel. You and your aides please join the other officers."

The colonel saluted his boss, started for the door, then turned back. "Actually, Baroness, there is one other matter. Can I ask why treasures have been removed from our evidence lockers?"

"Point one, they are not treasures. They are evidence in ongoing investigations."

"Yes, ma'am. But still—"

"Point two, this is happening under my direct authority and supervision. I personally signed the release form. Point three, soon as this operation is concluded, your *evidence* will be returned." When he remained poised by the exit, she snapped, "That is all, Colonel."

When the officer and his minions departed, she asked Kim, "Is he bent?"

"We have no concrete evidence, ma'am."

"Suspicions?"

"There are too many coincidences," he replied. "Regarding items that never make it to their related trial date."

Ricard focused on Eva. "Young lady, when this is done, I want you to go through all Fourth Ward records regarding seized assets. With a microscope."

"Aye, Baroness."

"Very well. Let's address the troops so we can focus on the night's true mission."

The meeting took place in the main conference room. Just Senna and the other eight coordinating agents were seated. Eva and Kim joined the colonel and his aides and all the other team members, standing crammed together around the rear and side walls.

Ricard began without preamble. "Now begins the night's true work. We are not after intelligence. Anything that actually comes from tonight's questioning is a bonus. The reason why the Council approved this emergency apprehension and temporary hold on nine senior Hawkins clan members all comes down to one thing. We want to spook Arno Held."

She gave that a beat, then continued, "You all have been given a list of recent Fourth and Fifth Ward unsolved crimes. Added to this are criminal activities we suspect are tied to the recently enlarged Hawkins clan. Your task is to request information about each and every one of them. And then you are to enquire what role Arno Held played in the crime. These questions are to continue until Director Kim says otherwise."

She took a longer moment this time, her gaze shifting around the table, then scanning the entire gathering. Taking note, Eva thought, of those who smiled in anticipation. "Our aim, as I said, is to drive the merchant from cover. Force him to sweat and, hopefully, to make a serious mistake. And once we have successfully brought his true actions and motives into the open, we are going to take him down."

A number of officers muttered approval. One woman muttered, "Finally."

Baroness Ricard glanced at the colonel, who cleared his throat and said, "You have your orders. Dismissed."

Ricard shook a few hands, greeted those she knew, offered quiet words of encouragement. When she could, she drew the three of them over to one side and said, "Now the real work begins."

Eva lagged a half-step behind the others as they tracked down the featureless corridor. Senna walked last of all, clearly spooked by being in the presence of their supreme commander. Eva carried one sack from the evidence lockers, Senna another, Ven a third. All but one of the headquarters' interview rooms were in use now. The two main bullpens were jammed with officers, everyone watching as Ricard stopped by several rooms and peered through the small windows, ensuring their suspects remained hooded. Ricard offered each senior agent now stationed by the door a word of encouragement. Eva watched and listened as from a great distance, remarking on how the Baroness handled authority. Making each and every officer feel truly important. Drawing them together as a team. Shouldering aside the questionable motives of their colonel and anyone else working under Arno's influence. The shackles were off. This was their chance to shine.

The enormity of what Eva had put into action grew with

her every step. What if she was wrong? She wanted desperately to speak with Kim, go through her strategy once more, make sure she had not overlooked something of crucial importance. But there was no time.

Ricard glanced through the small window. "Tell me why you think this is the one."

Eva opened her mouth, but was unable to make a sound.

Kim smoothly filled the void. "What's important as far as our aims are concerned, Baroness, is how this individual and two associates, both muscles for hire, left a tavern run by his former clan. They tracked a lone woman through territory they knew was firmly under Arno's protection."

"The Fourth Ward market," Ricard said.

"Just so."

"And the victim . . ."

"Was this young lady here. Who was in fact no victim at all," Kim replied, smiling at her. "She inflicted serious damage on all three. The injuries this gentleman bears are her doing."

Ricard glanced at Eva, then went back to studying the man beyond the window. "And this is important because . . ."

"What we need, Baroness, is not just to put the heat on Arno, but as you said, someone who can unravel Arno's web, who's ready and willing to break the Hawkins clan's rules and defy Arno's hold over the Fourth and Fifth Wards." Kim stabbed the window. "Caspian is heir apparent of the Allard clan. Or rather, he would have been, except his uncle, the clan's chieftain, agreed to merge with the Hawkins. Which has left Caspian stripped of everything that mattered, even his former name."

Ven offered, "Soldiers in the Hawkins clan will never follow Caspian, as I said before. He and his clan were deposed. He is nothing in their eyes."

Ricard stepped away from the window, turned, and inspected Ven. Eva expected the baroness to ask if the agent was OK, confronting the leaders of her birth-clan. Instead, she said, "We are very fortunate to count you among us, Captain."

"Thank you, Baroness."

"All right. I've seen enough." She nodded to Eva. "You may proceed."

But Eva's fear had built to a point where it threatened to engulf her; a great looming force, some unseen behemoth ready to swallow her whole. All the agents who were to handle the other initial interviews stood up and down the corridor, watching her. Just the same, she could not reach out and open the door.

She did not murmur so much as breathe around the acidic fear. "Am I making a terrible mistake?"

Kim was so close she could feel the man's heat, his strength. "We'll soon see. But I think not." He waited, almost smiling. "You remember what I say about fear, yes?"

Of course she did. "An excellent stimulus to right action, if taken in small doses."

"Very good, partner." He hefted the first of three containers leaning against the corridor wall. "You heard the Baroness. Begin."

The instant Eva appeared in the open doorway, Caspian jerked to his feet and struggled against the manacle holding his wrist to the table. He shouted at Kim standing behind her, "No! No! Get her out! She's crazy, that one!"

Eva shifted to the room's corner and watched as Kim upended a sack of currency taken from the evidence lockers. Caspian gaped at the money, demanded, "What's that got to do with me?"

Kim smiled at the man, went back outside, and this time returned with a canvas carry-all which he unzipped and dumped on top of the cash. A mass of small gold bars and coins spilled out. Much of the hoard fell onto the floor. The coins landed with the sound of muted cymbals.

A third exit, and this time Kim spilled a smaller sack of jewels and ornamental treasures on top of the pile. Caspian was so mesmerized he forgot all about his shock over Eva's appearance.

The man was not in great shape. His right arm was held by a splint, and this was attached tightly to his lower ribs. His face was heavily bruised. His left thigh and ankle were both trussed. A cane with wrist-guard lay unnoticed on the concrete floor.

Caspian asked weakly, "What is this?"

"We are here to offer you a new life," Eva replied. "Why don't you sit down and make yourself comfortable. This could take a while."

Kim stepped back, placing himself in the open doorway. Caspian looked from one to the other, then back to the wealth on display. "You're telling me this is mine?"

"Not this specific pile. We brought this to show you we mean business. But if you are willing to do what we ask, then we will supply you with all this and more."

He settled into his chair. Caspian tried to sneer, but the treasure clearly rattled him. "How do I know this is real, you won't just pull it all away once you get what you want?"

Eva turned and nodded to Kim, who stepped back into the corridor and said, "We're ready."

Baroness Ricard entered the chamber, waited until Kim sealed them in, then demanded, "Do you know who I am?"

"The boss lady." Caspian was severely shaken but did his best to mock. "Baroness somebody."

"Everything you are about to hear carries my approval." She turned to Eva. "Proceed."

Eva pointed to the blank screen imbedded in the wall above her head. A few seconds passed, then it came alive and showed eight different pictures; eight other captives with their wrists manacled to tables, only these others all wore sacks over their heads. They watched as agents entered the chambers and swept off the coverlets. Caspian gasped when he realized who the others were.

"The senior leaders of the Hawkins clan including your uncle were brought in for questioning tonight," Eva told him. "All so we could mask the conversation we're having with you. You will all be reinserted into the Fifth Ward together."

Caspian's eyes were round, but his surprise did not erase the man's hard edge. "Same question. What's this all about?"

"We want to employ you for the next ninety days," Eva replied. "At the end of this period, you will be given wealth plus a new clean identity. You will then be relocated to Spaceport Island."

"Ninety days. That's the Council elections." His features tightened into a feral grin. "I got it now. You're after the goods on Arno Held. You want to keep the rat in his burrow. I'm right, aren't I?"

Baroness Ricard said, "Pay careful attention to what the captain is about to tell you. This offer is available tonight only."

Kim opened the door. Ricard departed. He closed it and resumed position by the other wall. Eva went on, "The question you need to answer is, will you be our man on the inside."

"This is real, what you're offering." He studied the treasure, the cash. "Real."

"It is." Eva went silent and watched as Caspian reached out his free hand and toyed with a jeweled bracelet, a handful of gold coins, a wad of cash. Abruptly she became encased in a brilliant awareness. She was in control of this moment. It was hers to direct. Then the moment passed, and she was back inside the featureless interview room, the air thick with odors from a thousand arrests.

Caspian leaned back. His face twisted, only now it was to reveal fury. "Clan Hawkins robbed me of everything. All because my uncle didn't have the spine to go it alone."

"Is that a yes? We need to hear you say it."

"Absolutely. I'm done with them." Dark eyes glittered. "I'll walk away and never look back."

"In that case, you start tonight." Eva nodded to Kim, who described in specific detail what they were looking for. Anything that would connect Arno directly to the clan's next move.

When Kim went silent, Eva added, "If you can supply us with useful information that leads to an arrest, our need for you to remain imbedded comes to an end."

That brought him to full alert. "You're saying I can get out early? I don't have to stay there for the full ninety days?"

"Soon as we have what we need," Eva confirmed. "Soon as Arno Held has been arrested, you're free to start your new life."

The man's expression said it all.

"Tomorrow night, go to your regular tavern by the Fourth Ward market," Eva said, and opened the door long enough for

Caspian to get a good look at Senna. "This lady will come to you."

"Don't try any moves," Kim warned. "She bites."

"She will give you a dedicated commlink," Eva said. "One touch and either this man or I will answer."

She and Kim were in rhythm now, moving in close synch, like they were back on the practice mats. Kim said, "The commlink will be manned day and night."

"Soon as you have what we need, as quickly as we can confirm it's real, we pull you out," Eva said.

"You will be free to start your new life," Kim said.

"A rich man," Eva said. "On Spaceport Island."

Caspian looked from one to the other. "That's it? We're done?"

"I said you start tonight," Eva replied. She drew a photograph from her pocket, an enlarged version of the corporate ID. Eva settled it on top of the wealth. "Tell us what you know about this woman."

It seemed to Eva that Caspian barely looked for a moment. Then he leaned back, this time grinning for real. "The Barret girl. We always wondered if she was Arno's lady."

Eva forced herself to remain calm. Not showing Kim her electric thrill, suppressing her astonishment, took some doing. When she was fully in control, she asked, "Her first name?"

"I dunno . . . Kirra? Yeah, that's it." He picked up the photograph and drew it closer. "So she's his fancy lady. For a fat old man, Arno's got class, I'll give him that."

Less than an hour later, Eva and Ven traveled to the mines by way of hired transport. At Ricard's order, one of Tanner's minions had set up an appointment with the oddly named Elder Barret, who held a manager's position in the mines' central offices. As Kim put it, their approach needed to be as blandly normal as they could make it, while still insisting their arrival be front and center on the target's agenda. Kim stayed behind in order to supervise the return of their nine detainees.

Eva was exhausted from the sleepless night and the action. Yet the tension stayed with her, the electric thrill of handling a mission of such importance. She knew it was only a matter of time before she crashed and burned. But just then she moved forward on a wave so strong she could set her weariness to one side. "Elder Barret," Eva said, scanning the skimpy file the agency had on her. "Strange name for a woman."

"It's a tradition," Ven replied. "Barrets are known for that."

"Strange names?"

"Traditions. They're by far the strongest of the Fifth Ward clans. Almost legendary." She was silent a long moment. "We've met."

"Really?"

"When I was a kid I played in their front square. Elder introduced me to the stallholder who got me hooked on reading." Ven's features softened, a look of such vulnerability Eva was rendered uncomfortable. As if being allowed to glimpse beneath the woman's protective covering. As if Ven might at any moment grow angry with herself, and with Eva for looking where she shouldn't. "I fell in love with a Barret. Elder met me a second time, making sure I would prove a good mate. I liked her, the way she cared for her young men, the time and work she put into keeping them straight. There was a moment, I thought I could join this clan and be . . . I don't know, happy. Content. Safe."

Eva sensed it was the right point to ask, almost as if Ven needed to hear her say, "What happened?"

"A mine accident. Killed him and his father and two others."

"I'm so sorry."

"At their funeral I decided I was leaving. There was no life for me in any Fifth Ward clan and never would be."

Eva studied the older agent, and knew it was time for a confession of her own. Reveal her secrets, share and build a new bridge, all with a few feeble words. "I've never known a relationship like that. Where love might redefine me. I probably never will."

Ven's gaze was splintered by liquid she refused to shed or swipe away. "A beautiful lady like you? Give me a break."

Eva told her about the way she had been forced to erase her former existence. She tried to keep it cool, no big deal, just shedding the garments of youth. The three empty years that followed. Forensic accounting. Kim. Her grandmother. Tanner. All done in a dozen sentences. Less. Just the same, when she went quiet Eva felt as if her throat and heart had been scalded. She finished, "I date. Some. Not a lot. I'm always ready when the evenings end. It's like my ability to feel much of anything has been surgically removed."

Ven examined her for a long moment, her eyes clear once more. "We make quite a pair, you and I."

Eva nodded. She had been thinking the exact same thing.

They remained silent as they passed through Fifth Ward, then showed their badges and IDs at the mines' main gates. From there it was a quick transit through nearly barren scrubland. Clearly some effort had been made to plant and groom along the road. But the trees were stunted and the growth so uneven it almost heightened the vista's grim nature. As they halted before the mines' office complex, Eva asked, "Did you ever meet this Kirra?"

"Hard to say. She's what, twenty-five, twenty-six?"

"All we have to go on is the corporate application for Kirra Eblon, which we already know is bogus. That puts her age at twenty-three."

"That would make her seven years my junior. I might have met her at some point. If it's her."

"It's the first hard evidence the woman actually has an identity. If what Caspian says is true."

"He looked to me like a man on the level," Ven replied.

"I thought so too. Still, there's the issue of a missing ID, file, photo, the works."

"There are reasons why certain people in power could have made that happen." Ven was definite. "A lovely woman who is enticed into going off the straight and narrow, you understand? We have records of other ladies who took the protection of a powerful First Warder. Part of their reward for becoming a courtesan was a new ID."

"So maybe she entered Boaz's group as Arno Held's lieutenant," Eva said.

"Exactly. Arno Held would then have scrubbed all official

files, make it harder to track her once a new identity is in place. But you heard Kim. Apparently, this ID change takes the process to a whole new level." Ven opened her door. "We'll know once we have the lady in shackles."

The mines' central office complex showed a façade of pale colors. They were surrounded by a carefully tended garden filled with walkways and sculptures and flowerbeds. Yet somehow the result was little more than a temporary defiance against the surrounding grey plains. Beyond the office complex stretched an array of the largest buildings Eva had ever seen—warehouses and giant equipment sheds and dozens of refineries.

They entered the central offices' cavernous lobby and gave their names to one of the guards. The high-ceilinged chamber was modeled after the surrounding garden, with metal sculptures of indifferent quality and boxy stone flower boxes forming partitions for clusters of chairs and benches. A dozen or so people were scattered about, their conversations echoing off the hard surfaces, the sounds little more than a constant rush.

Ven pointed with her chin and said, "Here she comes."

Elder Barret was a thickset woman of indeterminate years, big-boned and square-jawed, intelligent and aware. She stopped and inspected them and asked, "Can I see your IDs?" Polite, but nonetheless a statement. Elder Barret was a woman clearly accustomed to being obeyed.

She gave their badges a careful inspection, then told Ven, "I remember you."

"Ma'am."

"You've done well for yourself." She handed back their ID wallets. "It doesn't say what rank you've earned."

"Captain. Provisional."

"Very well indeed." She cast Eva a single glance, and dismissed her just as swiftly. Her expression said it all. Eva was not of her world, and thus was not worthy of her time. "What's this about?"

"We're interested in what you can tell us about one of your clan," Ven replied. "Kirra."

The woman showed emotion for the first time, an agony that fractured both her gaze and her voice. "Why, what's happened?"

"We're simply trying to obtain a clear idea regarding certain events," Ven replied.

The Barret woman demanded, "Do you know where she is?"

Ven started to look at Eva, but caught herself. "We were hoping you could tell us."

Elder Barret staggered to the side wall and collapsed on a bench. "I knew this day was coming. I just knew it."

"Ma'am, what is the relationship between Kirra and the merchant Arno Held?"

"I wish I knew." She twisted her hands together. "Something terrible has happened. Go ahead and tell me what."

"Not to our knowledge," Ven replied. "But Arno Held—"

"You're lying!" Her voice rose to a wail. "Oh, this is my waking nightmare come to life!"

Barret's cry silenced the lobby. Eva halted the guards from moving in their direction by opening her wallet and showing them the badge. But there was nothing she could do about the heads that rose and stared over the shrubbery.

Ven's only response to the woman's keening grief was to settle on the bench beside her, calm as Elder Barret was frantic. "You've been waiting for us to show up?"

Elder Barret might have whimpered a yes. Eva could not be certain.

"Tell us why."

"First it was Madame Silver."

Ven glanced at Eva and explained, "The most powerful Fifth Ward courtesan."

"That's a fancy word for what she is." Elder Barret used her sleeve to wipe her face. "Silver lined up some First Ward scum who wanted to make my little girl his private plaything."

"How does that relate to—"

"I contacted Arno. Asked his help finding some job that would stop Kirra from making that terrible mistake."

"What did Arno do?"

"I don't know!" Elder Barret began rocking, tight motions, all her tension allowed. "My little girl vanished!"

"And the First Warder?"

"Arno claims that scum never met Kirra!" She stared at Ven, but Eva suspected the large woman did not actually see the agent. "Arno's always been a friend to our clan. Why would he lie?"

"How long has it been since—"

"I begged Arno to help us find my little girl! He swears he's checked everywhere!" She clutched Ven's hand with white-knuckled intensity. "She's gone! I know in my heart! My poor baby girl is lost to us all!"

Eva followed Ven back to their waiting transport. She felt like Elder Barret's wails still beat at her, tight impacts that made it difficult to maintain her balance. She settled into the seat, closed her door, and waited while Ven gave the AI their destination.

As they pulled away from the office complex, Eva realized Ven was laughing.

"What's with you?"

"That woman should be on the stage," Ven replied.

"What, she was lying?"

"With every breath." Ven glanced back. "You just watched a pro at work."

"I don't . . . I thought it was real."

"Of course you did." Ven settled back, smiling at the featureless Sixth Ward plains. "The question is, why did Elder Barret go to all that trouble?"

Eva did not realize how utterly exhausted the night's and subsequent day's activities had left her until she fell asleep in the shower.

She had stopped by the kitchen and spooned out samples from several dishes kept in the cooler, not tasting anything, just feeding her belly's empty void. Then she had leaned her head against the shower's tiled surface and closed her eyes. Brief flashes of memory crowded in. One by one she released them and allowed the emotions and stress and fleeting electric pulses to flow down and pass through the drain. She might have stayed there all night, under that cascading flow, if the water had not suddenly gone cold.

Eva shut off the taps, wrapped herself in one towel and used another for her hair, then stumbled into the bedroom. She was vaguely aware of her grandmother standing in the doorway. Salma spoke to her, a question regarding the mission and its success. Good, Eva replied, or wanted to. It went well. She then collapsed on the covers and was gone.

It felt as though Eva had only been asleep for a moment. Not even long enough to formulate a half-decent dream. The commlink's normally gentle chime impacted her like a drill. Eva fumbled, connected, and muttered, "I thought I cut this thing off."

"You did." Kim sounded impossibly awake, incredibly cheerful. "My temporary designation comes with powers unknown even to me, a former director. Can you imagine?"

"Kim." She spoke the word, not to identify him, but rather to try and nudge her brain awake.

"I requested an emergency override and poof, it happened before I could download the proper form. I really must come up with more interesting ways to use all this authority, don't you agree?"

She gradually became resigned to the man's real message, that her night's rest was over and done. "What time is it?"

"Don't know, doesn't matter. There's a car waiting downstairs. Leave Salma a note, give her my best, tell her we'll be gone six days, perhaps longer."

"I . . . What?"

"Hurry, my young friend. The convoy leaves in less than an hour. There is coffee and yet another dreadful sandwich waiting in the car."

Eva forced herself from the bed and searched for clean clothes. "Convoy?"

"To the lab! Yesterday a convoy left for the frontier lab, only to return that very same evening. They were attacked!"

Her only hope of maintaining balance while fitting on slacks was to lean against the wall. "I don't understand. What does that have to do with us?"

"Who knows? I certainly don't." Kim actually laughed out loud. "You'll never guess whose name was discovered on that convoy's manifest!"

"I'm sorry, I don't . . ."

"None other than Kirra Eblon, the woman who does not exist! Who promptly vanished the instant she emerged from the depot! Which means we have been handed yet another of those impossible mysteries. And even our dear Baroness now thinks there is a tiny shred of hope that you are right."

Shoes. She needed shoes before she could leave. And a pad and pen. And fingers that worked. "Right about what?"

"That these absurd mysteries are actually connected. Hurry now, the convoy drivers are leaving the ready room. Oh, and don't bother packing. We're only permitted a featherweight sack and no electronics." Kim laughed a second time, and Eva felt as if her entire body resonated to the man's joy. "Make haste, my dear! Regardless of what we find, this should be fun!"

Eva scribbled words she hoped her grandmother would be able to read and rushed for the door. Kim's joy was so potent it actually began invading her weary brain, offering an unexpected gift of energy and something more. Hope, perhaps. Or anticipation. Something.

She was going to the lab.

The convoy was already idling by the compound's main gate when Eva's ride pulled up. The vehicles could not depart, however, because Kim stood directly in their path, wearing the gentle smile Eva knew all too well. It was Kim's expression when preparing his most severe take-down.

A slender woman confronted him, her fists clenched by her sides and her precisely cut silver hair shimmering in the compound's exterior lights. As Eva rose from the vehicle, the woman turned slightly as she jabbed a finger in Kim's face, and Eva realized it was her mother.

Eva knew a remarkable mixture of pain and anticipation as she walked over. As if she could script the next stages. As if she approached a stranger who was about to be confounded by the force Kim would now reveal.

When Maxine realized it was her daughter who approached, she shouted, "You!"

Eva tried to recall how long it had been since their last meeting, and failed. "Hello, Mother. You've changed your hairstyle. It suits you."

"Very fetching," Kim agreed.

Maxine's ire swiveled from one to the other. "Please tell me you're not associated with this Guards' officer and his travesty of a demand!"

"It so happens," Kim replied, "your daughter serves as lead agent."

"Oh, that's rich." She now had a reason to sneer at her daughter. "Your grandmother must be so very proud."

The mix of nervous exhaustion, a too-brief rest, and Kim's good humor left Eva utterly immune to her mother's blistering wrath. She asked Kim, "What seems to be the problem?"

"The good doctor is reluctant to have us join her convoy."

"You *cretin*! Did you fail to hear what I just said? *You are not coming!*" She flung an arm at the guards observing from the gatehouse. *"Now open these gates!"*

"Unfortunately, Doctor, they have been informed this won't happen unless I say so."

"By yet another cretin! You and your ilk have no jurisdiction over my lab! Now get out of my way!" When Kim's only response was to wave at an arriving vehicle, Maxine rounded on her daughter. "You should be ashamed of yourself, consorting with cretins!"

"Director Kim is one of the finest men I have ever known."

"Then I pity you for the company you keep." Then she recognized the woman on approach, flanked by two uniformed guards. "What now?"

Kim saluted Baroness Ricard and said, "There seems to be a question regarding our right to travel. Doctor Fourier claims the power to deny us access. She says the lab does not fall under Florian's jurisdiction."

Ricard's voice remained bland, calm, frigid. "You are correct only so far as it goes, Doctor. Unlike the lab itself, however, your warehouse and supply lines are most certainly within my authority. Or Florian's dominion, if you prefer. And as of this moment, I am shutting it down."

"You can't do that!"

"I just did."

"My research is at a crucial stage! I've just spent *four days* collating—"

"Excuse me, Doctor. It is your research only so long as the Council grants you permission. Just as this consent is required for you and your convoy to pass through Florian's gates." She inspected the doctor, her gaze tight, her own ire revealed now. "Perhaps it is time your entire operation underwent a complete financial review. Top to bottom. Which of course would require your staff to return here, and remain here, until I and the Council are fully satisfied."

Maxine's mouth opened. But no sound emerged.

"I can only see two alternatives, Doctor. One is, you retire. Here. Tonight." Ricard gave that a beat, then continued, "That seems to be the most logical step, wouldn't you agree? After all, you are now in the process of alienating the Council's representatives. Perhaps your workload and the related stress has caused you to lose sight of just how precarious this entire operation remains, how vital good relations are to your future."

"I . . . No."

"In that case, the only alternative is to grant my two representatives full and unfettered access." Baroness Ricard's expression and softly spoken words carried an implacable force. "Make no mistake, Doctor. Your future hangs in the balance. Upon their return, these two agents will answer to me, and through me to the ruling Council. I expect nothing less than the news that you have answered their every question, and opened every door. Do we have an understanding?"

Maxine did not respond.

"Good. Now as you say, dawn approaches. I suggest you and your convoy get underway."

SEVEN
Kirra Barret

The instant Kirra's convoy had passed back through the veil, her commlink chimed. She checked her screen and found three messages.

The first, from Elder Barret, read: Black Watch and worse are hunting you. Don't contact me or Arno. Don't enter Fifth Ward.

The second, also from Elder Barret, contained just two words: Good luck.

Interestingly, the third message was not from Arno, but Dell: Hunters are closing in. Remember where Quinn took you? Go there. Don't use transport. Don't speak to anyone. Hide your face best you can. Use cash only. Hurry.

Kirra rose from her place in the front compartment and thanked each of the people in turn—pilot and relief driver and Marcel and finally Clarissa, who remained slumped against the side window, a pale shadow of the formerly cynical lady. She stepped back and started to settle in the seat next to Adeline, the surgeon from Corinth. Then she noticed the elderly woman two rows back was leaking tears. She slipped into the seat next to her and asked, "Would you like some company?"

The woman took hold of Kirra's hand. "How can you be so calm?"

"Inside I'm quaking with fear."

"I don't believe that for a second."

"It's true," Kirra insisted. "I'm sitting here because I need you to cry for both of us."

"Now that's a load of old rubbish." But the woman was smiling now. "Your fingers are like ice."

"See? Just like I told you. Frozen solid with fear."

"Such a sweet girl. Especially for such a liar."

"I'm shocked you would think such a thing of me."

"With every breath," the woman replied. She closed her eyes then, but still maintained her hold on Kirra's hand.

Kirra remained where she was, ignoring the fearful, almost angry chatter coming from the seats further back. She stared at the grey wasteland, what was soon to become Seventh Ward, and she planned.

The way ahead was treacherous, but Kirra was not so concerned about capture. She had just witnessed the power of her winged allies. The question was not arriving safely at her temporary haven. The real issues were how to do this and go unnoticed? And even more important, what next?

When she was certain the elderly woman had fallen asleep, Kirra returned to her seat next to the doctor, who greeted her with, "You have the calm and steady strength of a good surgeon."

Kirra had no idea how to respond.

"That's the first thing I look for in my students," Adeline went on. "They all know the books, else they wouldn't have made it this far. But when the crisis strikes and a patient's life hangs in the balance, how do they react?"

"I can't imagine myself in such a situation." Kirra punctuated that with a momentary silence, then asked, "What is life like in Corinth?"

"You really must come," the doctor said. "See for yourself."

"I would like that. Very much."

"Then it's settled." Adeline gazed at the featureless vista. She mused, "One of the reasons why my family traveled with me, we've been talking about moving back."

"To Florian? Why?"

"Rumors have been swirling for years. We now know there is more than a shred of truth to the fears. Our mines are playing out." She pointed at the grey void. "There are eleven untapped mineral sources in this region. More than Corinth had at the outset. Our Regent has requested access, co-ownership, some shared arrangement so our city-state can continue to exist."

"How do you know this?"

Adeline shifted around so as to smile at Kirra. "And there is the primary reason why my husband does not want to relocate. Not all city-states are governed the same. Corinth is by comparison an open city. All citizens are involved in the democratic process. Our Regent is an elected official."

The acidic bile of her early years filled Kirra. "I can't imagine what that would be like."

Adeline studied her. "You come from hard beginnings?"

"I don't want to talk about that."

The doctor nodded slowly. "For what it's worth, Corinth doesn't have anything like a Fifth Ward. Oh, there are bad areas. Life in Corinth is far from perfect. But a couple of centuries ago, a miner was elected Regent. He served three terms, eighteen years in all. Our First Ward bears his name."

There in the older woman's gaze was the answer. "Florian's rulers can't risk our Fifth Warders learning how life might be. That's it, isn't it."

Adeline turned her gaze back to the window. "You really should come for a visit."

The sun had fully set by the time they arrived back at the depot. Kirra took her time, allowing the noisy flock to depart first, then helped the elderly woman down the stairs and along the corridor and into the women's locker room. Kirra was very tired, the fatigue a weight she felt in her bones. But the night was going to be a long one, and every step had to be taken with great care.

She and Adeline shared weary smiles as the tall, narrow woman and two men shouted their annoyance over needing to shower once more, despite not having left the vehicle. The same tourists complained louder still over the money they had lost, with no chance of a refund. Yelling and slamming and stomping away, their voices echoing down the empty hall.

Kirra took her time in the showers, willing the heated water to ease the ache in her bones. Every connection to the diddybirds left her weary, but this was different. She felt wounded, as if the bond had sapped away something essential.

And before the night was over, she would have to do it again. She had no choice.

Money was not the issue. Fifth Warders always carried cash. Most banks didn't offer them credit rings. There was simply too much risk of fraud. Of course, she had a new ring along with her identity as a Three. But the habit of keeping cash on hand at all times was too ingrained.

The problem was staying invisible. The clinic, the haven where Quinn took her after the first assault, was all the way on the Third Ward's opposite side. A straight-line distance of some twenty kilometers. But Kirra could not risk traveling in a straight line, not with watchers or hunters or whoever they were monitoring every passage through the city-state's heart. No, her journey had to be all the way around the immense Third Ward, skirting the inner rings, doing as Dell and the others had commanded. Staying invisible.

Unless . . .

When she emerged from the depot, she found Adeline standing on the curb. "I decided not to share the Crillon transport with that lot." She pointed to a private hire approaching through the gates. "Can I offer you a ride?"

It was such a temptation. And perhaps she could have managed to hide her face from the cameras flanking the Second and First Ring gates. But the risk was simply too great. "That's so kind," Kirra replied. "But I live just a short distance from here. And to be honest, I could use the walk and the air."

"I understand." Adeline offered her a handwritten slip of paper. "My contact details."

"Wonderful. I will need to send you mine. Hopefully my new home will be ready in a couple of weeks." She played at a light, excited tone. "I'm moving into a Second Ward apartment."

"The lady is coming up in the world." Adeline offered her hand, then changed her mind and gave Kirra a quick embrace. "We'll be here for another few days at least. Everything depends on how long my husband needs to make up his mind about our moving back, you understand? Do be in touch. I'll probably need your help to convince him what just happened."

Kirra remained standing there as Adeline started to slip into the passenger seat. Then the surgeon rose back to full height as Marcel and the drivers basically carried Clarissa out and settled her into a waiting hospital van. Adeline and Kirra shared a long look, then the doctor slipped inside, her vehicle pulled through the gates, and was gone.

Kirra walked over to where the three men stood. The pilot and Marcel looked grim, exhausted, but steady enough. The relief driver, however, looked close to the same state as Clarissa. "I just wanted to say thanks for bringing us back safely."

The pilot inspected her, his dark eyes glinting in the depot lights. "Do you know, this is the first time a traveler has ever spoken such words to me."

"A day for firsts," Marcel agreed.

She wished them a pleasant evening, and set off. When she passed through the gates and started down the sidewalk, Kirra glanced back. All three men were still watching her.

Now that she had decided on her next move, Kirra felt encased within a shell of weary certainty. Everything up to that point had been taking one step after another into the unknown. To all the risks the night contained, all the hidden terrors, she had just one answer: *Why not?*

As she walked away from the depot, she decided that one response was enough.

The lab depot was located at the fringe of a commercial district. This time of night it was fairly easy to find an empty lane. Identifying what precisely fit her needs, however, was far more difficult. There could be no cameras, no risk of passing transports, nor people. Kirra walked long enough for the exhaustion to add a leaden weight to her limbs, when she stopped and peered down to her left. She crossed the avenue, stepped into the shadows, and spent a long moment studying the fetid alley. Finally, she spoke her decision aloud. "This is perfect."

The lane ran between two structures that were ratty with disuse. Fifteen steps further back, the way was barred by a high wire fence. Two streetlights flanking the fence were dark. Midway between the fence and the avenue was a narrow alcove leading to a locked steel door.

Kirra entered the alcove, lowered herself to the damp concrete, closed her eyes, and called.

She set up three teams. The first cluster were placed on the rooftops to either side of her hideaway, keeping watch. The second started looking for flying eyes, the drones used by Guards to watch over areas where it was deemed unnecessary to keep human forces on duty.

The third team were sent up, up, and away. Flying fast, farther and farther.

She was fairly certain she knew exactly where the clinic was located. When she and Elder Barret had departed, Kirra had taken careful note of the surroundings. The question was, would she be able to recognize the place from above.

The Third Ward version of an outdoor market sprawled between the nearest ring gate and the medical clinic run by Elyria. She flew her team high above the Third Ring, switching back and forth between her guardians and the spotters, when she realized what dominated the sky below her birds.

So many flying eyes.

Dozens of the mobile watchers flittered about. The diddybirds had excellent hearing, and these mobile units buzzed an angry note. Drones flittered back and forth over the inner three Wards, their presence forming a constant and threatening blanket.

Then Kirra spotted the clinic. Its exterior was in a fairly wretched state, similar to Arno's office. She recognized the battered steel portal through which she and Elder Barret had departed, confirmed by the three taverns directly across the main thoroughfare.

She pulled all her birds back, rose to her feet, stepped into the alley, and took a long shaky breath. The thrill and the danger of what she was about to attempt left her giddy.

Kirra lifted her arms, closed her eyes, called, and . . .

The birds attached themselves to her with a lithe and gentle grace. Where they gripped her flesh and not just clothes, Kirra felt a warm and comforting strength. She'd had no idea their talons could be retracted until that very moment. They lifted her, higher and higher, while hundreds of others enveloped her in a living cloud.

The lab technicians had said it themselves. They had no idea who these birds were or why they had suddenly appeared twenty years back. The frontier lab was expressly forbidden from investigating them further. There was every likelihood this cloud of alien beasts would be noticed by a passing drone. But who was to say this was not merely part of the diddybirds' nightly routine? Besides, when had they ever posed a threat to anyone?

The strangest part to her journey was how Kirra could not observe through her own eyes. The sharp-edged diddybird visuals heightened the absurdity of what she was attempting, soaring over the Third, then Second, and now even the First Ward. High, high up, far above the surveillance machines, making a straight-line journey from the lab depot to the clinic.

Kirra was almost sorry when the clinic's rooftop came into view. They hovered far up, waiting in cloudlike ease until that patch of sky was free of all drones. The birds then set her down, their wings a leathery chorus.

The roof held a single access point. The steel door was padlocked shut. At a command, the birds tore through the lock and handle. Then they departed.

When Elyria arrived around dawn, she found Kirra asleep on a gurney outside her office. The clinician drew an unsteady breath, then asked, "Are you a ghost?"

"Tell Arno I need to see him," Kirra replied. "And Dell. And Quinn. And Elder Barret. All of them together."

"What you're asking is nigh on impossible," the nurse replied. "Arno is under constant surveillance."

"Tell them to come only when it's safe. But they need to come. And soon as possible."

Elyria looked ready to argue, but in the end merely said, "They'll want to know the reason for taking such a risk."

"It's time they meet my crew." Kirra rolled over, setting her back to the corridor and the lights. "Tell them to come the hour before dawn."

EIGHT
Eva Fourier

Their transport traveled near the convoy's center, eighth of fourteen vehicles. Eva's mother isolated herself at a table intended to hold six. Maxine was seated with her back to the others. She spread out her work and did not speak a word. Eva found it easier to dismiss Maxine's smoldering presence than she would ever have thought possible. As they passed through the Sixth Ring and entered an utterly grey void, Eva knew a fleeting moment of regret. As if what she saw in the first glimmer of daylight was a reflection of their relationship. She wished the two of them could share this incredible moment. Then she pushed the yearnings aside. Eva had a lifetime's experience at enduring her mother's rejection.

The young man seated opposite her, Dr. Marcel Obon, asked, "Am I in trouble?"

"Certainly not," Kim replied from the seat next to hers. "Our interest in that day pertains to something entirely removed from your professional responsibilities."

Eva decided it would be best to add loudly enough for her words to carry, "If you even suspect that you face a downside to speaking openly with us, we will bring the Council's power to bear."

"This promise is open-ended," Kim agreed. "There is no time limit. If you have a question, a worry, anything at all, please reach out to us."

Eva took a moment to review the information on her tablet. "Dr. Obon, may I call you Marcel? You are a specialist in alien microbiology, correct? How long have you worked at the frontier lab?"

"Six years."

"And your associate from that most recent trip, she isn't with us today?"

"Clarissa is on sick leave. For how long is anyone's guess. Can I ask what you're investigating?"

"We are interested in aspects of that recent convoy," Kim replied.

"You mean, the attack."

"Yes and no," Eva replied.

"We will gladly answer your questions," Kim said. "But we would ask that you be patient and allow us to complete our own questioning first."

"It would help immensely if you try and answer fully," Eva said. "Once we have covered the issues that interest us, we will do our best to respond to your questions."

Kim's tablet pinged. He told Eva, "That will be Ven."

Marcel said, "Travelers to the lab aren't allowed electronic equipment of any kind."

"Ah, but we are not making this journey as tourists," Kim said.

Eva told Kim, "Perhaps Marcel should stay and observe. Allowing him to witness the interview would state in no uncertain terms that our investigation is not about him or the lab."

Kim looked up, studied her, then nodded. He told Marcel, "Agent Ven Hawkins has completed interviews with, ah, let's see, three of the travelers in that ill-fated convoy. I understand the pilot from that day is driving the second vehicle today, correct? And the relief driver . . ."

"Sick leave," Marcel replied.

"I asked our agent to send us what she had," Kim went on. "I understand connectivity becomes less dependable once we pass through the cloud."

"It's hit or miss," Marcel agreed. "But the link is stronger during the dry season."

As Kim drew up the downloads, Eva asked, "Do you know why?"

"Some airborne microbes carry such a powerful static charge they play havoc with satellite feeds. Convoys communicate by way of short-range microburst transmissions."

"So much we can learn from you," Kim said. "Very well. Let us observe together what Ven has learned."

Eva rose to her feet and motioned for Marcel to take her seat. "Any comments or input you can offer would be most appreciated."

Her intention was to stand by Kim's shoulder and observe Marcel as well as the screen. But the first interview was of a husband and wife who insisted on speaking together. Eva found their stream of complaints to be tedious, and clearly Marcel felt the same. The couple considered the interview an opportunity to list grievances. Their treatment at the hands of Marcel and Clarissa, the clothes, the lack of servants, the dangers no one warned them about, on and on and on. Eva straightened from her crouch and studied her surroundings.

The pilot's station flowed freely into the main cabin, offering everyone on board an uninterrupted view both of the road ahead and the vista to either side. Eva spent a long moment studying the approaching cloud, its mountainous swirls of muted colors, the incredible alien forces on display. A lance of regret struck unexpectedly, a sincere desire to share this moment with her mother. The stranger.

Eva turned away from the view and shoved the futile wishes aside.

Their central quarters contained four tables rimmed by swivel chairs and then a kitchenette and fresher. The two stations between them and her mother were empty. Maxine remained with her back to them, typing furiously. Beyond the kitchenette was a glass partition, and behind that a mobile lab. Eva watched a pair of technicians work in easy tandem at a vast array of sophisticated equipment. The pair studiously ignored the world beyond their glass wall.

She was drawn back to the table when Kim cut off the interview mid-complaint and told Marcel, "I assume you've heard enough from that woman. I certainly have."

"We get at least one of that type every trip," Marcel said.

"Rich, entitled, dumb, insufferable," Kim offered.

Marcel coughed. The relief driver laughed out loud.

From Maxine there was no reaction.

Kim sighed. "I suppose we should press on with the next."

As if in response, his tablet gave off a series of six pings, like the chimes of a nervous electronic bell.

Kim leaned in closer as he scrolled. "Now this is interesting."

A man's voice came over the transport's intercom. "Chief here. Veil entry in ninety seconds. Transports sound off."

Everyone on board stopped what they were doing and turned toward the pilots. As their driver chimed in with his terse report and they entered the unquenchable gloom, Eva found it interesting how all these professionals froze. Even the lab technicians. Even her mother. In the transport's interior lighting, Eva thought she actually glimpsed the real woman. It was the briefest of revelations, tragic and sad and weary and resigned. Then they were through, back in full morning sunlight and . . .

Eva was surrounded by an alien world.

Eva had no idea how long she stood gaping at the vista until Kim took hold of her arm. The director appeared unaffected by the impossibilities that now surrounded them. "Ven says her latest interview may hold something significant."

The chairs surrounding their table were attached to pillars that swiveled but did not shift position. Eva gestured for Marcel to stay where he was and did her best to focus. Ven identified herself and the woman now shown on the screen. The palatial Crillon lobby could be seen in the background. Eva heard the woman reply to Ven's question with, "I am a pediatric surgeon in Corinth."

"But you were originally a native of Florian, is that correct, Doctor?"

"Please call me Adeline."

"Our time is unfortunately limited. Before this interview began, you mentioned something. With your permission I would like to jump straight to that point."

"All right. Fine."

"Adeline, you say there was one individual in particular among the travelers who caught your attention."

"Kirra. Yes. She certainly did."

"Kirra," Marcel muttered. "Sure. Absolutely."

Eva dropped to her knees between the two chairs as Kim froze the interview. "Marcel, what was it about her that stood out?"

"Other than the fact that she's one of the most beautiful women I've ever seen?" He looked from Eva to Kim and back. "This is about her?"

"Answer the question, please."

"She was totally *on*. From the moment she stepped out of that hotel vehicle."

Eva demanded, "Which hotel was that?"

He pointed to the frozen screen. "Right there. Crillon."

Kim glanced at Eva. "We checked the registers, correct?"

"Of course."

"Crillon included?"

Eva nodded. "No one by that name has been registered anywhere."

Kim turned back to Marcel and said, "Please explain what you meant by that word, *on*."

"Very aware. Intent. Absolutely on target the whole time."

Eva asked, "Can you tell us Kirra's last name?"

Marcel reached for his own tablet, searched, then replied, "Eblon. Kirra Eblon." He looked from one to the other. "Why are you asking about her?"

Eva received a confirmation from Kim, and replied, "Kirra Eblon is a ghost."

"She appears, she vanishes," Kim said. "Poof and gone. There is no official record of Kirra Eblon ever having existed."

"This disappearance is not something that happens just once," Eva said. "It is an ongoing process."

Marcel showed confusion. "How is that even possible?"

"We have no idea," Kim said. "Shall we continue?"

They turned their attention back to the screen, Kim touched the tab, and they heard Ven ask, "Tell me what it was about Kirra that most held your attention."

The surgeon's response was immediate. "The word that comes to mind is *prescient*. She was more than simply intelligent. Or aware. Kirra saw what others missed. Myself included."

Marcel said quietly, "That absolutely fits."

Ven asked, "Can you give me a specific example?"

As Adeline described the conversation that took place in the locker room, Eva sensed her mother rising and stepping forward. Marcel tensed to the point where his entire body became rigid. But none of them glanced up as Ven asked, "What about once you began the journey. Do you remember anything specific that made Kirra Eblon appear to stand out?"

"Oh yes. Absolutely. I'm telling you, this went far beyond any one moment. The young lady was simply remarkable." Adeline described Kirra's entry into the pilot's cabin. Then, "My most lasting impression of Kirra Eblon was how she responded to the attack on the convoy itself. The rest of us were utterly terrified. Screaming, yelling, a total panic. Kirra was . . ."

"Yes? How did she respond?"

Marcel said, "Calm."

"She showed nothing at all," the doctor replied. "Kirra might as well have vanished."

"That's it," Marcel said. "That's it exactly."

Ven pressed, "Kirra disappeared?"

"Effectively, yes. Not physically. But she closed her eyes and very calmly went away."

Ven hesitated, then said, "I have witnessed some people handling panic in that manner. Just folding up inside themselves. Their calm is not so much a mask as a waking sort of faint."

Marcel shook his head, back and forth, as Adeline said, "No. That wasn't it."

"Then can you please help me understand—"

"The diddybirds attacked. You already heard about that, yes? Those little beasts saved us. When it was over and they vanished, Kirra opened her eyes and just went back to watching the scenery. Perfectly calm." Adeline turned away from Ven and searched for what only she could see. "You know what it was like? I had the impression she knew what was going to happen, how the alien birds showed up and saved us, before they arrived. Prescient, like I said. Aware of the events in advance."

The screen went blank. They watched as Marcel leaned back in his seat, nodded slowly, and declared, "That actually makes perfect sense."

They arrived in dusk's lingering light, the setting sun a faint sliver on the horizon. For the past hour, tension inside the transport had risen in time to the convoy's acceleration. They raced, they pushed. Maxine stood behind the two pilots now, watching, silent, rigid. The tires whined, the transport rushed and rumbled, the engine shrilled. Eva swung her chair around so as to watch the blurred landscape, and thought about what they had learned. The woman who did not exist, Kirra Eblon, the woman who was missing, Kirra Barret, her reaction to incoming danger and possibly death, the way the convoy had been saved by diddybirds. She was missing something. Of that Eva was absolutely certain.

This was where she excelled, distancing herself from the immediate and looking beyond. She reflected on the word that surgeon had used to describe Kirra. Prescient. Perhaps that was something she had in common with this woman they could not locate.

The convoy chief interrupted her thoughts with, "Midway Station five klicks. Hold steady."

The near-rictus fear did not fade until they pulled through the wire fencing and parked. Marcel sighed, an exhaled breath shared by all the regular travelers. As a collapsible tunnel extended out and attached itself to the transport's main door, Eva thought she heard Marcel breathe a few words, too soft for her to catch. A prayer, perhaps, or some litany against the night.

Maxine stood by the exit as the door swung open. She glanced back and announced, "There'll soon be a miners' convoy making the return journey to Florian. You can ride back with them."

There was no logical reason for the words to burn like they did. When Eva did not respond, Kim glanced over. He wore what Eva had come to know as his attack-smile.

She gave Maxine what she hoped was the same attitude.

Cold, implacable, holding enough force to declare she was the one in charge. "We are continuing to the lab."

"Why! There's nothing for you in the lab! The convoy you're interested in didn't even make it this far!"

The exhaustion and tension and weight from the past few days left Eva with a burning desire to destroy bridges, wreak havoc, put her mother and this absurd conversation behind her once and for all.

For reasons she could not fully explain, not even to herself, Eva rose and headed for the exit. "Get out of my way."

Maxine stepped back, furious. "If we had been five minutes later, we'd be *dead*! And it would have been *your fault*!"

The tunnel was floored in the same flexible material as the walls. Eva tread slowly, carefully, keeping both hands on the side-rails as the way ahead swam in and out of focus. Kim waited until they became isolated by a curve in the tunnel to say, "You have shown a wisdom beyond your years."

As she settled into her bunk after a heated ready meal, Eva cast back to the confrontation that had stained their arrival. Only now she did not revisit her mother's acidic comments, nor how Eva had responded by walking away. Rather, Kim's softly spoken words were what settled and comforted.

Eva woke very early and lay in her bunk, staring into the darkness. A dream she could not recall whispered to her. A tendril of fear drifted through her mind, so faint and indistinct she could not even say if it was actually the dream that left her so afraid.

She was surrounded on all sides by the sounds of slumber. Quiet as she could, Eva rose and took aim for the light spilling around the fresher's door. She had slept in her clothes and had nothing else with her except the nearly empty backpack. Midway through her shower, Eva realized she had no towel. Only then did she recognize how exhausted she felt, as if the disturbed slumber had only magnified the slow and muddled nature of her thoughts.

A frantic search revealed shelves hidden behind sliding partitions, holding not just towels but stacks of neatly folded coveralls. Eva sorted through the contents and came up with a set that, when donned, fit well and felt clean.

She left her clothes on the bunk and entered the silent foyer, which also served for after-hours socializing. Broad front windows showed a dozen or so mine transports, massive vehicles whose domed containers shone like khaki hills in the exterior lights. Beyond the fence, there was nothing save impenetrable night.

Eva followed the scent of fresh-brewed coffee into the dining hall. Her mother was seated at a table by the side wall, her back to the room, a tray pushed aside to make space for her tablet. Eva greeted the convoy drivers sharing a table, then prepared a tray.

She stood holding her breakfast, debating.

In the end, she decided it needed to be done. What exactly 'it' entailed, she had no idea. Only that this conversation was necessary.

Eva thought sitting across the table from Maxine would only add to the risk of confrontation. So, she sat at the table's end with her mother to her right. Maxine did not even glance up, she just continued typing furiously, pausing now and then to inspect her work, then her fingers flew once more. Eva took her time, extracting the ready meal from its warming wrapper, eating in small bites, studying this woman who insisted on maintaining such a distance. The coffee was strong and black and just what she needed. Eva finished her meal, drained her cup, and pushed her tray to one side.

"It doesn't have to be this way," she said. "We could use this as a chance to rescript our relationship. One adult to another. Talk about our worlds, our lives."

"You want to know about me?" Maxine's typing slowed gradually. She still had not met her daughter's gaze. "My life, my world, all I am, begins and ends here. In this lab. And you threatened to take that from me."

"Only because you acted like the queen of all she surveyed," Eva replied.

Maxine's expression turned flinty. She shoved the tablet aside. Stared down at her hands. Sighed.

Eva said, "Tell me about my father."

"What?" Maxine jerked around. "No!"

"I know about his relationship with the lab technician. And the child who died with them when the convoy was attacked." Eva held to a calm and level tone. Like she was interviewing a suspect. Rather than her own mother. "Tell me about him. I have a right to know."

Maxine's mouth opened, but she made no sound.

"What was his division called, Communicators? What does that even mean?"

"Salma should never have told you about that," Maxine hissed. "Never!"

Eva could see the portal slam shut in her mother's gaze. "All right. Fine." Eva rose from the table. "Have it your way."

She was midway to the hall's exit when Kim approached and said, "The lab convoy is loading up."

"Good," Eva replied. "I'm all done here."

The morning light had not yet reached full force when the road split. The main highway continued arrow-straight toward the island spaceport. Through their transport's right-hand windows, Eva watched seven heavily laden vehicles continue on south by west. Once they reached their destination, Spaceport Island, their loads would enter the final stages of refining. When these precious elements had attained a nearly pure state, they would be packaged and shipped off to worlds Eva was destined never to visit. She continued watching long after the convoy had vanished into the golden-hued dawn.

Kim had requested both Marcel and the travelers' pilot to journey with them. Eva sat at their table and listened as her boss went over the same material again. The pilot's attention had been focused on the road and the danger, and had very little new to add. Mostly Eva played tourist. The road leading to the lab was much narrower and in places made for rough going. Their two companions, pilot and technician, paid the bumpy ride no mind. Soon as Kim thanked the pilot, he rose and shifted to a fold-down seat behind their two drivers.

Maxine worked in the glass-fronted mobile lab, her back to

the main cabin. Now that her boss was ignoring them, Marcel became almost talkative. "Until this most recent convoy, the alien realm has always followed a very strict series of cycles." He pointed to the vast stretches of viscous earth, made almost beautiful by the illuminated rainbow waves. "These swampy regions serve as birthing pits. In the days leading up to each rainy season, those vibratory patterns increase in frequency until their color patterns blur. When the rains begin, little baby beastlings begin to emerge. The veins of hard earth like the one here to our left, see? They shine with an almost blinding illumination throughout the stormy periods. We assume it's to help the young remain on stable ground until they're able to fend for themselves. By the time the rainy season ends they're almost fully grown."

Kim appeared to be as utterly mesmerized as Eva. "What do they eat?"

Marcel nodded. "For years we had no idea. But with our new infrared long-range systems, we can pierce the storms enough to watch them consume the swamp itself. The slime is filled with nutrients."

"What about the other things mentioned by the travelers," Eva asked. "The trees."

"Mountains with eyes," Kim added.

"They both appear in the dry season's final days," Marcel replied. "Our observations suggest the trees act as mobile watchers, sort of like babysitters, during the beastlings' very earliest days. The hills we call sentinels. They rise up along certain lines of hard earth, regions where the new births don't populate for some reason. As the rain begins, those great eyes pop open. They remain there and monitor the birthing cycle. The trees come and go, we watch them drift around, then when the new aliens slip into the swamp they both vanish."

Kim asked, "And the caves?"

"Until yesterday, all we had were reports from the few survivors of convoy attacks. These reports match what passengers from the recent convoy witnessed. And we also now have video footage. Everything we witnessed was a mystery. Trees chasing the convoy, mountains rising in parallel to the road."

Eva repeated, "The caves."

Marcel nodded. "There is so much we don't know. Do some of these beasts exist for part of their life cycle inside caves we've only witnessed during such attacks? Are they a permanent fixture, buried somehow except for times of supposed danger?"

Kim asked, "Can we see the footage captured by that transport?"

"I suppose." Another glance. "Will you tell me why you're here?"

At a nod from Kim, Eva replied, "We'll tell you everything we know."

"Our mystery is not as big as yours," Kim said. "But close."

Treaty's only laboratory for alien studies was a campus of seven single-story buildings forming nearly a complete circle, with two towers anchoring the north and south points. The interior space was large enough to hold their convoy and more besides. The structures all had windows facing outward and were connected by passageways built from the same grey stone. Each of the transports became connected to the lab by collapsible tunnels. Marcel served as their guide, his manner distant and formal now, as their arrival was observed by dozens of personnel. And Maxine.

Eva and Kim endured a three-stage body cleansing, something normally applied to technicians who were returning from outside. As the case with all visitors, they dwelled apart. Their dining facilities, miniature rec room, freshers and bunks were all separated from the staff. Their boundaries were firmly established by doors bearing 'Restricted Zone' signs and which only opened via wrist IDs.

Eva welcomed the separation. Over a bland ready meal, Kim asked, "What do you want to have happen during our time here? It seems to me, our goals for this journey have been accomplished. All our next steps are back in Florian. Radio communication is out for the duration. I checked."

A glass wall separated the travelers' area from the main dining room. Any number of technicians and convoy drivers filled the dozen or so tables. No one even glanced their way. Eva knew he was asking about more than their investigation and replied, "There's nothing for me here. I was wrong to think there ever was."

"You have visited a part of your own beginnings," Kim said. "Who was ever to say this would ever be easy or pleasant?"

There was no logical reason why being understood would cause her eyes to burn. Eva swallowed hard and did not respond.

"Still, this has been an important journey," Kim said. "In time, you will see. I am certain of this."

Eva woke from a dream she could not remember. Just the same, it terrified her. She lay in the open-sided cubicle listening to Kim's soft breathing and waited for her heart to stop pounding.

In her sixth year of school, she and several other high achievers were invited to spend a day at the Second Ward's main hospital. Maxine had of course been thrilled, thinking this opened grand prospects for Eva—medicine, biology, all the directions over which her mother cast an approving gaze.

The compassion and care the hospital staff showed the afflicted and their kin had touched Eva at a very deep level. On the other hand, she had been invited to suit up and observe first-hand as a surgeon performed an abdominal procedure. The surgeon had sliced open the patient's stomach and delved with both hands, describing in clinical detail what she found, and what must be done to save the patient's life. The surgeon's utter lack of emotion, the aggressive way she invaded the patient, the bloody scalpel, all of it left Eva determined to avoid the healing professions. She had not thought of that day in years.

Yet Eva's nightmare carried that very same sense of clinical invasion. As if something or someone had plunged deeply inside, hunting Eva's most precious secrets. The search had not been painful, yet the dream left her aching. She rose from the bed feeling like she had been violated at a level she had not known even existed. Because of a dream.

Eva padded down the central corridor and entered the fresher. When she returned, Kim murmured, "Are you all right?"

She had always appreciated what honesty meant to them both. "I'm not sure. It might have been just a bad dream. But I don't . . ."

Kim rose to a seated position and shifted his feet to the floor. "We are surrounded by every imaginable reason for nightmares."

"I think it might have been something more," Eva replied.

Kim waited, and when Eva did not supply more, he asked, "Do you want to tell me about it?"

"I'm not sure I can. Maybe later."

He slipped his feet into the lab's canvas slippers. "Breakfast, then."

As they entered the travelers' side of the dining hall, Marcel offered them a minute wave through the plexiglass divider, his hand scarcely rising above waist-level. His smile was even smaller. Eva understood and responded with a nod. Marcel was among his tribe now. The terms and conditions governing their interactions were dictated by the lab director.

She and Kim ate in comfortable silence. Eva finished her decent ready meal, then spoke what had been on her mind since their arrival. Releasing the words carried a scalding force. Just the same, it felt right to ask, "Could a different daughter have developed a decent relationship with Maxine?"

Kim ate with almost dainty motions. Only the rough scabs over his knuckles, the thickness of his wrists and neck, the scars running up his right arm, attested to the man's hidden nature. He lifted his cup and pushed the tray to one side. Taking each motion slowly, adding a formality to his response. "What I hear is different from what you say. I think what you mean is, if *you* were different."

"You hear correctly."

"Then the answer is yes. Perhaps. With two caveats. First, it would not be you. It would be the woman designed by your mother. Who would perhaps please her. And perhaps not. You understand?" When she nodded, he continued, "The problem is you are too strong-willed to be so pliant. And the risk would be very great that even after making this soul-twisting effort, the result would still not achieve your desired goal."

"And the second?"

His dark eyes showed a singular warmth. "My life would be much poorer, not knowing the woman you have become. It is a selfish thing to say, I know. But there you are. I would miss you terribly."

Gradually a second wave of technicians filled the main dining hall. Eva's mother appeared, gathered up her breakfast, and seated herself at an empty table. Very few if any of her subordinates even glanced her way as Maxine ate and worked her tablet. Eva found a bitter satisfaction in how she was not the only one isolated by her mother's attitude.

She turned away. "Change the subject?"

"By all means."

"I'd like to go through recent events. All of them. Right back to when we met for lunch at the Crillon and Tanner stormed out."

"Interesting." Kim leaned back. "To what end?"

"We keep suggesting all these unexplained mysteries are somehow connected. What if the answer is right there in front of us and we don't see it?" She stopped, then, "Why are you smiling?"

"I like this very much." He motioned to the glass divider's other side, where the room was filled with people determinedly not looking their way. "We are as distanced from everything as we could possibly get."

"A day without pressures," Eva said. "For the first time since forever."

"You have your tablet with you?"

"Always."

"Good. One of us should make notes, and I left mine . . ."

That was as far as they could proceed, for at that moment the whole world changed.

Shouts and yells bulled through the glass partition as a crowd stormed into the cafeteria. The tableau held such a bizarre quality that Eva's thoughts froze. She felt as if her earlier nightmare had been given life.

And yet all these new faces looked beyond happy. So full of joyful excitement some of them even wept. A dozen people, more, shoved through a crowd of frantic technicians as if these other people did not even exist. They only had room for one thought, one aim. To cross the dining hall and approach her. Eva Fourier.

Maxine rose from her table and began shouting. Her fury was not directed at this newly arrived crew, however. Instead, she yelled angrily at a heavyset woman in a lab coat who, along with four others, attempted to shepherd this crew back in the direction from which they had come.

Only this woman was having none of it. She wheeled around, stomped over, pushed the lab director so hard that Maxine fell. The woman bent over, her face inches from Maxine's, and yelled more loudly still. Maxine scrambled back to her feet, tried to shout back, but the woman just kept growing louder, forcing Maxine back and back until she was crammed against the rear wall.

The newly arrived crew paid them no mind whatsoever. This dozen or so people were at complete odds to the growing number of lab technicians who now surrounded them. They were dressed in a rainbow assortment of clothing, almost as if they sought to mimic the alien terrain. They were all shapes and aged from late teens to a pair of men in their dotage.

All of them were singularly focused on Eva.

She was all they saw. Nothing else entered their consciousness, or so it appeared. Not the technicians tugging on their clothes and arms. Certainly not the screaming match between Maxine and the other woman.

These newcomers came forward, determined.

When the crew arrived at the glass partition, they spread themselves along its length, forming a human barricade between Eva and the main dining hall. She stepped closer, studying them. They did not appear threatening. Instead, they appeared happy. Excited. They greeted her approach by smiling and pressing their hands flat on the glass. Several shed tears.

Kim said, "Perhaps you should go to them."

"No," Eva decided. "I'll wait until I'm invited."

In the end, they sent Marcel.

The dining hall had become so crammed Eva suspected most or all the lab's technicians were present. Maxine hovered by the open lab door, arms crossed, watching. The larger woman stood at an angle, so as to observe her crew and still block Maxine from inserting herself any further. Eva could feel the women's electric tension radiating through the plexiglass divider.

"Humankind's first exploratory vessel was in the process of mapping Treaty and identifying surface-level mineral deposits when the ship's captain made contact with the master aliens," Marcel was saying. "That is to say, the master aliens contacted her."

"Telepathically?" Kim stood well removed from where they helped Eva prep for what was about to come.

"Correct." Marcel pointed at the group still clustered by the glass divide. "Since the five colonies were established, our only communication with the planet's original inhabitants has come by way of that crew."

Marcel had arrived accompanied by a female technician named Brisa, who added, "Every now and then another individual announces they're in contact with friends beyond the veil. Our communications crew sends someone to test their abilities. If the contact proves both strong and constant, they're invited to join our team."

Kim pointed through the glass. "Are they always like this?"

No one felt any need to ask what he meant. Marcel nodded. "Since the ship's captain passed on, always."

For the first time since humanity's arrival, an invitation had arrived by way of the communicators. All of them. Had it come any other way, the message would have been discounted as absurd. But the message had been unanimously received, and unequivocal. Eva had been summoned to meet the aliens.

She was to travel with Jon, a tall young man whose hair was shaded a translucent brown. He stood on the glass partition's other side, with all the other communicators surrounding him in a tight semi-circle. Jon only spoke when someone interrupted his view of Eva. Otherwise, he was docile and happy, like all his crew. Ready to face the unknown.

"Everyone knows what happened next," Marcel continued. "The ship's crew identified the virus that threatened to wipe out the world's entire population, and the treaty was signed, and humanity's island communities were established. The city-states and the spaceport were up and running within decades."

The woman assisting Marcel added, "The original settlers were frantic to get things in place before the master aliens changed their minds." Brisa was a lovely blonde in her late twenties. She pointed through the partition to where the communicators clustered around Jon. "That crew are our only assurance that the treaty still holds on the other side."

Eva felt as if the conversation and the communicators' welcoming smiles were knitting together a second partition. One that shielded her from the grim frustration imbedded in Maxine's every glance. As if Eva was stealing something of value. As if this was all her fault. She shifted slightly so as to not see her mother any more, and did her best to focus.

"We actually have no idea what is going on," Brisa was saying. "Even to guess why they've finally made this contact is an act of absurdity."

"We know a lot," Marcel softly insisted.

"Everything we receive from the master aliens is filtered through the communicators. As a result, all too often the information is difficult to comprehend," Brisa went on. "We call them the master aliens because records from the first ship contain that title, and it works as well as anything."

"Over a thousand years, no one has actually made visual contact," Marcel agreed. "We don't even know if they are actually an alien species, or simply a component of a planetary consciousness. We ask questions. A lot of them. And mostly what we get back is gibberish."

"Or maybe you just don't know how to interpret what they're saying," Brisa said.

"Oh, and you could do better?"

"If a certain someone actually requested my assistance, absolutely."

"Ha," Marcel said. "Double ha."

Eva told Marcel, "You should smile more often. It suits you."

"I keep telling him that," Brisa said. "He doesn't listen to me either."

Eva liked how the conversation was making Marcel

uncomfortable almost as much as how it eased her own heartache. "Maybe if we shout it together, he'd hear."

"Doubtful," Brisa said.

"Really, really loud."

"Worth a try, I suppose." Brisa began fitting the internal belts intended to keep the suit from shifting. "Too tight?"

"No, it feels good."

Marcel slipped her gloves into place and said, "If you two are finally done having fun at my expense, we're under time pressure here."

Eva countered, "How much time does it take to smile?"

Brisa adjusted the water-tube so it was there by her left cheek. "With Marcel, we're talking years. I should know."

Eva thought of it as a space suit, despite how she and Jon were not leaving the planet's surface. These two technicians, Marcel and his lovely paramour, appeared ignorant to the irony of fitting Eva inside her mother's suit, all while Maxine continued to blister them with barely suppressed ire. Or how the name 'Fourier' was inscribed by her left shoulder. Under different circumstances, all this might have made for a laugh. Instead, Eva heard herself murmur, almost as if the words were drawn out, against her will, "What is wrong with her?"

Marcel started to turn, then caught himself and kept his back to the main hall. Brisa accepted the helmet from him and pointed to the dispenser tubes for liquid sustenance and water. But what she said was, "Not a lovey-dovey mother-daughter relationship, I take it."

Marcel muttered, "Brisa."

"What. Just making an observation. That's what we do here, right? We observe."

Marcel sighed, shook his head, pointed to the helmet's exterior. "Stereo cameras are placed directly above both eyes. An exterior mike is positioned in between. Interior mike and camera above your left eye. Video screen above your right. Audio feeds through your earpieces. Everything controlled by the monitor in your left sleeve."

"We've been through this four times already," Brisa said, rolling her eyes in Eva's direction. She mouthed the word, *men.*

Which was the best possible way to refocus Eva's attention away from the smoldering lab director.

One of the people helping Jon into his suit tapped on the glass divider and showed them three fingers. As Marcel settled her helmet into place, Maxine started to reinsert herself into the process, only to be halted by the woman Eva now knew to be head of the Communicators division. The position her late father once held. Eva found it mildly interesting how none of the others even glanced at their boss.

As Jon started toward the building's front lobby, the other communicators patted his suited arm, shoulder, helmet. Eva had the impression they were not saying farewell so much as participating in whatever was about to happen. Marcel followed her gaze and asked, "Do you hear me?"

"Loud and clear."

"Jon has been their de facto leader since forever. We're all very glad they chose him to accompany you."

"Some of the others can be difficult," Brisa agreed. "Especially if they're stressed."

Kim drifted around the periphery, a silent observer until they entered the front lobby, when Eva heard him declare, "I should be the one accompanying Eva."

The entire group paused. Then Eva heard Jon reply through her earpiece, "Just her."

Kim shook his head. "Eva Fourier and I are a team."

"My friends say, her and me," Jon said. His voice carried a soft lilt that fit his cheerful demeanor. "One and one."

Eva heard all the other communicators chime in, "One and one."

"One, two, what does it matter?" Kim demanded.

Marcel replied, "You think all of us wouldn't beg to be included? That we haven't dreamed for years of doing this?"

"It's our life's work on the line here," Brisa agreed.

"We're excluded," Marcel said. "It doesn't matter what we're thinking. Or wanting."

"Why her?" Brisa said. "Why now. Why not all of us?"

The communicators responded with another chorus. "One and one."

Any further objection was halted by Jon heading for the airlock. "They are waiting."

The suit made for clumsy going, but not overly so. Eva thought it felt like wearing two sets of sweats, one on top of the other. Marcel came over the earpieces. "One more soundcheck, Eva."

"You're coming through perfectly." The helmet was a marvel. The glass portal extended almost as far as she could turn her head, left to right and up or down, granting her a marvelous view of the airlock's exterior door opening. She did not even need to bend at the waist to see her feet, make the step over the portal's ledge, and enter the alien realm.

"The communicators are getting antsy," Marcel said. "They insist the master race want you to speed things up."

"Patience!" Jon almost shouted the word. "We're coming!"

Marcel said, "Jon is on a separate feed to his counselor, but he can also hear you and me. If you want to close that link, touch the first blinking light on your monitor in the block marked 'commlinks.'"

"Understood." They had been through this twice while suiting up. The monitor screen wrapped around her left forearm. Eva knew Marcel was talking mostly to keep her company, and she appreciated it.

"Check your system," Marcel said. "Make sure you're recording."

Which meant stopping. She could not yet be certain of her footing and remove her gaze from the path. The external cameras and microphones imbedded in her helmet were backed up with another external set at the center of her ribcage. All input fed to the recording system in her helmet. There was also a small screen in her helmet's upper-right corner, on which she could see Marcel. Behind him stood Kim, and farther back was a view of the lab's crowded dining hall. They had shifted the communication system in there, as it was the only place large enough to hold the lab's entire population. Eva said, "Visual and audio lights are all green."

Jon was now half a dozen steps ahead. He called, "Summoned! Hurry!"

The lab's boundary perimeter was marked by a ring of grey earth-stones, reduced by time and neglect and countless rainy seasons to stubby posts. Eva followed Jon and asked, "Where are we going?"

The communicator pointed to the undulating vista. "To say hello."

As they trundled along the convoy road, Eva asked, "Marcel, how far are you normally allowed to go?"

"We may travel out, walking only, dry season only, so long as we return by sunset." The static began building, eating into his voice. Her internal screen flickered, faded, then sharpened once more. Eva felt the distance between her and safety grow much faster than her careful footsteps.

Gradually Eva caught up with Jon, who was now humming snatches of some melody she did not recognize. Then . . .

Up ahead the road intersected with a broad vein of stable hard-packed earth. As they approached, the vein began to glow, brighter and brighter, pulsing in time to Jon's footsteps.

Eva asked, "Do you have visual?"

"Barely." Marcel's voice broke through the static. "This is definitely new."

A mini mountain rose at the vein's center, perhaps twice Eva's height.

"Transport," Jon said. "Yippee."

The hill itself sloped and reshaped like melted tallow, forming a bench at head-height; small indents open along the hillside.

"They look like handholds," Marcel said.

Jon showed no hesitation. He clambered up, slipping and struggling, until Eva stepped forward and shoved him. Jon settled on the bench, then yelled, "Not comfy!"

Eva watched as the bench flowed and molded to his form. Jon shifted about, yelled, "Too hard! Too hard!" He appeared to sink partly into the rock. He pushed back, and the hillside sank with him. "That's better."

As Eva climbed up, she heard a click and then Marcel asked, "Can you describe what is happening?"

"The bench has molded to my form," Eva said. "It's like there's a thin sheet of padding over stone."

"Swing your helmet so we can take a look at the surroundings. Good." As they remained stationary, waiting, Marcel continued, "Jon often serves as our key link. One communicator receives the input, the others serve as echoes. Or confirmation. We ask our questions, sometimes they respond, mostly not. We're not even certain our requests for information are being properly communicated."

"Frustrating."

"And that defines my life's work," Marcel agreed. Then, "Are you moving?"

In response, Jon clapped his hands and said, "Off we go!"

"It's like riding a sled," Eva reported. "Incredibly smooth. I can't tell if the sled is moving over the path, or if the path itself is moving. OK, we're accelerating."

Faster and faster their mini vehicle proceeded along the vein. Dust motes sparked in the air, plinking against her faceplate as they flew along the road. Or perhaps they were some form of living organisms; Eva was about to ask Marcel when the screen flickered and went blank, and then her earpiece began emitting a soft hiss.

Marcel's voice emerged long enough to say, ". . . Losing you."

She wanted to turn off the audio feed, but was worried about stopping the record function. As they continued to slide along the illuminated path, though, she decided the sound was a little reassuring. As if this soft constant hush remained a final link to everything she was leaving behind.

Several times since they'd received the summons or invitation or command, Eva had wondered at her lack of fear. Perhaps it was due to how happy the communicators had remained, genuinely delighted with the prospect. All is well, this is fun, it's a grand and wonderful moment—that was their universal response, so cheerful it was infectious.

Then a thought struck. "Kim, can you hear me?"

The response was simply more of the soft background hiss.

Eva decided to say it anyway. "What if this trek is tied together with all our other mysteries? Last night's dream, remember? It felt like I had been internally frisked. Like they searched me. Not rough, but very impersonal." She paused, then added, "Somehow it feels like I'm now connected to whoever or whatever did that body search. And somehow that forms part of everything we're facing."

"Connected!" Jon almost sang the word. "That's who we are."

She turned so as to inspect the young man seated beside her. Through his faceplate Eva could see tears streaking down his face. "You realize that makes no sense."

He shouted more loudly, "Connected!"

According to the timer set in Eva's left sleeve, they traveled on through the silent, alien landscape for ninety-seven minutes. Long enough for the undulating rainbow vista to gradually shift from hypnotic to colorfully monotonous. The alien world was so silent Eva could hear dust pellets strike her faceplate, and the soft hush of their sled rushing along the illuminated trail.

Jon grew impatient and began shifting restlessly in his seat. Finally, he announced, "OK, that's far enough now!"

As if in response, their sled slowed. A few minutes later, they came to a full halt. Eva started to ask if Jon had spoken because of some incoming message he'd received, when he said, "Oh boy."

She waited, but as far as she could see nothing changed. She looked at the man behind the other helmet, saw his happiness, the childlike wonder shining in his eyes. Then Jon clapped his hands and pointed straight ahead. "Here they come!"

Eva followed his hand, and saw nothing different. The trail glowed softly, the liquid earth continued moving in silent rhythms. Far in the distance, more illuminated veins formed boundaries around the unstable terrain. Both moons were present, one rising and the other setting, ghostly half-shapes bound to opposing horizons. Overhead the sun shone in an empty dry-season sky. It was the perfect day for journeying through alien terrain. If such a moment actually existed. Beside her, Jon began humming again.

Then everything changed.

The undulating earth stilled, the rainbow colors vanished.

The illuminated lines of hardened earth joined to the broader swaths now, all sharing the same soft light. The silence held a potent force that was only magnified by how Jon kept humming his little tune.

Hills began rising on all sides, silently transforming the illuminated veins. They grew taller and taller still, gradually darkening as they rose so high they obliterated both moons. They formed a valley whose interior became cast in shadows. Or rather, it would have, except for how a narrow three-sided pyramid rose at the valley's heart, burning so brightly Eva lifted one hand to shield her eyes.

Taller and taller it grew, high as the surrounding cliffs, an illuminated spike jutting into the sky.

The surrounding cliffs grew eyes.

Great globular entities, dozens of them, adorned the valley on all sides. All of them observed her.

"Just like my dreams," Jon announced, calm now. "It's time for you to go."

The pillar dimmed slightly, as if in confirmation.

Eva managed, "Go where?"

Jon pointed to the pillar. "They want to say hello."

She was about to ask if it was safe to cross, when an illuminated path opened up by their sled. "What about you?"

"Not me," Jon replied. He curled up, or tried to. "Make it softer and flatter." The seat extended, the back folded down. Jon curled up, closed his eyes, and went to sleep.

Walking in the clunky suit-boots was a talent Eva did not have time to learn. The distance from their sled to the narrow pyramid was about three hundred meters. Eva had only covered about ten when the path began to crawl forward. She extended her arms out to maintain balance. But her passage remained steady, like traveling along a moving sidewalk.

Up ahead a second three-sided pillar rose immediately in front of the first. Only this one showed a trio of humanoid faces. This second pyramid was only slightly taller than Eva, and rotated—not continuously, rather it showed one face, shifted, showed another, shifted again. The faces remained partially imbedded in the stone pillar, and their shading was the same as the hills, a hundred colors, all gold.

A voice came through her headset. "Can you understand me clearly?"

"I can, yes."

"It is important that I am clear. Or we. Selecting words in your language is proving difficult. We feel we must choose between speech-patterns that do not truly apply."

Eva indicated the young man now slumbering in the stone sled. "Why do you limit your contact with humans like you do?"

"Human visitors are allowed to see, hear, witness, observe, learn about my-our planet only what I-we wish." The pillar shifted, and the new face looked beyond her, back to Jon. "For a thousand of your earth years, these have been our dearest and only friends among your race. With them we can be open. Welcoming."

"Are you the master aliens?"

"I am. We are. But not of this form. Our true physical nature would only terrify. Do you wish to be frightened?"

"No, thank you. Did you invade me in my sleep?"

"We inspected." The pillar shifted and revealed another face, this one covered in what appeared to be stone scales. "We thought you were the correct member of your species. But we had to be certain. This message requires precision."

Their conversation carried the lyrical quality of a verbal ballet. Two different species seeking to understand what both united and divided them. That was how it felt. Seeking to move beyond the patterns that had defined their relationship for a thousand years. "What is your message?"

The pillar swiveled. The new face was cold, implacable. "It is time for humans to depart."

The words jangled inside her brain. "Excuse me?"

The pillar shifted again. This face held such a potent force Eva found herself being invaded again. Just like the previous night. "All humans must leave this planet. Now. It is not yours. It never will be. The bonds defined by our treaty have been broken. You have invaded the forbidden zones. You must depart."

In the days and weeks that followed, in multiple conversations with Salma and Kim and Ricard and Knowles and the entire Council, even with Tanner, Eva described that precise moment as her breaking point. There was no other reason for the chilling certitude that filled her body and mind. A clarity as solid as ice. An electric fury. Meeting this member of the master aliens with her own cold and implacable force.

The three faces, their voices matching the latent power that had reshaped this region and formed a valley rimmed by giant eyes, had no right to declare an end to humanity's time on Treaty. It sounded precisely like the sort of demand her mother would make. As if their voice was the only one that mattered.

Eva replied, "You and I both know that is not going to happen."

The pillar shifted, revealing the face of a general preparing for battle. "In that case, we have no choice but remove the veils, as you call them. We must take responsibility. Your race will be obliterated."

Her response might as well have been scripted in the sparkling air. "In that case, the ships encircling your planet will release a cascade of viruses. The ones which would have destroyed life on this planet, without our intervention. Remember that? Not to mention new strains we've developed over the past thousand years."

The pillar shifted. Again. Another time. And another.

"Your demand is idiotic." Eva marveled at how musical her voice sounded in her own ears. As if she had gained the ability to sing her fury. "I suspect you already know it."

Shift. Shift. Shift.

"This is *my* planet too. *My* home. And it's time you accept this as fact. Which means dropping your absurd demand."

Shift. Shift. Shift. "We demand to be left alone and isolated."

"We demand to live!" She waited through another trio of shifts. Each face was slightly different. All showed confusion. Uncertainty. Eva continued, "Here's an idea. Why don't we both forget you even mentioned this ridiculous, idiotic ultimatum. We'll pretend it never happened."

Shift. Shift. Shift. Faster now.

"So, let's start over," Eva said. "You brought me out here because you have a problem. Tell me what it is, and together let's try to find a solution."

NINE

Kirra Barret

Waking in the silent clinic held a surreal quality. Kirra had apparently been so deeply asleep she had not even noticed when Elyria had pushed her gurney into a neighboring room and then settled Kirra into a full-sized bed. She rose and showered and dressed in the same clothes, for they were all she had. Kirra could see subtle indentations around the shoulders and both sleeves where the birds had held and lifted and carried.

The thrill of what she had accomplished, and all this signified, stayed with her through the long and empty days that followed. Kirra settled into a comfortable if lonely routine. Elyria had a clinic to run, which meant only occasionally having time for her unexpected guest. Kirra was impatient to meet with Arno, and yet somewhat glad for a forced break. She spent hours in the main office, hunting what little she could find about Corinth. All sources available to her were heavily redacted. No mention was made of the city-state's recent history, or their government, or their mining methods. Which only heightened Kirra's excitement about an idea that gradually took hold.

Six mornings later she had finished an early breakfast when Elyria entered and found Kirra washing her plate and cup. "Leave that. Arno and the others should be here shortly. He said to tell you he's hoping Elder Barret can join them. But with security so tight no one can say for certain."

"Ask them to meet me on the roof."

"Should I come?"

Kirra had been debating the same thing. "Are you certain you want to? What I share with them carries risks."

"But it's my choice?"

"After all you've done for me," Kirra replied, "I couldn't refuse you anything."

When she emerged on the clinic's roof, the sky was awash with the vague grey pastel of early dawn. Kirra brought up chairs and formed a makeshift circle. She settled down and turned her face upward, reveling in the day ahead.

So much had happened to bring her here, a fugitive trapped on the roof of a semi-illegal clinic. The triumphs and pitfalls stretched back in what now, looking back, appeared almost orderly. As if all along she had been destined for this place and time. The late dry-season air held a bitter flavor, like tinder ready to explode. She could almost see the spark of seasons rubbing against one another, taste the sweet release of those first raindrops. Kirra breathed deeply, drawing in all the unseen changes held by this new day.

"Kirra?"

She opened her eyes and rose to her feet. "Thank you so much for coming."

Kirra took her time settling her guests into chairs, then seating herself. The sunrise was still a half-hour away, but the heat was already dense, the air thick with dust and the nervous friction of coming storms. Kirra had no experience at gratitude. Yet her world had been defined by these four, Elder Barret and Arno and Dell and Quinn. They represented far more than safety and wealth. All her opportunities, her chances to rise beyond the Fifth Ward upbringing, these four were as responsible for Kirra being in this place as the birds.

"It could all be so different," Kirra began. "If clan Barret had not been there to protect and raise me. If Arno had been someone who didn't build his empire on a genuine respect for his partners—"

The chair squeaked noisily as Arno shifted his considerable weight. "Is this what we came for, your idea of a final farewell?"

Kirra had to smile. The old man was as uncomfortable receiving gratitude as she was shaping it. "No."

"Then get on with it! I've dozens of questions that need answering—"

"Hundreds," Elder Barret said.

"And the longer we stay here the greater the risk!" Arno waved both arms at the sky overhead. "There are watchers everywhere!"

Kirra nodded. So be it. "Trust for trust," she said. "I want you to meet my team."

With every bonding it became harder to draw in a limited number. Instead, she sent all but a trio out on a city-wide mission. Even so, she had no idea how many would appear.

The moment of binding and instructing took the span of three breaths. Less. When she opened her eyes, they observed her with nervous apprehension. Clearly, they wondered if the strain and pace of events were breaking her.

Then a dozen or so birds settled on the walls bordering the roof, while the trio of her childhood fluttered down to the tiles by her feet. Kirra reached out, and two settled on her forearms while the third took up position on her right shoulder. "From time to time I'll need to close my eyes so I can bond with the others. Be patient with these interruptions. They're necessary for you to understand."

"So you can *bond*." Interestingly, it was Quinn who said it.

"Yes." She exchanged a look with Arno's protector. She had so much in common with this slender assassin. Kirra allowed herself a moment to wonder what it might be like, starting a relationship with such a man.

Quinn must have detected a hint of her thoughts, for he offered a tight smile and repeated, "You bond."

In reply, she closed her eyes and reached out. "Observe."

She refocused on the gathering dawn as a cluster of birds deposited a mangled collection of metal bits in the center of their circle. The diddybirds then joined their mates on the perimeter wall.

Quinn lost his smile. "Is that . . ."

Elder Barret leaned forward, squinted, said, "Great heavens above."

Kirra paced around, closing her eyes and bonding and

waiting as yet another demolished drone was dropped into the growing pile gradually encircling their little group. These punctuations helped frame her description of the depot assault, her silent scream, the birds, the realization of what had taken place. Then in careful detail she described learning how to bond, to see, to fly, to steal.

By this point so many birds had arrived, the roofline could hold no more. The metal rubbish now encircling them was almost waist high. And still more came.

She asked them, "Have you heard about what happened to the frontier lab convoy?"

All four shifted as if coming awake. Elder Barret said, "The attack."

"It's all anyone is talking about," Dell said. "It's been the main point of Florian's news alerts."

Arno asked, "That was you?"

"No," Kirra replied. She gestured to the birds that now blanked the entire roof. "It was my army."

There was a shared tension now, an acceptance of truly a new day. Arno and Elder Barret both rose to their feet and then were joined by Dell and Quinn, all of them walking slowly about the rim of destroyed drones. The birds' only motion was to track their movements, a leather forest of heads and spear-like beaks. The four's movements formed a woven tapestry of footsteps as Kirra repeated, "Trust for trust. I want to make a suggestion. Nothing more."

"You have a plan," Arno said.

"I think so. Yes."

"We're listening."

"It all comes down to Corinth wanting access to Florian's undeveloped mineral deposits."

Arno froze in place. "Yes," he declared. "Yes."

It was precisely the response Kirra had hoped for. Such a swift sharing of her vision confirmed she had found the way forward. Grant herself the life she dreamed of and longed for. Permanently establish a better life for the Barret clan. Strengthen and expand Arno's hold on power. She asked, "You are their representative?"

Arno smiled. "My secret of secrets now revealed."

Kirra could almost hear the crystalline fragments meld into place. "How long have you been their ally?"

"Since the very beginning. I was a small-time merchant struggling to become what Florian's rulers would never allow," Arno replied. "Corinth has known for over a generation that their mines were failing. Their requests for Florian's help were flatly rejected. Corinth's rulers decided they had no choice but change the status quo. They offered me the chance to break free."

It was Dell who said, "To become the leader you were meant to be."

"They gave me the resources I needed to redefine my world," Arno agreed. "What is more, they gave me a purpose."

Kirra closed her eyes and bonded and sent her birds away. They needed to vanish before the city awoke.

Growing daylight was momentarily filtered through thousands of leathery wings. When Kirra opened her eyes, Elder Barret and Quinn and Dell were all gaping at the empty sky. Arno, however, was watching Kirra. He told her, "Tell us what you have in mind."

By midday, everything was in place.

Their planning became so swift, Kirra felt like they all could hear the same subtle drumbeat, marching them forward.

Early that afternoon, Elder Barret traveled alone to the First Ward. She passed easily through the First Ring gates because Arno had forged a certificate naming her as the Corinth embassy's new head cleaner. They all shared a bitter humor over what this represented. Their anticipation of what was about to happen left Kirra incandescent.

For a calling card, Elder Barret carried two items: Baron Knowles' diamond-studded timepiece taken in Kirra's first foray, and the tiara taken from the Crillon suite, intended to adorn the head of the spaceport ambassador's official reception hosted by Florian's Regent.

Kirra's first and dearest friend stayed inside the embassy until nightfall.

Finally, Dell arrived in the gathering dusk, bearing the news, "It's all arranged."

Kirra waited until just before midnight, when the surrounding Third Ward was quiet. Dell accompanied her to the roof. As she watched the cloud of birds descend and gather, she said, "I would not have missed this for all the jewels you've stolen."

"Stolen for us," Kirra corrected. "I hope you and Arno never forget that."

"Stay safe," Dell said, and embraced her for the very first time. "Our friend and partner."

The cloud condensed and gripped and carried her aloft. Higher and higher, then across the immense distance separating her from everything the First Ward represented.

She landed in the center of Corinth's largest courtyard. When the birds rose and vanished into the night, the ambassador stepped forward, bowed low, and said, "For years we have sought a lever to pry open this door." He studied the sky as the birds vanished into gathering clouds, then said, "I welcome our newest and most valued ally."

TEN
Eva Fourier

By the time the alien sled arrived back at their frontier lab, Eva had fashioned a step-by-step method of moving forward.

Maxine was of course furious when Eva refused to disclose what had happened. But her mother's ire remained nothing more than a storm on some far horizon.

Eva ordered Marcel and Maxine to travel back with them. She decided to include Brisa as well, then opened the invitation to the lab's entire population. Everyone who felt a need to learn what the master race had told her were welcome, Eva made that as clear as possible. What she had to say would result in significant changes to every level of their work.

In the end, only a reluctant skeleton crew and the entire Communications team were left behind. Jon spoke for the others when he said they already knew everything. When Maxine tried to probe them for information, Jon and his mates only laughed and turned away.

Eva offered Kim a few sentences, enough to forge the special bond this incredible moment required. She had made direct contact with the master race. Their discussions were both enormous and far-reaching. It also confirmed direct links between every mystery they currently faced. The threat Florian's Council feared was very real.

The entire journey back, either Kim or Eva kept hold of her space suit's helmet and the recordings. No one was allowed to access the memories until she addressed the full Council. And fulfilled one other vital task.

Soon as they were through the veil, Kim alerted Ricard and Knowles, and through them the Council. Eva limited her own messages to the other duty. Her grandmother was to be ready for her arrival. That had to come first. She owed Salma this and far more besides.

As they approached the depot, Eva drew in tight to Kim and whispered, "A request."

His response was even softer. "Anything."

"I'm assuming Arno Held has remained under surveillance. I need to know everything that's happened, every move taken by everyone connected to him and this investigation."

"Consider it done."

Four vehicles and a bevy of uniformed Guards awaited them at the depot. Eva ordered Marcel and Maxine to accompany her, and sent everyone else to the Council headquarters. Her mother was by now utterly cowed. She had shrunk in on herself, clearly frightened by the sweep of events and how her iron grip had been stripped away.

Maxine was right, Eva decided, to be worried.

Salma wore the same grey suit she had donned for their first meeting with Tanner, all those many eons ago. She greeted them as she would a gathering of senior officers, escorting them into her parlor and offering tea which everyone declined.

Eva handed Marcel the helmet and ordered him to set it up so they could view her journey on the wall-screen. Once it was in place, she thanked Marcel and told him to leave the room.

When the recording ended, Eva said, "I wish I could offer you more time to absorb the news. But the Council is waiting." She rose to her feet and studied the two women. Salma remained as she had been upon their arrival, grave and thoughtful and sternly aware.

Maxine looked utterly shattered, her features an ashen mask.

"You are welcome to stay here if you want," Eva told them. "But if you're coming, we need to leave right now."

In the end, both women accompanied her.

Salma served as her daughter's guardian and companion both. She remained tightly fixed to Maxine's side, there to help steer, ready to catch her if or when Maxine's strength gave way entirely.

The entire Council was gathered, even the Regent. Eva

wished she could have paid more attention to the august surroundings. But she found herself unable to absorb anything at all. When they seated her at the huge oval table, while Marcel made things ready, she promised that one day soon she would return and give this palace a proper inspection.

The Council remained breathlessly silent through the entire viewing.

When the huge front screen finally went blank, no one moved or spoke, until Ricard asked, "You have made an initial assessment?"

"I have, Baroness."

"Very well. The floor is yours."

The words might as well have been scripted into the table's surface. "The issue we currently face has its beginnings in humankind's earliest days on Treaty. A thousand years ago, when the virus threatening all alien life was finally vanquished, the master aliens discovered they had lost control of the diddybirds. This was very worrisome, because of the role these birds played in the planet's overall structure."

Ricard asked, "And that role was?"

"The same as it is today," Eva replied. "The diddybirds were intended to serve as the master aliens' private army.

"For a thousand years, the issue was both unsolved and not especially critical," Eva continued. "Because the birds were rendered harmless by the absence of another controlling force.

"Then a pregnant lab technician from the Fifth Ward Barret clan went into labor on the journey back to Florian. The convoy's chief, a mother herself, elected to pull the convoy off the road long enough to allow the woman to give birth. The aliens viewed this as a breach of the treaty and attacked. Only one transport managed to make it back to Florian. The official records state that everyone else, including both parents and the newborn, were all killed. But it seems the daughter survived. Her name is Kirra, and she was raised by her mother's Barret clan."

Ricard offered, "Records of the Fifth Ward are spotty at best. This woman's existence only recently became known to us. We thought she had died with the others."

Kim said, "You should know, Kirra of clan Barret is responsible for the unsolved thefts."

One of the other Council members said, "What, all of them?"

"Not her," Eva said. "The birds. And this leads us to the matter at hand. Somehow Kirra Barret has become the birds' authority. She controls them utterly."

"To understand what this means," Kim said, "you only need review the slaughter of eleven men at the Fourth Ward transport depot. Which is what happened when they tried to assault this woman."

The same Council member declared, "This Barret female must be destroyed!"

"Even to consider this would be disastrous," Eva said. "Strip away her control of the birds, and the same thing could happen to Florian that occurred to the marauding aliens when Kirra's convoy was attacked. Not even the aliens' combined might could stand up to the diddybird army. The birds could potentially destroy our forces just as they did the aliens who assaulted the convoy." She gave that a beat, then added, "There is every chance the birds would destroy this entire city-state."

Ricard added, "These same birds have taken out every drone the city possesses. Our skies are unmonitored for the first time in centuries." She nodded to Eva. "Tell them the rest."

The Council member was aghast. "There's more?"

"Indeed," Ricard said. "The worst is yet to come."

"Kirra Barret is allied to Arno Held," Eva told them.

"Their alliance appears to be so strong, the man now effectively has his very own private army," Ricard said.

As the Council's table became enveloped in worry and shouts and frustrations and fears, Eva pushed her chair back to where she was now planted on the side wall. She looked down to where Salma and Maxine sat, both women now pale and shaken by the need to accept that this child both lived and threatened Treaty's entire power structure. Beyond them, Kim offered Eva a nod of approval.

It was enough. Eva rose to her feet and waited.

When Ricard finally managed to silence the gathering, Eva said, "I have an idea as to how we might proceed."

When word came that Elder Barret had entered the First Ward using false papers, then spent the afternoon inside the Corinth embassy, Eva was ready.

The Council of course wanted to arrest the clan leader and imprison her. Ricard and Knowles together shouted them into submission. Which made Eva's job much easier. When the Council then insisted she be accompanied by a full Guards convoy, all Eva needed was a few quietly spoken words to describe how that was the worst possible response. What if Kirra released her winged army? What if the convoy was torn apart with the same ease as her attackers at the depot, or the alien force, or their own drone forces?

In the end, Eva traveled in private transport, accompanied by Knowles and Ricard and Kim. When they pulled into the Corinth embassy forecourt, Eva said, "All this started with Director Tanner's aim to insert me secretly into the Corinth city-state."

"Actually, the idea was mine," Knowles said.

Ricard smiled. "Hard to believe, but true."

"We knew they were going to come after us," Knowles said. "If it were me in their terrible position, I would find a strong ally who was hungry for more power, and who held no allegiance to the Florian power structure. I insisted to the Council that we determine what form this threat might be taking. And that required an ally within their financial system."

"And look where it brought us," Kim said. "Forging a young woman into a ghost. Someone whose disappearance from Florian might go unnoticed. A financial analyst who could be secretly inserted into the Corinthian realm."

"I was opposed to Tanner's methods," Ricard confessed.

"As was I," Kim agreed.

"But I must say, the end result may actually have prepared you for this role."

"The only person in Florian who might save our city-state," Knowles said.

"Regardless of what happens," Ricard said, "Know you will be well rewarded."

"Baroness, I am not after rewards."

"Which only heightens your qualifications," Kim said.

"And our determination to elevate you," Ricard said. "As you well deserve."

She took that as her cue and rose from the transport.

A uniformed guard stood by the open door as Eva crossed the forecourt and climbed the embassy's broad front stairs. She halted one step from the pillared veranda, so that she needed to look upward. It was best, she decided, to show as much respect as possible.

Eva said, "I would like to speak with my sister."